NATIVE
INVISIBILITY

NATIVE INVISIBILITY

DARRIN "1831" COLLINS

MYND
MATTERS

Published by
Mynd Matters Publishing
715 Peachtree Street NE
Suites 100 & 200
Atlanta, GA 30308
www.myndmatterspublishing.com

978-1-948145-25-1 (pbk)
978-1-948145-26-8 (eBook)

FIRST EDITION

To Kimbra, my mother,
you are the closest human to God.
My Pope.

Contents

CHAPTER 1

Day of Judgment

Cleanse my heart, Father. Cleanse my heart. Let Your covenant be manifest. Let Your will be done. My breathing got more intense.

As I prepared, I found myself in a meditative state. I prayed more for myself than for Chris. I was anxious. *I ask only that You consummate your message through these actions. I do not act in defiance. My life, my body, my soul belongs to You. I seek nothing but Your approval. Oneness with the whole. Bless my actions.*

I paid my fare, swiping my bus card. I ran up the steep concrete stairs leading to the train platform.

There is a time for everything. I am Your soldier in this time of war. The enemy will feel Your strength through me, Father. I was holding the chaplet loosely. The dangling of the beads composed the beat to my stride.

My eyes met those of each person on the train platform. They offered me nothing. I saw through it all. I saw their sin and their privilege. Their disdain for all things holy. They love the devil and to the devil they shall return.

Give me Your hand, Father. Give me your hand, please. Let my faith stand as my living testimony. May the glory of Your KINGDOM shine through me. Cleanse my heart.

Two workers in bright yellow vests stood against a nearby wall. A loud and muffled voice came through the small two-way radio attached to one's side.

"BRRRRKKK Brown line BRRRRKK early BRRRRKKK."

The red line showed up at the Sheridan stop. As it slowed, everyone jockeyed for their spot. No one cared about the woman with the stroller or the crippled man with the cane three cars down. Each person pushed and looked over their shoulder. All they wanted was to get to their destination. They desired as little human contact as possible. It was clear. Each was attached to some type of rectangular electronic device. Some shiny piece of plastic that owned their senses. Because of this, they were less human. In a Confucian way, you know? Real recognize real. Well, human recognize human. Why else are we here? *We must do unto others as we would want them . . .* My thoughts raced. What did Confucius say? These people were crazy. Everyone knew it. Who has to reiterate it? Bruce Lee? Marcus Garvey? Marley?

God, who am I to judge? Who am I? Please order my steps. Instruct my hands and bring clarity to my decisions. I paused. *Bless them Father for they know what they do, I know it. But show mercy on them. Please do not let their children drown in the same fire. That's all I hope. Do not let the innocent...do not let them destroy new life. Give us three hundred years of glory. Show them their fault and they will have no choice. They must change!*

As I traveled south towards the center of the city, my

anticipation grew. I was excited to be doing God's will. There is no answer for the atrocities of the past. There is no answer for the present transgressions. There is no subtle response to the preparation for future transgressions—the strategic dismantling of certain peoples. *God, today the meek shall inherit the Earth. Today we shall negotiate our freedom as equals. You gave us Your WORD to empower us. Not to defeat or humble us. If we believe in You, we shall live forever and a day. I will live through You!*

The automated voice on the train announced, "Fullerton is next! In the direction of travel, doors open on the right at Fullerton."

It was almost time. I scoped the train again. By this point, I was standing next to a tall mulattresse. Her hair was curly, maybe more like wavy. She was pretty. Her eyebrows and lashes were thick and black. Some might mistake her for white. But they'd be way off. I'm sure she absolutely hates when people think she's white. "Ha!" I laughed aloud at the thought. I often think for people I've never met. Especially for pretty women, which was my only vice. She looked up at me, threatening to remove her noise-canceling headphones. She raised her hand inquisitively then dropped it dismissing the notion.

Focus my mind, God. Focus my heart on Your will. Take my eyes off of any distractions. Take away all weakness from this vessel. I am Yours and You are mine.

I looked at the girl again. She had her ears gauged. They were like saucers. When we got to Fullerton, she took the recently vacated seat in front of her. I stepped over to let others by and found myself directly in front of my mulatresse. For a moment, I was in a Harlem Renaissance novel. Her perfume hit me as I slid in front of her. She smelled familiar, almost too familiar. My brain would forever remember Simmone. Her perfume had autographed my olfactory glands. Sweet Simmone. We made eye contact momentarily. She smiled to break the awkwardness. I stared back. On any other day, I would have asked her name. "Sweet Smellin' Simmone," I said inaudibly. But today was different.

"North and Clybourn is our next stop! Doors open on the right at North and Clybourn."

The stops were coming quickly. I had to get off soon but I wanted to remember the experience. I wanted to recount each step. This story would have to be told and I wanted to be the one to tell it. I would write my name in history. This is the day life changes. Today, the last become the first. Today, God's covenant is realized. Pan-Africanism. Birth of the Melanoid Nation.

A hollow bell went off announcing the opening of the doors at North and Clybourn. My eyes were locked on the doors. A flood of bodies entered. Several times, the conductor overshadowed the muffled voices and announced, "Please use all available doors." Nobody heeded the advice. They simply dumped into the doors by some form of diffusion. The doors opened, and without thinking, their bodies naturally sought out the equilibrium. Some came in and others went out. Never seeing one another, never making the experience any more than impersonal.

"Doors closing," the automated voice was back. "Use all available doors," the conductor bellowed in frustration.

There was no "please" this time. He was clearly talking to the homeless man still struggling to board the train. Bill Clinton, I instantly named him. Not because he was white, he was actually blacker than purple. But because he seemed to have an arrogance and an aloofness to him that made him presidential.

Bill made his way onto the train carrying his life along with him. He had four big garbage bags, a crate, three book bags, and a half-dead dog. The train was packed. But everyone was aware of this one man, even if they weren't aware of anyone else. People moved without communication. Bodies simply spread, opening a path for Clinton. Bill walked towards me, but I didn't move. His dog wore a bright orange harness. It seemed pretty mild-tempered, but I learned a long time ago never to trust other people's dogs. If you did not train him, he's not loyal to you. I stared the dog down. His attention went directly to the floor of the train. He was mine.

Bill bumped into me as he passed but I didn't mind. He said, "Excuse me brother." I nodded with acceptance. It was the first real interaction I had that morning. It did not have the same distrust held by Simmone's smile. No. It was human contact. Genuine and simple.

As Bill took his seat, the entire section moved. Agreeably, his smell did overwhelm my Sweet Simmone's perfume. But, it was not enough to clear an entire section on a crowded Chicago train. Admittedly, the entire station smelled like urine. The train car itself smelled of cleaning solution and white people. But Bill's presence made everyone shift and retreat. Each at their own pace. Some waited for Bill to decide where he was going to sit before they gravitated to the door. Although their stops may not have been fast approaching, they hated seeing themselves in the mirror: his outward appearance a.k.a their inward appearance. So each and every one of them moved.

Even my Sweet Simmone, when the time was right. Without a word, she elegantly stretched her body like a lovely giraffe. She placed her left arm across her chest, slightly bending at the wrist, she was telling me "excuse me." She didn't say a word though. I moved slightly to the right. Her body brushed mine. I was given a quick waft of her morning routine. I loved it. I caught the sweet scent of her hair too. I could imagine what she tasted like. A brief fantasy. Without words, she had wiggled to the other end of the car. I was glad we never exchanged words. *Maybe she does like white people?* I asked myself.

I do not know anything about this man, Father. Please protect him as You protect all of Your children. Let him know that the pain is temporary. Speak to him. Let him know that today Your will is revealed. Let him know that today he is the chosen. He is the sign. Today he shall be resurrected." As I spoke, I moved closer to Bill.

Suddenly I became aware of increased shuffling around me. I lost Simmone momentarily. Bill was reaching into his bags. I had no idea for what. When he didn't find what he was looking for in the first bag, he began to mumble to himself. His dog hadn't moved. I think it was a girl. I wasn't too interested in the dog except for the obvious: why did he own a dog but not a house? He continued looking through the bags. He frantically searched all of them. Then, he moved onto the book bags. He searched with great enthusiasm for his lost item. He threw one of the book bags down. The dog was startled, but still only slightly picked up her head. She appeared used to his spurts of frustration.

He found it. To my surprise, it was a piece of gum. Just a piece of gum wrapped in aluminum foil. I was amazed. Immediately, he looked around the car and saw everyone looking in his direction. Everyone. Especially me. I was sitting across from him now. The seats had opened up, and I figured it was comical. This entire section of the train was empty all because of one homeless man.

We passed Clark and Division. People were getting on the train and instinctively avoiding our section. Several of them actually sat down before they realized what they were sitting next to—this obnoxious image of human decay. Either they were wrapped up in their cd players, or novels, or whatever it may be, but they missed him. When they realized, though, they shot out of their seats and moved. Their eyes bucked, revealing their hearts. Windows. One man even went to a completely different car.

Suddenly Bill flung his head back. The three hoods that were previously covering his head came off. He uncovered a mangled head of salt and pepper hair. It was a mix of matted locs and bald patches. His face was covered in hair. Hiding what I assumed to be a formerly handsome and promising image. But this face was worn with anguish, worry, and a whole lot that I had no clue about. But I kept my eyes on him anyway. *The world belongs to you, Bill. It belongs to you.*

The train lurched. The contents of his gum wrapper were revealed. Powder fell from his hand onto the ground. He looked alarmed, and immediately sniffed the remainder of the cocaine in the wrapper. At this point everyone on the car was looking down acting like they didn't see it. I looked around at this point for some sort of response. None. Bill was in complete control. Bill and his dog.

Bill jumped up. The dog moved slightly out of the way. He began to pace up and down the car. His clothes hung off, swaying as he bobbed from left to right. His pants fell lower and lower. He stumbled as the train rocked. The train stopped, sending him halfway across the car. He caught himself on the seat. Grabbed the waist of his pants. The car pulled up to the platform.

A derelict was in the center of the car. The crowd didn't know which way to turn. They were afraid. So, they did what they knew best. Some jumped cars while the majority sat in the first empty seat, hopefully as far away from the human decay as possible. But Bill continued to pace the aisles, shouting and murmuring.

"You think you're big time?!?" I was nearing my stop. But the entire time you're on a train, I guess you're nearing your stop. He paused in front of me, hesitating momentarily. I wanted to figure out if he was high or not. I couldn't tell. His eyes were clear. He was acting, I thought.

"Ali said, 'I'm the greatest.' Well, I'm here to tell you, aint no man the greatest. Aint no man ever gonna be great. Not even yo motha-fuckin daddy."

We came to the next stop. Bill was still pacing. He had made it back down to our end of the car. The dog stayed still. Only lifting her head up when Bill made excessive noises. He whispered something inaudible. As we pulled away from the stop, the man sprinted to the other end of the car letting the pants that he had previously held up drop to the ground. All I could see was his thigh and knee. The baggy clothes covered the rest. I could not tell whether he had on underwear. But it honestly didn't matter. It especially didn't matter to the other passengers, who at this point began to yell "sit down" and "let me ride in peace." There were three women seated at the far end of the car. At this point, many of the passengers pulled out their cell phones to record the affair.

One man stood up as if he was the CTA citizen appointed Security Guard.

"Hey man, put your clothes back on." He was thirty-something, white, and wore cargo shorts, flip flops, and a Jonathan Toews jersey. He walked toward Bill, bracing with each step as the train swayed. When he reached Bill, he attempted to guide him back to his seat with the unamused dog, without touching him. Gesturing, like a miniature bouncer, he tried to control Bill. Bill ignored the man and continued on his merry way. They grazed each other as Bill tried to walk around Toews. Toews was appalled at Bill's audacity and appeared disgusted by his touch not in any way accepting that he had in fact approached Bill. But the unacceptable part must've been that Bill didn't listen to his authority, which pissed young Toews off. Although he had spent so much effort not touching Bill, the man lunged for him now. Both hands, in the shape of a U, were positioned for Bill's neck while rage filled his eyes.

It was funny to think of him lunging at a half-naked homeless man. I bet he never thought that would happen. Bill shifted his weight to his back foot and ducked out of the way. He was ready for the attack. I was impressed. He had clearly been in a number of scuffles in his day. Toews looked like a fool stumbling into two women who were tucked in the fetal position atop their seats. His face hitting one of the lady's knees and causing a cut above his eyebrow. His Blackhawks hat flew off. He was in a fight. There was no turning back now. Blood streamed down the right side of his face. It started slow and picked up speed.

The other passengers jumped from their seats and ran toward the doors as Bill and Toews rolled from section to section. There were about twenty people on the car at this point. Everyone was headed downtown for the parade. Toews found himself on top of Bill. Bill was seated. Toews mounted, with the guillotine in position. The car lunged once more. This time we weren't at a stop. Instead the train was stalled.

"Sorry for the inconvenience passengers . . ." the conductor apologized as the train lunged.

The momentum tossed the men. Now Bill was on top. At this point, his dog was aware of the imminent danger. As Bill raised his hand to Toews, the dog latched onto the exposed white drumstick. Bill dropped his hand but missed the punch as the train moved forward. His weight carried him forward, exaggerating the strike. Toews was overwhelmed. Bill regained his composure and began mauling Toews. He landed elbows, hammer fists, slaps, closed fists, it was the most unorthodox display. He may have bitten the man. I think I intentionally forgot about that. He definitely bit his nose.

There was blood—a lot of blood. Finally, Toews worked his way free, but the dog was still attached to his leg. She went straight for the Achilles. Toews snatched away, exposing his wound. All of the blood appeared to be his. His slipped in the aisle, allowing the dog to catch him and latch onto his left thigh. He shook the dog off and struggled to open the emergency door as he switched cars.

Bill took a breath as he let Toews run away. He was not quite seated, both knees were in the chair. His arm held up his head. Finally, he rose and walked toward the end of the car where Toews had retreated. When he got to the final seat, he squatted behind it. Holding onto the headrest and the windowsill. He ducked behind the seat, face straining, fist clinched and biting his bottom lip. The twelve or fourteen people left on the car with me, my fellow witnesses, all had a quizzical look on their faces.

What next? Mouths open. Bodies leaning forward. They were all asking themselves, "What is this man doing?" But I knew instantly what he was doing. We have all done it thousands of times. Sometimes even in our pants. He was taking a dump on the train car. As each person realized what they were observing, one by one, they ran toward the exit door on my end of the car. Sweet Simmone fell but no one cared. One man stepped directly on her spine. Another woman tripped over her in the process. The whole affair was messy to say the least. I reached out to Simmone as she tried to get up. She didn't see my offer because she was too focused on this crazy start to her day. I should've protected her. My sweet Simmone.

As we approached the Grand stop, Bill and I were the only people still on the train car. The twelve apostles left me to be crucified. I was only one stop from getting off myself, and the smell hadn't hit me yet, so I figured I could bear it.

Bill rose from his squat. His goal was accomplished. Or at least I think his goal had been to clear the car. He walked slowly back to our end of the car. He looked at me, questioningly, his face saying, "I just took a shit on the train, why are you still here?" He brought the smell with him. It was strong. It punched me in the nose. It was like the feeling when you realize that you're driving behind a garbage truck with your windows down. You can mildly distinguish the odors: milk, cooking grease, dead animals. I was really not ready for the odor of a homeless man's naked body coupled with the stench of human waste. I'll never forget that odor.

I assumed his goal was to clear the train. If so, it hadn't been accomplished. As he crept down the aisle, he removed his sweatshirts, all umpteen of them. He stood in a Smurf t-shirt. Grouchy, I think it was. Ripping the shirt from the collar, like some Hulk Hogan wannabe, he searched for my response. Now, he was completely naked. He still crept down the aisle though. Judging from his body, he looked to be about forty years old. He was slouched as he walked. His toned frame still showed through the ravaging of drugs and years of neglect.

He was long. His penis hung loosely. He had not been circumcised. And now the smell hit me even harder. It felt like I had run into a wall of moose ass and cab driver B.O. But he came toward me. At this point he had made it to the second entrance: about two seats distance from where we had originally been seated. I watched him as he came forward. Not overly concerned, I was just weary of his nakedness. It was loose and nasty. I also wanted to be poised if any fecal matter were to fly off of his body. He was like a sea monster. A giant squid. I did not want to touch him.

As he returned to his seat, back across from me, he looked forward and resumed his original posture. Only his clothes were missing at this point. We sat in silence for a moment. The dog joined him moments later. I really was wondering what this man was thinking. And, in fact, he was thinking about the last subject I would have imagined: me.

"Why didn't you get off the train like everyone else?" he asked me with a little chuckle in his voice. But I simply stared at him.

"Well, that's just about the perfect answer," he responded acknowledging the pause. "My stop was coming up before all them people made me miss it." Again, he had that little chuckle in his voice. I was still silent. "Well I aint really miss my stop, see? I'm riding to the end. Caint miss your stop when you're riding to the end. But I did want to sit downtown for a second and catch some of that lakeside breeze. Them goddamned white folks made me miss my breezy downtown living. Now I gotta go out south and sit in my own shit," he spoke with utter frustration. I wondered why he didn't chuckle then, but I guess he was being figurative. I was wondering who he was frustrated with. He did, in fact, shit on himself.

"Well, them white folks will make you miss out on a lot," that was all I could think to say to the man.

"Aint that the God-fearing truth. A job. A car. A house. They'll make you miss out on freedom if they catch you off your P's and Q's. Boy them white folks is something else." He paused and thought sincerely about what he was going to say to me. "But you aint like them white folks. And I know cause you still aint got off this train. You aint like THEM! You aint like them cause you don't think you better than nobody. I am sitting here naked in my own shit, and you having a full out conversation with me. If I wasn't me, I woulda been left the car."

I hadn't thought of it that way. I hadn't even thought of that as the problem with white people. Well if that's the problem, it seems like it would be pretty simple to rectify.

"Lake is next! In the direction of travel, doors open on the left at Lake," the automated voice rang out. I was pleased. My stop was coming up. I debated whether to take Bill with me. It seemed fitting. God sends signs of his favor. Bill was a sign.

Suddenly he changed the subject. "My name is Garvey. Sergeant Garvey Pearce Belly is my God-given name. Not the sergeant of course. I got that in the Marines. Green Beret. They certainly didn't think they was better than me when I was killing them Vietnamese for Capitalist freedom!" He stopped momentarily holding an intense gaze at the floor. Then he broke the gaze. "With that said, you can call me Belly." He was older than forty. Closer to sixty if he served in Nam. Melanin is a wonderful thing.

Belly was very close to Bill. He looked more like a Jerome or a Thomas or something.

"Well, I don't think I'm better than you, Mr. Billy." The humor of the name hit me after I said it. I pronounced it like Billy. And so, the name stuck. His name was Bill.

"Naw, naw, naw don't call me no mista nothing. That's all part of us being equals you see. I learned that in the military. We all alive and we all dying. Death really do come to all. In that way, you an me are eternally and permanently equal."

I continued with what I was saying before.

"Well, Billy, like I was saying, I don't think I'm better than you."

"But," Bill filled in for me.

"But, I really don't know why you did what you did," I secretly wanted him to explain.

"Ha!" Bill let out one big cackle. "Ha!" he let out another. Then he collected himself. "It's simple son, I shit on the train because they turned me into a scene. I can't ride the train without a bitch saying "Yuck" or a mom telling her kids not to sit near me. I didn't ask for these people to look down on me. I just want to get to my stop—just like you and just like them. But they look and they point, and they spit on me and run me off of corners. They have no respect for me or you or anyone. But least of all for us. And do you know why that is?"

I sat silently. Bill continued without delay. "Because they don't know the truth."

"The truth?" I said before I could catch myself.

"The truth that they did not create themselves. You see, they think they did. How could they? They think they are alive because of favor and not grace. But you and I know. We know young man. We know. I have killed too many men to believe that they could not have killed me. I did it to show them that we are all equal. And to get them off this mothafucking train and away from me with their mothafucking judgments."

"This is Lake! Transfer to orange, purple, and green line trains at Lake. Doors opening," the automated voice said one last time.

I got up and grabbed Bill by the wrist. "Come with me. Leave your possessions and come with me," I said. "Heaven awaits us." We got off the train and made our way toward the street.

When we made it to the street, there was a thunderous boom. The earth shook slightly. Everyone stopped and moments later, I heard sirens. They were rushing to the Lake stop. Something happened in the subway below. Nobody seemed to notice either myself or my new sidekick. They were consumed with fear. Earthquakes in Chicago. "We will move mountains, Father. Thank You for protecting me thus far. Bless Your Prophets and arm Your soldiers."

CHAPTER 2

Communion

Bill and I walked down Lake Street. The sirens growing more distant with each step. Bill followed me like a naked shadow. *Are all shadows naked?* Thoughts like that consume me. Turning down Michigan Avenue, there was no more commotion, no more sirens. Making a right turn, we ran directly into a melee of people. The Blackhawks had just won the Stanley Cup. There was a sea of red on their way to Solider Field. But my people were ready. WE had been free for a very long time. In all the distraction, nobody seemed to notice Billy's looseness. His nudity was purloined in the hustle of Michigan Avenue. Everyone was looking up. Tourists took pictures of the floats and buildings. They had no time to notice their neighbor.

As we turned, I was consumed by the pitter patter of drumsticks on buckets. Three young men encircled a light pole. They were banging in rapid rhythmic formation. They were uniform: white t-shirt, jeans, Air Force Ones, and dingy dreadlocks. But they all possessed a different spirit and level of enthusiasm. Their dreads were shaking rapidly. I focused on the one in the middle. He tossed his stick in the air. It spun like a propeller. He caught it without hesitation, without bobbling. Clearly, he had spent hours upon hours developing his craft.

Deservingly, a small crowd gathered around them blocking the walkway. Maneuvering through the crowd was no easy task. As usual, there was a ton of crazed tourists and suburbanites whose eyes, cameras, and cell phones were all pointed upward in their efforts to immortalize each and every experience in downtown Chicago. Because we all know the rule—*it didn't happen if you didn't take a picture.*

Their bodies and the bodies of their children moved in and out of the sidewalk traffic aimlessly. In groups of five or six they cut you off in your route simply to go slower than you. The children with their sticky ice cream-covered fingers darted behind their parents like tadpoles. A little Mexican girl, wearing what looked like a quinceañera dress, stepped on my toe. She looked back for a second with deep black eyes but said nothing. I smiled back. Her face looked to be sticky and her mouth was big and red. She grinned, shockingly revealing four silver teeth across the top of her mouth.

The Bucket Boys still banged on their instruments. They nodded as onlookers gave donations. They played harder and harder as the crowd gathered, sensing that this was their opportunity to rack up on some tourist change. I stopped before I had completely walked through the crowd and turned back to the performance. Reaching in my pocket I grabbed a hundred-dollar bill. I had no use for it where I was going and I couldn't resist the urge of pride swelling inside of me. Still, nobody noticed my naked sidekick. I could tell these men, these Black Men, had accomplished so much with so little. They turned buckets and drumsticks into classical instruments. It almost made me turn around and go home. But I had a mission to attend to.

Bill placed his hand on my shoulder, probably to keep up. I didn't mind. He had become my companion. Maybe even my conscience at this pinnacle in my life. He was the type of freedom I wanted one day. Today.

"Dem boys is amazing! Give em anything and they can make music! Making so much outta so little. That's colored folks for you!" Bill shouted in my ear over the bucket boys.

We kept moving. Swiftly, we cut through the crowd. The hand on my shoulder appeared to lose itself.

"What am I gonna do with what the Father gave me? How far can I make it stretch?" I shouted uncontrollably, knowing that God will multiply what He pleases. I looked at the solid black Kenneth Cole watch on my left wrist. It read 15:14. There was another huge explosion behind me. It was on Lake. I didn't turn around. I stumbled slightly as the earth moved under me. I was surfing on dry land. The scene was surreal. People scattered everywhere. But ahead, everyone was calm. I walked to the calmness. Looking down again at my watch, there was a third earthquake. This time at Roosevelt. It was muffled. But the chaos had reached us. People were running. Cars were honking. The sound of panic was deafening.

I couldn't resist. I shouted the old Wolof proverb, "If you support yourself, HEAVEN will help!"

We walked forward. Traffic was at a standstill. People were running in every direction. I made it to Congress. The light was red. We waited. Obviously, we were the only people who waited. Sirens were blaring. Babies were crying. The walk sign appeared. What a relief.

Trying to ignore the terror around me, I couldn't help but think how history would depict this day. If everything goes as planned, I will be rewriting the annals of time. How will I write the story of this day? The birth of New Africa—place your money on Black.

As expected, no one was ready. They had enough manpower for a small terrorist attack. Police and firefighters were the first responders. But the situation clearly required a more aggressive response from the state. I took off my bookbag and pulled out my two-way radio. Looking down, I briefly turned on the walkie. I knew there had to be some action. The black knob turned in my hand. It felt like a levee was breaking as the voices came through frantically. They had no idea what to do.

"We need National Guard . . ." one voice rang through the mic.

"Medical! Where is Medical?" another voice shouted. "We've got at least ten dead. Maybe more at the State and Lake Stop . . ."

They were all talking over each other. There was no coordinated plan. The voices seemed to fade into the background as I saw my opportunity approaching. National Guard had been called. They know nothing about combat. It's amazing that the world played by their rules for so long and used their terms. We were brainwashed. Scared of the myth of the U.S. military. The world's strongest? A myth. But no more. Technology doesn't make you strong. I end this today. Today the Black Man's cancer goes into remission. Sergeant Billy and myself.

I looked down at my phone at a message from Chris. *We slowed them down at Roosevelt. Three Hulks headed south down Balboa.*

Billy and I waited for the tanks to show. The opportunity was beautiful. They were falling into our web. Three massive metal green

Hulks pulled down Balboa.

"They sent the tanks for us. How stupid could they be?" I let the words slip out before they were even thought. I had figured they would come off of Roosevelt, off of Lake Shore Drive, but I was wrong. The explosions sealed off the highways. They chose to take the streets. Either way, there is only one way in and out of the downtown area now and that was along the waterfront. Can't account for the human variable. That's why you have to build contingencies in your plan. Now we wait for them to come by air.

My crew was in tight formation to seize the Hulks. There were three tanks which would have to do. I wondered momentarily why they didn't send more. But how could they? Who was attacking them? They still had no clue. The real question was, how do you send tanks for an imaginary enemy? Seems a little aggressive. I was counting on them being aggressive and it worked.

"What you waiting for?" Bill shouted in my ear. "It's time." Suddenly the hand on my shoulder fell off. I turned toward Bill and could not find him among the crowd. There were people everywhere. Some were screaming and running. Some were statues, paralyzed by the incident. While many others were trying to help. They wore the blood of victims on their shirts, faces, hands, and jeans. Blood has always represented the United States, its valor and hardness.

"Bill! Where'd you go? I need you!" I shouted. "I need you?!" I shouted inquisitively now. I didn't understand. But I knew that our encounter had given me the strength to found New Africa today. New Africa will be founded on June 19, 2015.

Looking up, I spotted my muse, the one who gave me the courage. Bill was on top of the rear tank. Skinny, naked, and Black, he was atop the tank prying the hatch. Every muscle in his body was exposed. His skin glistened in the sunlight.

"What courage!" I said under my breath. With one inhale, I joined Bill in the fight. He moved in before Shannon and Chris had time to put our decoy into effect. The plan was to stop the convoy via distraction and not to deal with them head on. Plans change.

I ran to Bill, but my feet never touched the ground. It was as though I floated on the pavement. In two moves, I scaled the Hulk. Bill and I were side by side as the Turret Gunner popped the latch. Still in the tank, the gunner fumbled his pistol. He wasn't prepared for today. None of them were. Pop! My ears rang. The gunner had shot inside of the tank. Amateur. Bill grabbed the gun, as I punched the gunner in the mouth. Feeling a slight pinch on my hand, I pulled the gunner out before he could fall backwards into the tank.

Bill jumped in. The gunner held onto the side of the Hulk. We moved forward. I looked down to my hand. There was a tooth, an incisor to be exact, stuck in my knuckle. Ignoring the tooth, I found the weapon and fired. It was a nine. A very familiar model. I missed on purpose. My goal was to get him to let go, as no more than necessary had to suffer. He lost his grip, crashed into the pavement, and I entered the tank.

Chris messaged me, *What now?*

He and Shannon were perched adjacent to one another atop two high rises. They were in sniper position. The plan had changed. We no longer needed the decoy.

Bill was in the driver's hatch. That old man was a very capable ally. I couldn't tell whether it was anger, frustration, or sheer opportunity that I was witnessed, but we were one. I had long wondered what my spirit animal was. Once, a lover of mine told me that my spirit animal was a fox. My reply was no, it's stronger than a fox, it's a leopard. But we were both wrong. Bill's my spirit animal. Alive or dead, Bill is my spirit manifest.

"Follow them, Bill!" Knowing that I could achieve my goal with only two tanks, I sent a shell out of the cannon. The explosion lifted the tank to the right. The driver rode on. Both tanks rode on. Communication was ridiculous at this point. There was no direct command. Bill and I listened to the conflicting orders. We listened as the soldiers prayed for the military to save them. The world's mightiest military is completely offensive. They cannot defend the third largest city in the nation. Forget 9/11. I am taking your land. WE will own something.

"We take two of the Hulks and grab Keith. Shannon takes it. You stay watch. Snipe freely." Opening the latch, I pried the hatch open and raised the sign of OUR freedom. OUR new flag. The crew was signaled, as we turned down Roosevelt. Over the radios, as we listened in, the police were now having trouble keeping people away. Thousands of people stayed to take footage on their cell phones and tablets. They had no clue what they were witnessing. We had even gained fans. Our Melanoid Flag waved in its jet-Black glory. The silver fist in the middle standing proud. Our slogan branded the flag. The flag was already a symbol of freedom on Twitter and Facebook, #Supportyourselfandheavenwillhelp.

After crossing the bridge at Michigan, the ground shook and the sun was no more. The city fell into complete darkness. The lights would not shine until freedom rang. I put that on everything I loved. The bridge was no more. Access had been shut off. The lights had been cut off. The sun blotted and the electricity to every part of the city was under OUR control. New Africa was ours for the taking.

The pursuit continued. We sent two more shells at the tank on the right. The second explosion was enough to flip the tank. Billy lost control momentarily. We felt each explosion because of the proximity. The soldiers hadn't been authorized to shoot. We were shooting at lame ducks. We rode over the tops of several cars to get around the tank. I aimed the gunner in front of the second tank. I wanted to stop it and give Shannon a clean opportunity to make his move on the lead tank. I shot slightly left of the tank. The impact leveled the road and caused the tank to divert to the right in Shannon's direction. We hadn't rehearsed or planned on taking over the tanks but they would help us once we got to the police station.

Shannon jumped from the third story of a high-rise onto the tank. He almost missed, falling clumsily onto the hatch but holding on for dear life. If he fell, there was no round two. Luckily, he pulled himself up.

"Do not open the hatch!" A voice came through the radio. This time we shot at the building in front of the tank. The explosion caused the oversized piece of machinery to stop. The east end of the building collapsed, causing structural debris to fill the street below. Shannon held on.

"Wait for back up," the voice came through again. The gunner didn't listen. He opened the hatch with his rifle pointed at Shannon and began to fire immediately. Shannon was forced to let go. Fortunately, it was at a complete stop, so he wasn't injured. He took most of the damage from the explosions.

Billy continued to drive forward, blocking the lead tank between us and the debris. The gunner came out of the tank.

"Why'd he go and do that?" Bill shouted with joy. "They don't train em like they usedta," he explained as he made his way to the hatch. As Shannon fired back at the gunner, his comrade came out of the lead tank. Except, he was not seeking battle. He ran off, abandoning his fellow soldier. The gunner fired at Shannon who hid behind a garbage bin. At intervals, Shannon returned fire.

Billy, with his flesh hanging loosely, jumped out of our tank holding an A-K that he'd found inside. Sneaking around the right side of the lead tank, he crept up behind the gunner. I saw him raise the weapon then I lost him. He let off five shots before the gunner came sprinting out. He'd been wounded in the lower body. I couldn't tell where but he was limping. Shannon let off two rounds, both head shots, and took him out. Shannon nodded at Billy and assumed his position in the lead tank. Billy returned, and we rode to the police station to free Keith.

CHAPTER 3

Original Sin

"*Mal*, get in here and clean these dishes! You always leaving dishes in the sink!" Aunt Sis yelled from the kitchen. I walked the short distance from my pallet in the living room to the kitchen. It was 5 a.m. I could barely hear her, let alone comprehend. "You got one job in this house and you caint never get it right."

I didn't look up. She was completely absorbed with the dishes. Which, I guess, was understandable. But at 5 a.m., nothing is worth arguing about. At least, not for men. I have since learned that distinction. Knowing women the way I do now, she probably had a dream about the dishes.

When I was twelve years old, after my family suffered our second eviction, we moved from Memphis to Chicago. Chicago, the name says it all. I loved my city and it loved me back, even though it didn't have to. For the first year or so, give or take two months, we lived with Aunt Sis and my two cousins. There was little space for us: Mom, Chris (my little brother), and me. We slept in the living room, Mom and Chris on the couch and me on the floor. I'd tried out the loveseat but it was too short.

There were so many distractions in that house. But Chicago opened up to me. She allowed me to live and be alone in person. I loved her because I knew her. West side, south side, north side— they're all mine. I learned the four corners of Chicago like a disciple. The city became my work of art. Little did I know my destiny, her destiny—founded by DuSable and taken back by Jamal Dale.

I learned from Chicago and take her everywhere with me. She gave me this story by way of Ellison and Wright's dialogue. Native invisibility is my curse. But not invisibility in the traditional sense. People still see me. I was reborn here. Opened up and dissected here. My face is as commonplace as the next, but invisibility in the truest sense, in never being recognized as a subject. I love my city, but she blasphemes. She whispers to me. She says that God himself wasted His time in creating me. With my whole being I have to rebut and simply say, "You know what, you're lying." My city was founded by someone who looked like me. Chocolate City from the very start. She is mine for the taking.

"You hearin me?!?" Aunt Sis stepped forward and cupped the back of my neck. She was strong. Especially for 5 a.m. and at the same time, too strong for 5a.m. We made eye contact as she leaned toward me. "Wash these dishes and get outta my face!" She pushed my head aside.

As I washed the dishes, all I could think about was how much her breath smelled of coffee, cuss words, malice, and cigarettes. At 5 a.m.

I don't remember much about growing up in Memphis outside of a couple of birthdays, a few Christmases, and my extended family, of course. But I do remember a lot about my transition to the north.

My mother, Chris and I left the rest of our family, including my oldest brother Keith, behind when we moved. I didn't have many problems academically. In fact, I was pretty advanced. But everyone at school thought my accent was a point of great amusement. Every time I responded to a question in class, for the first month or so, there would be fits of snickering. However, as I got older, I realized that after the first week, the laughs came from a group of girls that had crushes on me. But this truth didn't stop my feelings of resentment at the time. When we first moved, I felt uncomfortable and alone.

I was angry, not because of my troubles at school, but because I had to deal with them by myself. Keith decided to live with my grandmother in order to finish his senior year of high school in Memphis. So, I quickly became the oldest and all the burden was on me. Keith would have helped me. He would have taken the yoke off my neck. I couldn't have predicted the way it turned out. Three months prior when I first heard the news that Keith was staying behind, I was crazy excited. I almost cried literally.

Our separation meant no more noogies, figure-four leg locks, or "let's see who hits harder" competitions. By the way, Keith is six years my elder and weighed more in the eighth grade than I do as an adult. He always hit harder. My first thought was, "I'm free." But, I never knew how much he did and how much he saw. When we left, I assumed his responsibilities. I was forced to grow up in his absence. Deep down, I knew if he was there, he would have protected me. He would have said something. At least a muffled, "But it's five in the morning!" He was never one to bite his tongue.

There weren't many dishes in the sink. Just a couple of pots and spatulas from the night before that I was letting soak. I began singing to myself to avoid thinking about Aunt Sis's breath. That would be the only way to achieve sleep again. Otherwise, it was going to be a long day for no apparent reason.

Tossing the final spatula in the rack, I promptly went back to my pallet. My head hit the pillow and I fell into silence.

When we moved to Chicago, or rather Black Creek, IL, we lived with my aunt and my two cousins in a two-bedroom apartment. We were the second Black family to move to Black Creek. My aunt and cousins were the first. The landlord was pretty "liberal" for the time and for the small suburb of Chicago. He was open to renting to all kinds of people. Two or three unmarried couples with children lived in the building too, a pretty big deal in Black Creek. To this day, my aunt still talks about the day they moved in and how the sheriffs had to escort them. It was the same thing when we moved in. We had a convoy with our U-Haul truck and it was like the whole town was watching. People stood on their porches, not to water to their grass, just to be nosey. The sheriffs didn't lift a single box or open the doors for us though. They stood with their hands grasping their belts, poised to unholster the weapon and fire.

Chris, my youngest brother, and I started school immediately. He had a lot less trouble adapting than I did and I don't know whether to attribute it to age or natural disposition. Whatever it was, as we got older, he was definitely more temperamentally predisposed to new people and new ideas. It came naturally to him. Chris and I would walk to school together at the advice of my mother. We usually left our cousins because they were always late. My mom instructed us to do that. However, leaving Chris was mortal sin. We were to go everywhere together. But I didn't mind. We have always been a duo. We went to Ronald Reagan Elementary School and for the first time in my life, I was in a classroom with white students. There were even two or three students who were neither white nor black, and this concept blew my mind the first time I saw them. There was Eileen and Mike, two Asians who had been adopted by white families. There was Anna who I always thought was Mexican but later found out that she was some other type of Mexican (Latinx). She had also been adopted.

This was the most diverse group I had ever been a part of. In terms of numbers at least. Especially if you think of the white kids as different ethnicities. But they all acted the same. Well ... not all. They had their little clusters though. Tribes. Everyone who wasn't in the accepted tribes was trying to be in the accepted tribes. As an adult I identified it as a group conscience, but as a child I wanted to be included. I wanted to know what their interests were, what they found funny, I wanted a part of their culture. But try as I may, in the year that I spent at Reagan, I never could figure it out. The kids came back from breaks with tans, freckles, and sunburns, stories of their travels to Florida and other intriguing sounding places that I didn't know a thing about. Even in the same space, we lived in different worlds.

"KASSSSSHHHHHHH!!!" I jumped out of my sleep as shrapnel landed on my face and blanket. Instantly, I knew what was happening and who was doing it. After the shards of glass crashed, there was a brief moment of peace, and then I sat up out of instinct. I would've been better off staying down, pretending to be dead, anything but sitting up.

At that point, the entire house was awake. Not an eye was shut. I still felt the peace for a moment. I looked toward the doorway, seeing a petite silhouette. She stood there. Motionless. With her hands on her hips, super-villain-like. She was standing like the sheriffs.

I always wondered what she was thinking when she would overreact. I pitied her. She needed to be seen, felt, hugged. Something was void. But there were no hugs this morning. Not one. I remember. Not even a, "See ya later."

"Meisha! Gone from my child! Gone, before I flatten ya'!" My mother said, quickly hopping off the couch as Chris gracefully moved out of her way. She threw the blanket off like a cape. Her green pajamas, imitating the weakest of superheroes: the Green Lantern.[1] Who wants to be a lantern? She was wearing a onesie. It fit her loosely, as all of her clothes do. When she stood up, they were about five feet from each other. The tension was palpable.

They glared at each other as predators do. Aunt Sis backed down, like a defeated lioness. There were a number of factors working against her now: 1. No longer was the cub defenseless. 2. It was still early and she was ready for work, including makeup. 3. My mom fucks that lady up every chance she gets. It's an older sister thing. Plus my mom is like five weight classes bigger. UFC weight classes. Like from bantamweight to light heavy, seriously.

"Yall clean up after yourselves in my house. This is MYYYYYY house!" She emphasized the "my," letting us know our place. All of us.

---

[1] It hurt me to even capitalize his name. Literally, I want to edit this book and... Forget the Green Lantern.

My cousins had made it to the party. They were cool. We never had any issues, per se. They just had a crazy old lady. You can't help who you're born to. I couldn't. They saw their mother tuck her tail. There was a chink in her armor. The feud was temporarily muted. No truce. Ever. Both of them are too prideful. It's a sister thing.

CHAPTER 4

Hole to Whole

The move to Chicago took a major toll on my mother. As you can tell, Aunt Sis liked to argue. They fought a lot when we lived with her. There was constant feuding over money, space, the way my aunt treated us, and a number of other petty disputes. sister stuff, I thought. But, I think it is more accurately titled, poor stuff.

The first argument I remember was the day my brother and I came home with brand new roller blades. My mom saw the stress that the move was having on us. Mostly me though. Although, Aunt Sis had her own choice spats with Chris too, I was the focus of a lot of her venom.

My mom was concerned about my sociability in school and wanted me to be more active and make friends. The good old goal of life was make as many friends as possible, even if they're not real, even if you don't know them, and even if they are just a "Like" sign and a two-dimensional profile picture on your computer screen. So, she went down to the school and signed me up to learn how to play the saxophone. Later on we went to the park district where she signed Chris and me up for a roller hockey league. Those two "hobbies" cost considerable sums of money that we didn't have at the time. Who knew having kids was such an investment? Parents.

Needless to say, when my aunt found out about the expenditures, she was livid. I still never understood the bartering situation in the house. My mom collected Link, or government assistance, which meant she funded the food for both families. My aunt paid the bills. It seemed reasonable to me. Still does if you consider feeding six people, three of whom are males with bottomless pits for stomachs.

Either way, when she found them, like usual she brought a roller blade into the living room where my mother and I were sitting and threw it on the floor causing a dramatic explosion and shocking both of us. Before I knew it, they were in the middle of one of their classic arguments.

"What is this? Every time I come home yall done went and bought something new. Lawd have mercy! We gotta get some rules round here!" Aunt Sis said in her normal duh duh duh cadence. She was always trying to "get some rules round here." She waved her neck and right hand in unison pointing intensely at the roller blade.

"What you mean what is this? It's a gift for my children. Yo kids have shit. Why can't mine?" My mom already knowing where this conversation was headed. Her eyes wore the exhaustion of three weeks' worth of anguish and impotence, probably longer, but all I could see was three weeks.

"Imma just keep looking for my own place. A peace of mind is priceless and I sholl caint find it here." My mother talked about peace of mind so frequently that her search for it held a certain charm.

I never considered the implications of her search. Why hadn't she found the peace that seemed to occupy so many aspects of her life? Looking back, her misery was masked by her burden. Her failed attempts at love were disguised by parenthood. She poured her all into us, and we were her peace. Her children's success held the fruition of her worth. Her freedom did not await her death, it simply awaited my maturation. I am her retribution. We are her redemption.

"Aint it? You act like I'm getting on yo nerves or something. Yall is staying in my house affecting my peace of mind, my children's space, and everything else of mine."

Aunt Sis paused and looked at me. Realizing I had no control over affecting her children's space, she barked, "Boy what is you still doing here?" I just put my head down and left the room because the truth was I didn't know what was happening and I really didn't want to be there anyway. In all actuality, I had been trying to escape their argument. Even in the other room, I still heard them. Their insecurities and the anger they aroused filled every inch of the space.

For a while, I dreamt. But Aunt Sis's gaze brought me back and I understood the misery of ignorance. *Why is this a problem? Does she not want me to play roller hockey? I don't even have to.* At that moment I just wanted *it* to be over but didn't really know what *it* was. So I left.

Living with Aunt Sis was hell on wheels. There were many times where her glance caught me in mid-movement as though she was trying to pierce through my skin as I opened the refrigerator, cracked open a new set of colored pencils to sketch, ironed a shirt, or walked out of the bathroom after making one of my cousins wait. One time she even locked the refrigerator. The resentment was palpable. I felt like I was wearing her eyes and still could not see myself. However, I never felt it from my cousins since they were just happy to have their older cousin in the house. They always wanted to play, especially Ashlene the youngest, who was seven. She would show me off to her friends and say I was her older brother. Calvin, who was nine at the time, always wanted me to play basketball, not because I was good but because I was big. He would also ask me to walk with him to various places because he was too young to go by himself. We had a mutualism. I was his means of mobility and he was my means of escape. Maybe we represented the same things to each other. I mean it has to suck having a crazy mom.

The last fight my mom and Aunt Sis had happened on one such day. After school, Calvin asked, "Jamal you wanna walk to the Soda Quota with me, please?" Soda Quota was the local corner store and I knew the only way he could go was if I went along, so I obliged. Plus it gave me a reason to stop my chore of washing the dishes.

Along the way, Calvin talked up a storm about everything he was looking forward to in the future. He talked about everything from becoming rich when he grew up to what he was going to say to Stacy, his new crush, when he saw her at school the next day.

"You know I'm going to Peoria with my dad this summer?"

"Oh yea, why is your dad down there?" I said, not knowing where Peoria was at all, or for that matter, who his father was. "Down there" just seems like the right thing to say when you don't know where something is.

"He got put in jail for somethin but nobody tell me fo what. I bet he robbed a bank or somethin. Somethin cool! Getting money or something," He paused, pointing guns in the air to shoot at some imaginary target. His slim frame was accented by loose baggy clothes.

He was in a white t-shirt, shorts, and some beat up Air Force Ones. That was the uniform at the time. Then, he continued after receiving the awaited laughter.

"But my granny stays down there and he gets out in April, my mom says. So I'm going. I just wanna get away from Ashlene."

At nine he spoke with the experience and aloofness of a middle-aged man. It was as if there was a ventriloquist controlling him. I heard someone else when he talked.

"Why is Ashlene stayin? Aint she going to see him too?" I was a little confused. I assumed that Ashlene didn't want to see him. She can be mean, especially when she feels ignored.

"We got different dads. Ma says her dad live in the city," Calvin said, pointing back toward the house. Chicago was back that way. From where we stood, there was a clear shot of the skyline. I was part of the city at that point. Cleveland Ave, the street we stood on, lead directly to downtown. The houses along the block framed the skyline. The triangular Hancock was the most visible on that day.

"Why I aint seen em if he stays so close?" I already knew the answer. Parents are stupid. Why have kids if you refuse to raise them? Why? "He don't come round much do he?"

"Ashlene aint seen him in a minute either. I don't know why though he stay right up there, somewhere. My ma says she's the father and the mother though, so I don't think bout it much," he said with a shrug. It was clear he thought about it non-stop. There was no way living in Black Creek, with all of these, supposedly happy, complete white families that he didn't feel inadequate.

"Guess you bout right. Me and Chris got different fathers and I don't know mine either," I said with the realization that I hadn't even thought about my father since I left Memphis. But I constantly wished Keith was there. I now empathized. Partially because we were in the same boat. Maybe that's not empathy. But whatever it is, I understood him. It isn't that hard to unthink someone who has never been there. Their presence is never missed.

Calvin's eyes rolled. He desperately searched for something else to talk about. Our conversation had turned quickly. He wanted to keep it going. "Hey Mal…"

We got to Soda Quota and Calvin spent about fifteen minutes searching for candy and drinks. As usual, Ibrahim, the son of the owner, was standing at the counter. When we went in, Calvin went straight to the back and got two pops for us. He then went to the candy aisle and got two packs of Skittles and a Snickers. He danced through the aisles with joy, his own beat playing in his head. He went to the counter and told Ibrahim to give him two dollars' worth of Fruity's. Ibrahim obliged with a nod and a smile.

"I see djou will be going to d dentriste tomorrow, huh little buddy?" Ibrahim said with a thick accent.

Calvin continued to look over Ibrahim's shoulder. He always asked for unnecessary conversation. Calvin simply ignored him and requested more snacks. Graceful almost. He paid Ibrahim who was bagging the snacks.

"Three oh sethen is djou change."

On our way out, Ibrahim came around the counter possessed, and grabbed me by the collar of my coat—violently.

"What deed you dake?" he said with a thick Arab accent. "I saw you!" Before I could say "nothing" or "something," he had already unzipped my coat and was feeling the pockets. He was a certified

Black Creek officer that day.

I hadn't seen Boubacar, the owner, sitting behind the counter at the time, but he jumped up to watch the spectacle Ibrahim was making of me. "Ibra!" he called followed by a couple of words in their native tongue. "Let the little boy go. He stole nothing." Boubacar's English was much better than his son's and he was right. I didn't steal anything. Not yet at least.

"This is why we have nothing now," Ibrahim responded before returning to their native tongue. "You let these animals come in and rob us. But not me," he ended the statement in English.

Turning to me with a tone of residual dissatisfaction, he said, "I know you. You little djieve. Tell djou friends too I know they think we no joke anymore. Djou try next time, and I cut off djou hand. [I] dare djou. Try to steal [from] here, see [what] happens."

Still a little startled but moreso angry, I snatched my coat from him. Everywhere I went I was picked on. I couldn't understand why I was unwanted. The confusion of not being able *to be, simply to be,* created a panic, a crisis. I couldn't be quiet. I couldn't be honest. I couldn't even be sleep. I wanted to hide but I couldn't for some reason. I felt like a brown highlighter. People couldn't help but see me. It was hard to reconcile this ostentatious nature with my unwanted presence.

When we got home, I cried. I wanted to lose my face in my pillow. *Why me?* Why couldn't I be a child? At that moment I fell into a reverie. My frustrations had peaked and I was no longer aware of my surroundings. I wanted someone to protect me. My vulnerability surfaced in that store and it had to be submerged once more. I could not disappear. I could not die. I could not roller blade.

I could not go to the store. I could not fit in with my classmates. The world was doing a good job of telling me what I could not do. But they couldn't stop my thoughts. So, I trained myself to escape. I taught myself to actively dream until one day, they became more than dreams. I dove into my bed, buried my face in the pillow, and fought reality. On this day, unbeknownst to me, my purpose was revealed.

MY BROTHER'S KEEPER: *Where was Keith?* Where the fuck was my brother? There! In the distance I saw him standing at a podium of some sort. It was fuzzy at first but I found him. He was at the altar. We were at our home Church in Memphis. What was he doing? We weren't allowed to stand in the pulpit. The choir couldn't even cross the pulpit on their way to their benches. But he was there. Keith was even delivering a sermon. His dark skin glistening as the beads of sweat formed on his forehead. Without missing a word, he took a white cloth and wiped his entire face, forehead to chin, just like Reverend Trueblood back home. The sweat still collected on the blue collar of his oxford shirt, but the intensity of his gestures let me know that it was of no consequence. He signaled to the right, requesting a glass of water, just like Trueblood. There it appeared on the podium. Manifestly. The condensation collected on the outside of the glass of ice water.

We were the only people in the Church. Where did the water come from? I didn't know who he was preaching to, whether he was preaching to me or for personal edification, like a true egocentric southern evangelical. But it seemed a bit much if it was just for me. I wanted him to come down and talk to me. I wanted to tell him everything that I was going through. I wanted to take him to Ibrahim at the Soda Quota and have him lay hands on that asshole—*hands*

hands, not the casting off of spirits.

But as I walked closer to the altar, I saw my mother standing where the baptismal pool would normally be. Instead of a pool, there was an aquarium which took up the entirety of the far wall. A shark tank. She stood in all white with her hands outstretched towards me. As I walked past Keith towards her, he grabbed me violently by the arm and with a reverential enthusiasm, recited a verse that we read often in bible school.

"If you don't know how, find a way. Because it is said in scripture that, 'We do not wrestle against flesh and blood, but against principalities, against powers, against the rulers of darkness of this age, against spiritual hosts of wickedness in heavenly places. Therefore, take up the whole armor of God that you may be able to withstand in the evil day.' You've gotta find a way . . ." His face was even more intense than before. The sweat from his lip flew off as he spoke, accenting each word.

Before Keith could finish the scripture, I pulled away. His grip had begun to burn me and my arm grew darker in the very spot he held. His fingers imprinted on my forearm like a brand. When I broke free, I ran toward my mother, thinking she would soothe me. Her language was not cryptic like Keith's, it was simple. Direct. Her love was not burdensome like Keith's, rather it was light and nurturing. She was supportive but clearly panicked about something. Her body was turned away from my brother. She was not listening to the sermon. Instead, her attention was absorbed by the aquarium. Looking to me, she could only point at the tank.

When I reached the staircase, which lead to the baptismal aquarium, I saw Chris flailing in the water. He was in deep and couldn't swim, literally. His face pressed up against the tank, struggling with his own weightlessness. The water wanted him to float, telling him this is not natural, not where he should be. But like all frightened people, our instincts make situations worse. Fighting the natural pull of the water, his body sank and sank. After a slight hesitation, I continued up the stairs, arms stretched anticipating my mother's embrace. I tripped on the top step, falling flat. The fall knocked the wind out of me, and in one gesture, my mother picked me up and said, "Aint no time for clownin boy. You the only one that can swim." With that, she pushed me into the aquarium to save Chris.

While I swam toward him, my mother gave an account of Adam and Eve, her favorite biblical tale. Her voice quivered as she recited the story.

"God made me of the rib of man. From hole to whole. First him, then us." She paused and repeated with an authoritative tone, "First him, then us."

CHAPTER 5

Exodus

"Jamal, Jamal," Calvin yelled.

"Yea mane. What up?" I said groggily. He was hovering over me. I hadn't noticed his presence

"I been calling you for forever. Want some hot cheese puffs?" he said, holding out the dollar bag of chips, not noticing my rapidly drying tears. His whole being smelled spicy.

"Naw I'm good. Where's Ashlene?"

"I don't know. Prolly in mom's room," he said with a shrug and a hint of indifference.

"Go find her. Make sure she don't get us in no trouble," I said, both wanting to get him out of the room so that I could hide my tears, and to honestly make sure I would not get in trouble. The searing smell of hot chips left with Calvin. When he left, I put my face back in the pillow trying to retrieve my life-dream. It was just getting good. I told myself I was going to talk to Keith this time, but my efforts proved unsuccessful. The moment was lost and my frustrations had disappeared. I no longer had a reason to dream. Something was different about the dream though. It felt real, so prophetic.

Aunt Sis got home before my mother that night. She came in and performed her normal inspection to see if we had broken anything in her "god damned" apartment. Looking up and down the house like a crackhead searching for a lost bag. Her nose almost touching every inch of the house in her thorough investigation. She had become a bloodhound. It must have taken her fifteen minutes each night. She stormed out of the kitchen with an empty pack of Skittles in her hand. She was a garbage digger.

"Who the hell bought these?" she bellowed.

At the time, she was standing in the hallway, adjacent to both bedrooms, and it was not clear that she was talking to someone in particular—me. I thought she was going to ask about the unfinished dishes, and this unpredicted line of questioning caught me off guard. I didn't know the origin of her instant hostility. She was more angry than normal. Usually she's mad about a slight irritation. This seemed bigger. Way bigger than normal. I heard rage but I wasn't scared. I wasn't even startled. Just caught off guard. Over several months of cohabitation, I had been conditioned.

Slowly entering the hallway, I turned toward her. Again, she was closer than anticipated. She was still in her work clothes. Her heels made her taller, but no more intimidating. Her posture was completely erect. She was even looking up at something in the distance. She was mad. Too mad to make eye contact. I could almost make out a tear.

"Why are you coming out of my kids' room, boy?" She was furious. Her voice quivered and her hands shook. Did I mention that I wasn't allowed in Calvin and Ashlene's room? I am also not allowed in Aunt Sis's room obviously, neither is my mom. Basically, I can go to the bathroom, wash the dishes, and sleep on a pallet. Fuck the refrigerator.

"You just in the mood to touch shit that aint yours today, huh?" Her tone had cooled. It had become accusatory. She broke her glare. I was staring a hole through her. She stooped down, making eye contact now. The light was behind her head, making her face shadowy. Still she was not intimidating. She felt impotent.

I didn't know which question to answer. So I simply told the truth after coming out of the room. "I just wanted to be alone for a second." I felt a little Nietzschean—existential. Her grip was loosened on me. She was weak. Her life was weak, and she hated me for seeing it. All I had to say was "No." All I had to do was reject her reality.

"I just wanted to be alone, Aunt Sis," the bass in my voice more apparent. "It won't happen again."

"You damn right it won't happen again!" She was yelling out of confusion. Something was different but she didn't know what. I wasn't a kid anymore. She continued on her rant. Holding the Skittles wrapper in my face now, she repeated louder.

"Who the hell bought these?"

"Caaa-l-viin ma'am," I was confused now too. *Why is she holding an empty Skittles wrapper? Why did she go through the garbage?* After managing to get the words out, I was on the floor from the sternest closed-fisted right hand I've ever witnessed and let alone, felt. I say stern because I've definitely seen and felt harder punches, but there is something about that unexpected blow that cannot be mimicked. My eye was on fire. I couldn't open it. Her little knuckles got right under my brow. That first blow, the unanticipated one, when you were still kind of saying something. Ouch! Also, there is something stern about any punch being thrown with the understanding that the other person cannot hit you back. Or so she thought. It's perverted to start an unfair fight.

I landed wedged between the floor and the wall, laying on my right side. Instinctively, I bounced back up off of my right arm and hip. I was in survival mode. I was tired of people touching me. I was tired of people. Grabbing behind her knees with both hands, I tackled her into the wall before we fell to the floor. There was a crater the size of Aunt Sis's back in the drywall. You know who got blamed for that.

My head hit the ground but I didn't feel it. The Skittles wrapper flitted its way to the ground shortly after playing in the air. Aunt Sis was pushing and scratching me at this point. I climbed on top of her after pushing her knee out of my chest. She was going for my eyes using her manicured nails as weapons. I grabbed her hands and forced them to the ground. She was helpless now, squirming on the ground, fully mounted. I was tired of her. But I didn't know what to do. Should I kill her?

"You lie! Don't you go blaming my son for this," she yelled from underneath. Her voice was hoarse. Breathing had become difficult. I didn't know what "this" was. Was it really that bad for him to have eaten Skittles or any of the other snacks? Still stunned by the shot, all I wondered was why she hit me, but I dare not ask. I still wanted to respect my Aunt.

"Who do you think you are going into my room?" she said with an accusatory tone. She struggled underneath me as she tried to breathe. Aunt Sis was kicking and bucking once more to no avail. Her room was off limits to just my mother and me. Everyone in the house but us was allowed to enter her room, even company, like we weren't family or something. I didn't even want to enter her room. As far as I was concerned it was the devil's lair, where all the evil in the world was generated: world hunger, AIDS, Scientology, cancer, the Illuminati...

I said nothing in response to her question. It still had not dawned on me that Calvin had stolen the money for the trip to the store. My cheek jumped with a not-so-pleasant familiarity. A knot was already forming. By now, I saw Ashlene and Chris standing in the hallway watching me. I still had not gotten off of Aunt Sis because I didn't want to. She was trying to spit on me and I couldn't have that. What a disgusting trait. She might take my getting up as an opportunity to hit me again.

"Chris, grab the duct tape," I ordered. I had a plan. Even more than myself, I knew Chris was waiting for this day. He had discussed a coup d'état so many times on our way to school. Chris sprinted to the kitchen and got the tape from under the sink. He had already torn three long pieces off before I could tell him what to do. We worked well like that.

"Get the fuck off of me!" Aunt Sis shouted, squirming more. She was a feisty little something. Not strong though. She tried to spit at me again. Then she tried to spit at Chris. He simply punched her in the mouth. She was running out of hydration too. Spitting itself was becoming a struggle.

"Why would you do that? We aren't going to hurt you. You're the crazy bitch," he said in a very calm tone. Unexpected. I saw blood coming from her upper lip. It was on her teeth making them pink. For the first time, I doubted my plan of action but it was too late for doubt. We were committed.

"Get up and be a mane boy! You took my money so face up to it. It's already spent just face up to it." She managed to get those words out as she choked slightly on the blood and spit in her mouth.

Chris placed the black duct tape around her face from the back of her neck over her gaping mouth. She was mostly mute now. It was difficult to make sense of her mumbles. Holding her hands and feet together, Chris then taped both. She was calmer now. A lot less squirming but her eyes were locked on me. Her rage was always on me. *I must look like a man she hates.* Maybe I look like all of the men she hates. I laughed to myself, but there was nothing funny about this situation. Well it's still a little funny when I tell this story at the family reunions. Aunt Sis still gets mad. But Calvin stole the money. She should've done a more thorough investigation. He still had the change and receipt from the transaction. Shit. He was holding the chips, hands and mouth a dull red.

"Why me?" was the only question I had. Of the four of us, why was she so adamant that I was the one who took her money? I haven't done anything wrong to her. In fact, I'm the only one who contributes to the house. I was the babysitter, the maid, the errand boy, Mr. Reach-it, and the thief apparently. Fuck that house.

It hadn't crossed my mind that Calvin still had not come out of the room. He was guilty but I was punished. I started to get up after Aunt Sis was fully arrested. Her mood was mellow now. Tame. Chris and I moved her to her room and swept up the pieces of drywall from the floor. Then we all went to Calvin and Ashlene's room in silence. We knew the truth. We all knew. There was no need to talk. I had done the right thing. I knew that too.

I am not sure how much time elapsed between the brief brawl

and the time my mother got home, but it felt like an eternity. We sat in silence. Every now and then Calvin would look at me, catch eye contact, and then look away. He wanted to apologize and I knew he would. Now wasn't the time though. The wounds were way too fresh. I mean, I could still feel my face swelling up. I wanted my mom to come home and protect me. I needed to lay my bruised eye on her breast.

Chris looked at me, then walked toward me. Placing his hand on my shoulder he whispered, "Go to the bathroom. She scratched you pretty good."

On my way to the bathroom, keys jingled outside the door. I got scared. I wanted to run into the bathroom but there was no time. The door opened and there was my mom. She was crestfallen. The bags in her hands dropped with a thud. When my mother saw my swollen cheek and cut-up face, she rushed to me and fell to her knees. Then she barraged me with questions. I couldn't answer them. I didn't have an answer. What was the proper way to explain what happened? My aunt fought me like an enemy, like "someone on the street" as people say.

"Did this happen at school? Why didn't the principal call me?" she expressed in a panicked voice. My mom had gotten a job at a bakery near my principal's home and they instantly became bosom buddies, at least that's what it felt like. She was crouching down at this point, holding my chin. Her thumb lining the left side of my face. She rubbed the bruise. Her hands were warm, and they felt good. It felt like I was already healing.

A sharp pain emanated when she got closer to my eye. I jumped away. "No ma'am," I said softly. I was partially embarrassed and, even more, I wanted to avoid the confrontation which I knew was inevitable. She was going to kick Aunt Sis's ass on my account. I knew there was no reason for any more dramatics that night, but that didn't mean there wouldn't be any. I've learned, people do not desire peace, otherwise they wouldn't seek bullshit. My mom simply wanted a justifiable reason to hit Aunt Sis square in the mouth. Chris did too. This was their opportunity.

"So who hit you?" She began to get impatient. I knew she would not hit me again though. She wanted revenge. Someone had harmed her cub. But I knew she wanted to hit me. She was frustrated. "There's always something," she would say.

Low and behold there is, indeed, "always something." She felt like I was lying to her by omitting my abuser. I was really trying to keep the peace.

"Nobody ma'am," I wanted to say something else because I knew lying would warrant further punishment. I just didn't know what to say. I didn't want her to find Aunt Sis taped up in her room. I just wanted to hide. But before my mother reached her crest of frustration with me, Aunt Sis came back into the living room. I was taken aback. She had gotten out of the tape. I guess Chris and I weren't the most sophisticated kidnappers, but I was surprised at the time. Looking back, it was probably very easy for her to get out of an eight-year-old boy's handiwork. Chris is funny. That is honestly why she probably stopped resisting. She was like, "These idiots. Tape?"

"Yall have got to leave my house. I caint stand this no more," she said, calm now. Her voice like a river. Her lip was swollen as though she'd been dipping chewing tobacco. It set out there fat. She spoke around her lip in a Rocky Balboa manner. Aunt Sis still had some of the tape on her ankles. Her hair was disheveled and she walked with a noticeable limp. She wore the attack as much as me and she still had to go to work tomorrow.

"That's fine with me but who put they hands on my son?"

My mother asked rhetorically, quickly deciphering the answer to her question. Once again, she assumed the posture of a proud lioness, as she stood back to her feet. Her chin was high, shoulders back, and nose flared.

Aunt Sis put her head down. She was ashamed and insecure.

"It was an accid—" but before she could get it out, my mother tossed the coffee table, which was between them, aside, shattering the glass tabletop, and pounced on Aunt Sis delivering devastating blows. I did not know my mother could move so fast. I was so shocked, all I could think about was the type of fights they had when they were younger.

My mother honestly had the footwork of a Lyoto Machida. She bounced in and out on the feet. Aunt Sis was unprepared. She dragged Aunt Sis to the ground in a headlock, their bodies landing with a force that knocked the wind out of Aunt Sis. Once again, Aunt Sis was mounted. The second time in one day. That's low key impressive. Go team. But before she was able to hit her again, I threw myself over Aunt Sis's face and chest. Laying there, I wondered why I hadn't been hit. My mom stopped while Aunt Sis lay beneath me crying, jerking as she sobbed. She rolled over underneath me. Her shoulder pushing up on my chest as she rolled. None of us had the wherewithal to move. All three of us temporarily inanimate because what happened was too much.

Then she shouted, "Get out! Get out!" No one moved. After

noticing everyone's stagnancy, she yelled once more, "Get out of my house! Get out!" We got up slowly and cautiously. Not trusting each another's movements. Aunt Sis's insecurities were back but there was no one to call. We hesitated.

By now, Calvin had come out of the room. He wore his guilt as naturally as a smile. Maybe he was smiling but I didn't care about him. In that moment, we weren't family and I could have killed him. He let me take his punishment. Fuck him. More yelling followed the reanimation but it soon grew late and energies became exhausted. It's funny how fatigue brings clarity. If not clarity, it at least blesses us with neutrality. Aunt Sis realized what she was really doing by kicking us out and offered to let us stay. In her sluggishness she saw the error in putting out her sister and her two nephews in the middle of March in Chicago. The simplest answer is normally the best answer, and fatigue brings that out of us. But what do I know.[2]

My mother, however, had too much pride to stay. She simply said, "You can keep your peace of mind." After her words peppered the air, we all knew their relationship was forever changed. I never quite understood why it hurt so much when she wrote someone off, but it cuts like a razor. I think it's because her disdain is tangible, you really feel it. She is permanently crestfallen because those who are

---

[2] Maybe that's the secret to life. Exhaust all energies and resources, be on the verge of concession and defeat and then, and only then, will you realize what's truly important. Unless you've driven until the wheels fall off, you will not know how your car works. You must drive until your car is barely a car, until it is almost unrecognizable. In the same way, you must live until you become an animal or a god. We must live until what we stand for has caricatured us to the point of beasts or deity. Or you could just live and be human around other humans. Whichever you prefer.

supposed to love her treat her worst of all. With each trough, she loses faith in this world. The failure of the world has become her emotional burden. In this way, she is unmistakably feminine. All of those emotions were condensed and transferred when she cut a person off. A complete loss of faith, a questioning of humanity.

In the short time that we lived with my aunt, there were many explosions but none as visceral or relationship altering as this one. My mother's countenance changed significantly. I didn't know why at the time, but I came to find out that the fight was not simply about Aunt Sis hitting me. A couple of months after the incident, I learned that earlier during the day, my mother discovered that Keith had been arrested for possession of drugs. In retrospect, it makes perfect sense and is in alignment with my mother's character. Whenever she seems to be overreacting to an incident, there is always something more. But at the time, all I knew was we were moving. I knew Calvin hadn't been punished and whenever we saw Aunt Sis in Church afterwards, there was a profound tension which only she tried to hide.

For the two months before we moved into our own place, we stayed with Ms. Yvette, a young white woman who worked with my mother at the bakery. We lived out of large plastic totes. We had strangely enough become very accustomed to this mode of existence. Always prepared to pick up and leave. In fact, in the time that we spent at Aunt Sis's, we never fully unpacked. The night of the incident, it was extraordinarily easy for us to move out since were never truly at home. This genuinely affected me. Even in my familial space, I didn't feel welcomed. For the longest time, I had to build my house wherever I was. I became an emotional forest and the calluses of construction show, not simply physical scars, but most profoundly in my temperament. My arrogance was birthed through a forced and premature independence. I wear the stretch marks of my forced growth with pride.

Yvette was a younger woman, probably ten years younger than my mother. She was a perfect circle, just as big as she could be. She had a long mane of hair, maintained with the utmost decadence. She constantly brushed it like she was trying to get waves. Even though she was white, her skin was the color of a manila envelope, with a little more sheen. Most importantly, her immaturity was always on display, especially when she spoke to her children. Being around her, you could feel she was forced to deal with adult situations before she was mentally, and to an extent spiritually, prepared. She had eight daughters, the first of whom she gave birth to at 12:43 a.m. on her fourteenth birthday. She loved to tell people that. I found it weird. Even at the time, who brags about being pregnant at thirteen. Only three of the daughters lived with her. I always found the orders of the three confusing. For me it would only make sense to have the youngest three or some other consistent pattern. But Yvette only had custody of her first, fifth, and sixth born. What a crazy white lady.

CHAPTER 6

The Arc of the Covenant

We showed up to the police station on Cermak, near China Town. It was eerie. Not a soul was there.

"Nobody is here. Do we proceed?" Shannon called over the two-way radio. I hesitated. Looking at Bill as he drove the tank, I wanted to abort. We were so close to completing the covenant. But I had no clue. All I wanted was to go back home with my brother but that was no longer a possibility. We assumed a posture of war. There is no anonymity. All retreat must be tactical.

"Proceed!" I shouted back. "Proceed. We are ahead of schedule. Making great time."

Bill looked at me. "It's a trap, young sir. They're going to cook this goose if we run in there recklessly." He was a beret alright. I needed him for that. It felt off but I had no tactical experience, except for a bunch of war video games. They made me feel like a soldier. But in this time with bullets flying and bombs exploding, I was at a loss, relying on God. Running into Billy was divine intervention.

I looked to heaven. "I have supported myself thus far. I need a little help." Shannon checked in once more. His voice was strained.

"Proceed with the plan? You sure?"

He felt the same way as Bill—something was off. He called once more after a moment with no reply. His tank was approaching the east wall of the police station. The plan was to force our entry and grab Keith from his cell. Shannon was thirty seconds from plowing through the wall.

"Blackbird, it's now or never!"

"What do I do now?" I shouted, looking up. Bill looked up with me. Time paused. The tanks stopped moving on their own. Bill attempted to drive but the tank was halted. The engine growled but there was no movement. We jerked slightly forward like we were about to take off—but nothing.

Two people came toward each tank. Four people in total. They were dressed like Egyptian pharaohs. From the left came two women—slender, long, and chocolate. Their hair was cut low. Atop their heads were tall crowns with gold and purple jewelry adorning them. Their dresses flowed, draping their elegant frames. The purple and gold of the dress was only outdone by the gleaming gold sickles regally held in their left hands. The sickle floated as they walked toward us. I heard Shannon and Chris now on the radio. They were scared.

"I can't move. My body is frozen," Shannon called over the radio. I couldn't speak. My stomach was tight. I couldn't breathe. The tank felt like it was boiling. My ears were on fire and all I could do was watch.

The men approached from the right side. They too held staffs. Their crowns were purple and gold, except theirs were fashioned like lion's manes. They flowed, draping over their shoulders. Gold armor covered their shoulders and chests with purple chainmail holding it all together. I was about to pass out. My chest heaved. I exhaled. I lost sight of them. The hatch bust open. They were on top of us. All four of us were packed tightly in the tank. Bill turned around. He moved freely. He was unaffected.

"What have we got here?" He said without regard to the divine presence in front of us.

I looked into their faces. They were the same. One was masculine. One was feminine. But their features were the same. They moved in unison like synchronized swimmers. Each stood tall. She was slightly shorter than him. Their skin was dark and shiny. Their features indistinguishably indigenous. They looked like Black American Indians by cheekbones, noses, and mouths. I caught my breath. I didn't have anything to say.

They dropped their sickles in unison and began to speak. "We are the Lord your God."

Shannon's voice came over the radio again. "I knew God was Black!"

God continued to address us all. "You have done exceedingly well with the life you have been given. We do not write things down as your people think. You chose your path and it was just. You fought against evil spirits and wickedness in positions of power. This is why you have the privilege of seeing Our face. The faith you have shown does not go unseen or unrewarded. Continue along this path and you will receive heaven in this life."

I listened. Their voices sounded like a chorus. There was a harmony of voices that rang into my ears and filled my spirit. I was completely filled.

"What do I do now? Is this an ambush?" God looked through me. They smiled smugly, in a way that only God can.

"Hell yea, it's an ambush. Where could every cop in the district be right now?" Bill snapped in my ear before God could respond.

"The enemy is waiting on you inside. We have judged their souls. Their souls are tarnished. They have rejected humanity. Once the signs reveal themselves, you will be granted entry into the station and your brother will walk free. We have sole dominion over life and death."

God continued to reveal Their vision. I could see what was to be done without words or direction. Bill, Shannon, and I sat in the divine presence watching the future like a movie. It was simple. The struggle. Keith's spirit. Hope held out in his heart. The future required us to be chaste and to listen. We had to listen intently to the signs of God.

My Father and Mother reached out their hands. She reached out her left. He reached out his right. The gold bracelet gleamed in the dim lighting of the tank. I reached back. I grasped His hand. With my right hand I grabbed Bill's rough palm. He gripped tightly. Bill took Her hand into his completing the circle. They spoke to us.

"The world spins like a roulette wheel. In the beginning, Black is on top. The spiritual world is king. In the middle epochs, white holds the odds. The material world is out of balance. But soon Ethiopia shall spread her noble wings."[3]

Their words and voices sang a melody. I exhaled for what seemed like the first time. My chest felt empty. I listened. I understood. I was

---

[3] Invisible Man

scared.

"We are your guide in this life. Follow Our direction and never turn your face away from Us. Your path has been revealed." Bill held tighter. In that moment, others appeared. I knew them. We were familiar. They were the Prophets. All of them: Jesus, Moses, Muhammad, Mary . . . they were the chorus. The Messengers. Their mouths moved in unison with God's.

"Be swift and decisive in your steps. To you is the victory. For no weapon formed against you shall prosper. You belong to Us, and your soul will return to Us when we call it."

The tank jerked forward then stopped again. All was returned to present. Shannon shouted, "What's the next move? We are getting closer." He hadn't seen the vision. I thought we were all there. I wondered if Bill had seen it but there was no time.

"Left. Make a hard left. We have to wait. This is a trap!" I said, knowing he didn't care. We were almost there. Keith was seconds from being free. He was also seconds from being dead, depending on how we played it. Shannon turned late. Too late. He ran into the wall causing a crater-sized hole. He exposed wires and plumbing. The Hulk rolled on. We were in pursuit.

"What now? We just keep moving?"

We just keep moving. That was the vision. We circle. Just circle. "Yep." I thought of how to tell him. He hadn't seen where we were going.

"Shannon, we are going to circle the station for . . . uh . . . for three days."

Shannon shouted through the radio. His sarcasm and rage rang through the tank. "Circle? For what? We have to be at Soldier Field,

Chris is waiting for us. We have no way to communicate now!!!"

We needed to take action. The tanks might run out of fuel and be nothing more than million-dollar caskets. We needed to circle. God showed me the Way. But how could I show them the signs? We had gotten to the front door of the station. They could kill my brother any second, but we needed to circle at a steady pace with faith for three whole days. Starting with Shannon at the lead but he was irate. God hadn't shown me this part. I guess this was the work.

"Are you with me?" I shouted back. I had nothing else to give. I was scared too. He wanted more. I couldn't explain. There was no time. Was Bill really there with Them? Was it all a vision? How could I tell Bill and Shannon what I saw? There were so many gaps.

"Are you with me, Top Dawg?"

I called for Shannon's allegiance. That was all we needed. He trusted me. Without replying, the M1A1 tank took off fast. He was angry. Very angry and probably confused. As I was. Bill said nothing. Shannon crashed through the traffic on the street. The cars had been abandoned. Luckily.

"Slow down. We have to go at a steady pace, or the fuel will run out." Shannon again did not reply. He was angry but couldn't touch me. He wanted to fight. I could feel it in him—like we were of the same blood.

Shannon slowed down. The hours in the tank seemed like days. Nobody tells you how hot it gets in those things. We couldn't use the air conditioning for fear we would run out of gas. The day was winding down. Nothing seemed the same. The streets were torn up. Cars left everywhere. Downtown was evacuated. It was a ghost town. But we knew the police forces were in the station, ready to pounce on us, and we didn't have enough firepower to hold them off.

As we drove around, we looked for movement inside the station. We tried to plot where they were holding Keith in the building.

"I just want to bust down those walls. I'm tired, hot, and hungry," Shannon's voice came through the radio. He sounded fatigued. We'd been riding for just over a day. If the situation was less intense, the heat alone could have turned us around. It was becoming hard to breathe. But at least Shannon wasn't housed with a shitty homeless man.

"Stay strong. Stay strong." I was running out of motivation as well. The hunger was affecting me the most. Bill's overwhelming smell was turning my empty stomach. We'd exhausted all conversation. At this point, we sat in silence memorizing the route around the building. One right turn after another.

When we reached the halfway point, the sky changed color. The dust was in the air from the previous day's damage. The sky held the grayish blue of the destruction. Like the changing of hue in mixing water colors, the blue gray gradually turned to a deep purple. We continued our route as the sky transitioned like a desktop screensaver.

"These are the signs of God. Stay close to the faith. God's plan is almost revealed." I shouted through the two-way radio. Then the sky grew pitch black. The darkness spread from the center and crept outward. It sealed all of the light. All was blotted out. We were driving from memory.

At the same time, the sky opened from the center, as though someone unzipped the darkness. A gap was formed. Moments later, light flooded from the center. The light guided our path. It shined on the tanks. The heat was lifted from us. All discomfort left, including

Bill's fecal odor. We continued to ride, able to see once again. God was pleased. My stomach filled. I was satiated.

Four dark hands reached out of the sky. Each hand belonging to God. They grabbed the police station lifting it from its foundation. Debris fell from the building as the exposed concrete and wires flitted in the air. God shuffled the building like a Rubik's Cube—each floor and window shifting up or down at God's whim. As They manipulated the building, bodies fell to the ground hundreds of feet below. I could hear them yelling and landing. Their bodies crunched with impact. Bodies scattered about the tanks. We mowed them over. I could hear the officers yelling for their lives. It was too late to repent.

"We felt your weariness. We have given you this sign. We control life and death. All rewards and punishments come from Us. Fear none but Us. Listen to none but Us."

The faces of the Prophets appeared once more. Their voices in unison. A chorus. God replaced the police station. It sagged now. The darkness left. It was morning again. One step closer to fulfilling the covenant. We encircled the station. Our laps were smaller now. As we traveled around the building, each complete circle shaved off layers of brick, insulation, and concrete. After six laps, the building was completely exposed. We could see through the structure. On our eighth lap, the station continued to breakdown. A toilet fell from the third floor and hit Shannon's tank. Shannon halted, thinking he may have been under attack.

"You're clear. It was a toilet," I said, releasing my first laugh in several days.

"I can't. The tank stalled on me." It jerked forward. Bill pulled up beside it so the tanks were next to one another. The building toppled. I didn't know what to think. Dust filled the air. My brother! Where was my brother?

"Top Dawg!!! Shannon!!! You still there?"

"I'm here. We need to find—" Before he could finish, an army of men appeared in the distance. Fear overcame us. I heard Shannon's heart beating. Our hearts were in unison. The Army had arrived. The dust dissipated and we could see them more clearly. The Prophets were carrying Keith's bruised body. Malcolm X under his right arm. Bob Marley under his left. Nina Simone held her hand on Bob's shoulder.

My brother was free.

CHAPTER 7

From Dust to Dust

*M*y mother had a knack for finding young mothers who were searching for guidance and a little emotional support. She would often barter. She gave her parenting services in exchange for their (generally government-sponsored) material resources. The women formed a mutualism, each depending on the other with an unwritten contract of indebtedness. Of my mother's relationships, these were the unhealthiest and least sustainable. But they proved to be the most useful. These relationships served as bridges, never letting us drown in times of hardship. Keeping our head above water, making a way in the rain. Temporary layoffs. Good times.

"Did you get a newspaper on your way to work today? I gotta look at them apartments," my mother would say as Yvette settled in for the night.

"Naw, I forgot. We'll just figure it out. Tomorrow is Saturday anyway. I can just drive you around to the spots you done called already."

Yvette had a car, which was a huge perk. Even though it was rough fitting two adults and five kids in it.

"Yea, besides, we gotta go grocery shopping anyway. I got my Link for the month and Jamal can watch the kids while we out tomorrow." My mother would offer these two services for the aid that Yvette was giving.

"Jamaw!" she yelled.

"Ma'am?" I said, knowing I had been given another duty. I wasn't too concerned at that point. Yvette and her daughters were cool. The oldest one was cute. She used to let me kiss her when they were gone. She was a year older than me. I was only in charge because Yvette didn't trust her—for good reason. She was wild.

"You gotta wake up early tomorrow because me and Ms. Yvette is goin to run some errands in the morning. You gotta watch the babysit."

The words came out wrong.

"I mean watch the house, and make sure don't nothing happen." She smiled at me with a wink of her eye. She wore blue eyeshadow and kept thick mascara on her eyelashes. The wink was a bit creepy, but I had gotten used to her awkward gestures.

I was simply happy to be somewhere I was welcomed. It was nice being out of Aunt Sis's house and not being a burden. Family aint always blood.

"Yes ma'am. How early?" I said, knowing I was going to be up for Saturday morning cartoons anyway. My motivation for getting up so early on Saturdays was two-fold. First, I loved cartoons. Second, it was the only time I ever had to myself. I would have a huge bowl of Fruity Pebbles and watch the Ninja Turtles, Twin Dragons, Beast Wars, and, with some regret, Pokémon, with no distractions. Beast Wars was obviously my favorite. I mean, what's better than the combination of robot animals?

My mother didn't answer. But Yvette just looked at me curiously. She was admiring my responsibility but, in fact, she was preparing to launch an uncomfortable conversation for any pre-pubescent boy. Don't trust women when they get to staring, it is never a good thing.

"Boy, you don't never put up no fight. If my Ma was giving me all them commands at your age, I woulda been pouting and fussing and arguing and slamming doors," she said in one breath. Yvette had switched to her Black voice. I never understood why she wanted to be down so bad.

She paused for a second and continued, "You gonna make someone a good husband one day. You got a girlfriend?"

There it was. Why did it matter? She just didn't have anything else to talk about. I had my mission. Get up and make sure nobody dies— done. I should have left after "yes ma'am," but I trusted the stare. Thought she wanted to fuck. Nope. Don't trust the stare.

I didn't know the right answer. I didn't have a girlfriend. I had a crush, though.

"Yes ma'am," I said, trying not to extend the discomfort. Having a girlfriend felt like a status symbol. I wanted status. But I was unprepared for the questions to follow. She tossed them at me like a ninja wielding throwing stars. A barrage of questions hitting my shield, some getting through to slice a little flesh here and there.[4] Now I know the right answer to dissolve a conversation like that is "Um, I don't know." Actually, there is no right answer, and there

---

[4] It was then that I grew to hate questions. All types.

may not be a way to dissolve conversations with women. Questions, questions, questions.

"Is she white?" Her tone became serious. It was weird coming from her. She was clearly white but her daughters were all different shades of brown from tan to mocha. She had pictures sprawled through her house of all of them. Yvette talked about them nonstop, although I only ever saw the three. She was white. Why would she lead with the . . . the race card? It made me uncomfortable. The race card is ours. Somewhere along the line though, I think white people took it back. Maybe it was when she had those mulatto babies. "Is she white?" I repeated in my head. That's how they get us. My mother was burning a hole in the side of my head with her piercing gaze. At the time, I didn't know what else to do, so I told the truth.

The truth as far as the crush was concerned was, "Yes ma'am."

My response sent a crushing blow to both Yvette and my mother, which they hid with humor. Their faces went from shock to comedy once they made eye contact.

"That's what happens when we send our kids to they schools. All the good ones go to the other side," Yvette said.

She spoke of the "other side" as if some universal code had been violated. But she was white. My transgression was not one which warranted punishment but moral judgment. I had committed treason and my self-respect was the victim. But what about all of the guys who had slept with Yvette and left? Had they committed the same treason? Or were they alright because they left a white woman to be a single mom? I was confused. Her younger daughter, Tara, poked her head around the corner. She was the darkest of the three. Tara was nosey. She came into the living room and walked through the dining room to get to the kitchen. She took the longest route possible. Her objective was simply to eavesdrop. She didn't even come back with anything from the kitchen.

"What's her name, darlin?" Yvette said with a smile.

I knew immediately I shouldn't say anything about her original comments for two reasons. First, the longer she talked about it, the more aware of my mother's sentiments I became, making me feel uncomfortable and guilty for my fake relationship. The sharp end of the lie had become pointed at me. The more it was referenced, the more wounds I received, and I didn't want to prolong the anguish. Second, I didn't want her to open a new line of conversation likening me to her exes or others who had done her wrong. Honestly, I think she started the conversation to talk about herself. Women are funny in that way. By twelve, I was aware of the numerous scars which lie just beneath the surface of the conversation. More than anything, I wanted to avoid being clumped with the others who had hurt her. I couldn't bear that guilt too.

So I simply said, "Mel."

"What's her real name, boy?" my mother snorted.

She was growing more irritated. She really wanted to know. Yvette was asking the questions that she wanted to at heart, but we were dealing with so much materially that there was no chance to have these types of intimate and intimidating conversations.

"Melanie," I said reluctantly almost in rhythm with her question.

"Oh lawdy, she's real white. Girl, what you think?" Yvette said almost comically. Holding her mouth as she laughed. She loved to hide her teeth as she laughed. I think she was self-conscious. Her front tooth was slightly chipped. Nothing major, but enough to cause insecurity, I guess.

My mother woke from a deep period of introspection to say, "Well Jamal, as long as you're happy baby, that's all I care bout." I sensed a "but" coming. "But I sholl do wish yo happiness could be wit a girl who looks like me."

That was her concession. It was as comforting as hitting your funny bone. I knew then as I know now, I could not be my mother's redemption with a white wife. "You can't talk Black and sleep white," as the old folks would say. She did not want to raise someone else's husband. My wife must be a representation of her. From hole to whole, in His image. The declaration had been cast.

This was my first encounter with the phenomena of white women, but it was definitely not my last. I didn't understand it at the time and to an extent, the situation is still a little fuzzy to me. How could my mother send me to a school with three black girls in my class and expect an inherent race loyalty? Success, failure, education, love, and even vocation have to all be tailored to this skin. It's a beautiful thing this skin. It comes with a lot of responsibility. Someone should write a book, *Responsibility of the Oppressed*.

The next day in class, I was unhinged at the prospect of having a white girlfriend. The girls stopped looking so inviting. Their faces opened while mine closed. For the first time, I saw them without seeing them. Not because they hadn't been there, rather because I had been defined. I knew where I was in relation. I was feeling a sort of existential repositioning and that reassurance is priceless. It's peculiar how transparent people become when you view them objectively, without desire or expectation.

Class went more smoothly. I became more aware that Mrs.

Wells, too, was a white woman. Her face was also opened, exposed. I think part of the humanizing affect was that Yvette was white. I was living with a white woman and her white children effectively. Because I now recognized our common humanity, I participated more and was less intimidated about giving a possible wrong answer. I knew they could be wrong. Yvette was wrong all the time. She was even wrong about Mel. They were different humans. No worse or better. Different. Yvette was too.

A wave of love washed over me. The bond of Melanin. My family had been defined. I knew all of the possibilities of this life. My legend was already written.[5] I didn't think about my classmates anymore because I knew the possible relationships we could have were limited, disparate. I never really wanted friends because they would never be able to come to my house. I would never want a girlfriend, at least not a white one, because I just knew. I knew it wasn't right. I couldn't take her home either. So the day was going well. I felt freer than I had felt at any point since being in Chicago. My mind wasn't on her or him. It was on me and what I wanted out of it.

To prepare us for middle school, Reagan initiated a block class schedule. We had four classes a day: Science, History/Social Studies, Mathematics, and English. We would go to gym, music, and art once a week, respectively. On Tuesdays, we went to gym. If there was one thing I loved about the school, it was their gym. We could play anything in that gym. They had rope climbing, a rock-climbing station, basketball courts and tons of basketballs (good ones),

---

[5] The Alchemist

footballs, baseballs, softballs, badminton sets (complete with shuttlecocks and all), tennis equipment, Wiffle balls and bats, wrestling rooms, and all types of other stuff. There was so much to do at the school. Often at the end of the day, while waiting for Chris and my cousins, I would just be a twelve-year-old boy in there: climbing, jumping, falling, shooting, hitting, landing, missing. I was a verb. I was able to be alive in the gym. I didn't need a kid around me for miles to play. The gym was humongous. It was big as hell with high ass ceilings and shit. They had everything a kid could want, except personality.

"Duck!"

"Brrrrr, you're out!" Ms. Sornon blew her whistle, telling Corey he was out.

This specific Tuesday, we played bombardment. It's kind of like dodgeball mixed with basketball. Foam footballs, nerf balls, dodgeballs, and all the other soft balls are placed in the middle of the court. There are two teams and the objective is the same as dodgeball. When a player gets hit, they sit out. But if they catch the ball, the person who threw it sits out. However, if I am hit and my teammate catches the ball after it hits me but before it hits the ground, I stay in and the other person is out. The goal is to make a full court shot into the other team's rim. If the ball hits the backboard, then one player is released. If a ball gets thrown and it goes into the basketball rim on the opposing team's side, then everyone who was out on your team comes back in, and the person who shot the ball is hero for the day.

"Toss me a ball, Jamal!" Kristin called out to me. I was surprised she knew how to pronounce my name.

We had been playing for a while, and my team was losing badly.

Kristin, Will, and I were left to play against eight or nine people on the other team. Kristin was in the cool sixth grader crowd. I think her and Will might have dated at some point, I don't remember. I would remember if I was privy to such information. But I wasn't. So fuck them too.

I wasn't sure whether Dom was in the game or not and if he was, it was puzzling how he had lasted so long. At times, I wasn't sure whether he was alive or not. Dom was like 5'6" and bordering on three hundred pounds. He never said much and was like a blob in class, the only way I was sure he was there was because of his smell. It wasn't bad necessarily, it was distinct though. He smelled of mop water, lemon juice, and mayonnaise, if I recall.

There was one day, earlier that year, when I was sure he smelt like death. It seemed inexplicable at first, but soon the smell of shit hit me and the entire class. Our seating was arranged in alphabetical order and on the seating chart, Dominic Cristoicic was three seats away from Jamal Dale and I smelt every molecule of the fecal matter. I thought he was dead cause I only heard of people releasing their bowels to that extent when they died. You know everyone has a little follow through from time to time, but full out dookie, uh-uh.

The wildest part about it was that he sat there until the final period of the day, barely breathing, not noticeably blinking, or drawing any attention to himself. Then he raised his hand and asked to be excused. "Mrs. Wells, can I go to the nurse?" he asked without emotion.

I couldn't tell whether he was in or out. He was the biggest and slowest target in the game. If he was in, how did they miss him? Outside of being shocked that the biggest target in the room could perhaps still be in the game, I wasn't concerned with anything but the basket. I wanted to save my team and be hero for the day. I slipped the balls gracefully, allowing the poorly thrown balls a bounce and letting the others sail by. It was about moving your feet. They never aimed where you were going, only where you stood. It was weird. Like none of them ever played a sport.

I picked up a foam football, eyes locked on the net of the basket, I tightened my grip around the backend of the ball, cocked back, and I slung that ball with every muscle in my body. At the point of release, I felt the pressure of a dodgeball, which must have held a brick inside the way it connected. I had been hit. The ball hit the right side of my face, knocking me off balance as I followed through. It bounced high off of my forehead and Kristin, who was either strategically or cowardly, depending on your opinion, standing behind me, followed it in the air and caught it.

Based on the rules, we got one more student. Head shots were off limits. Besides that, Kristin caught it before it hit the ground. In one instance, Eric from the other team was sent to the sidelines and one of our players was brought back in. A number of balls were thrown in my direction. I dropped to the court. My torso hit first, knocking the wind out of me and releasing a premature exhale.

I searched for a ball and jumped back to my feet. I found a small dodgeball. It had some weight to it.

"Don't throw any more balls on their side!" I declared the new strategy to my teammates. The other team exhausted their reserves, and we held all the balls. I planned to get all of our team back in the game. Once they threw all of the balls on our side, there was a look of confusion on their faces. Then I slung the small dodgeball at the basketball rim, changing my reference point. The ball sailed over the backboard, bouncing off the wall, hitting the back of the glass, and finally falling dramatically to the ground. Kevin picked it up and held it. They had adopted our strategy—now it was war. Attrition.

Will, seeing my plan, yelled, "I got your backup! Don't worry about them throwing the balls at you! Just make the SHOT!"

He was holding two balls, one in each hand. Jason who had just come in, echoed Will saying, "Hit the shot, Jamal!" Kristin had relocated to standing behind Will, so our plan was foolproof as long as I made the shot. As long as I made the shot.

I grabbed a slightly larger dodgeball and set myself up in the middle of the court. There was intense pressure as everyone in the gym was watching me. All of the balls were on our side. Kevin was standing there waiting on my move. I hurled the ball with a major arc hitting the ceiling. The thunder of the impact reverberated throughout the gym. The ball shot like a laser from the ceiling, smacked off the square behind the basket, hit the front of the rim, shot up in the air once more, and fell directly into the basket without touching the net at all. All that could be heard was the boom of voices from the sidelines and the pounding of feet on the wooden court as my teammates returned to the game. Kevin launched the ball that he had been holding onto toward our side and Lindsey, the first person out of the game ironically enough, caught the ball and sent him to the sidelines.

There my team stood. We held all the balls, had the advantage numbers wise (like twenty to six or five by now, Dom had been hit), and we let it ride. I could have sworn Will had a Tommy gun, Gatling gun, rocket launcher, or something attached to his arm. He was sending the other team to the sidelines at will. He was throwing the balls like a major league pitcher. Everyone was throwing.

I got hit on the hip by an errant ball and looked up to see Eric, who had come back in after one of his teammates caught a ball, pointing at me and screaming, "You're out! You're out!" like I didn't know that already. He was excited. So I simply jogged to the sidelines and watched my team destroy theirs, sending them away one by one. Every now and then, my entire team would look over to me making eye contact. There's nothing like being on the winning team, as a matter of fact, there's nothing like victory period. Winning together always creates a bond.[6]

I rejoiced at lunch in my own happy solitude. Will decided to sit with me for the first time. The fifth and sixth graders ate lunch at the same time, and I always sat with two black fifth graders listening to the happenings in their class but more often than not, tuning out their conversations about the latest CD or movie. The two boys (Jason and Nathaniel) were currently engaged in an argument about their crushes. They couldn't decide who liked who and who stood a better chance with whom in their class. So Will and I were in an oasis of silence filled with white noise—literally, white noise. White people making noise.

We didn't talk much, in fact, we had never talked before. There was simply no interest before. I had come to the conclusion that he was a character though. In the silence, I analyzed him and how weird I thought he was. He hovered over his food while I stared at him. His bangs dangled over the lunch his mother packed and all I could think

---

[6] The Detroit Bad Boys are the best example of this.

about was how he managed not to get the spaghetti sauce in his hair. It was quite a spectacle. His bangs swayed pendulum-like over his meal and not one strand ever made contact. Back and forth. Back and forth. It was like watching a dog step around his own mess. The bangs were in a tenuous spot.

He was a blank canvas for me. My thoughts wandered, and all I had were questions because I knew nothing. *Why is his hair like that? Did his parents let him do that?* Yes, in fact, his parents had allowed him to cut all the hair off of his head and leave a set of bangs long enough to tickle his upper lip. He looked like, like all those girls with the undercuts.[7] *Why are his pants so big? And why doesn't he ever take them off?* He wore elephant pants or rhinoceros pants, I don't remember what they were called. They were these massive denim concoctions that served no real purpose other than to drag the ground. Each leg was about the size of four normal legs. The back heel of the pants was tattered and rode the floor like the train of a wedding dress. Even in gym he wore those pants, accepting the reduced participation grade for not putting on shorts. He wore those pants every day, the same pair. The weather didn't matter. Summer, Winter, Spring, Fall he had a ball. He did everything in those pants. As an adult I'm amazed, but as a kid, I was disgusted. *Why doesn't he talk?* One reason for the strained lunch dialogue was that Will normally sat alone at lunch. He never spoke really. The only class he participated in was Music and it wasn't clear why because he was always wrong, at least according to the teacher, Mr. Nemis.

---

[7] You know, the Rihanna undercut. Like, it looks great on her. But she's Rihanna. You know?

One time, Will made Mr. Nemis so flustered, he got sent to the principal. It was unheard of at Reagan Elementary to be sent to the principal's office. Nemis was giving a presentation about music genres. He had a fancy slideshow prepared. Like always. He never taught. We never played instruments. We just took notes from his decadent slides with the most obnoxious animations. He spent so much energy on the animations as if they helped us learn. After going over the most popular genres of music and their respective histories (Rock, Classical Rock, Heavy Metal, Soft Rock, and Jazz), he asked the class, "And the top five most popular genres of today are?"

Nemis stood at the front of the class flipping the purple highlighted bangs of his salt and pepper hair. The room was dark. The projector shown bright against the whiteboard. In the shadows you could still make out Mr. Nemis' thick black eyebrows on his pale skin. He waited on the answer to what seemed to be a rhetorical question. We all waited for an answer.

Will filled the awkward void. "Reggae! Reggae has to be number one. People all over the world listen to it."

Will never raised his hand. That was sort of his thing. Nemis stared at Will the way he always does. Will just wanted to play instruments like all of us. Nemis hated it for some reason, instead forcing us to learn the history of music and the origin of cultural instruments.

Nemis's response was classic. "Now everyone listen to me closely . . ."

We all leaned in waiting for the epiphany he was going to reveal.

"Reggae is absolutely not a genre of music. Reggae is a religion started by a bunch of drug addicts to promote anarchy."

The class seemed to look back at Will. Waiting for a response. He delivered.

"Reggae is not a religion. Rastafarian . . ."

Nemis did not let him finish before dismissing Will with a stern finger pointed at the door.

"You cannot preach about a pothead religion in this class!" he shouted. "Take your belongings and head to the principal's office." Nemis swung his bangs to emphasize the seriousness of discussing a "pothead religion." He still didn't look at Will.

To put this in context, Will was the O-N-L-Y kid Mr. Nemis ever put out of class. Nemis hadn't so much as shaken his head at another student. Grabbing his bag and putting his "belongings" away, Will made it swiftly to the door. Turning the handle, Will managed to sneak out a final cry.

"Rock and Roll has more drug addicts!" he shouted on his way out of the class.

We looked back at Mr. Nemis. First, I heard a couple of snickers. Then the entire class was cracking up, except Nemis. He was stone cold.

But the real question beneath all the others was, *Why had he chosen to sit with me today? What made me more inviting than the white students who I'd never really seen him talk to?* Will looked up and saw me staring at him. He immediately looked back into his lap, or wherever his eyes were, I couldn't see them for the bangs. They were his shield. He hid behind them. Unlike Will, I was comfortable in the silence. It was probably the second-best part of my day after gym. Simple silence, then I had to go home to chaos, personalities, and emotions. But I knew he would think something was weird if I didn't say something after our incidental eye contact, so I initiated the conversation.

"Where'd you learn how to throw like that? You play baseball or something?" I said, wanting to let him know that I was okay with him sitting there.

"Uh, I don't know. I just throw." He was happy that I had spoken but hesitant to show that he wanted to talk. Instead he waited for me to continue the conversation. It was a natural pause. His eyes were going back and forth between me and his plate.

"Do you play a lot of video games or something? Get your forearms stronger? Cause you was slingin them balls." I just wanted to hear him and pass the burden of conversation. Questions help do that. I thought if he said he played video games, we could talk the rest of lunch. He surprised me.

"Uh-uh, I play the drums though. Me and my dad play together." He paused again. This time to think. "We don't have a TV in the house."

His participation in music class now made sense. Waiting for a response and getting none, he continued. Most people find it weird when a living room is void of a TV. At this point, the two black fifth graders were listening. The no TV thing really got their attention.

"My dad, uh, he sings and plays the guitar. He wants my little sister to learn how to sing so we can have a family band. But I don't know cause I kind of like it being just me and my dad. We don't even know too many songs, we just play," he stopped.

"I play the saxophone," I lied. I didn't play it yet. Well, I owned a saxophone, but I didn't know how to play it, at all. Remember, my mom bought it with the roller blades. I didn't know much about music or how long I could keep up the conversation. That didn't matter though. I figured he'd be able to talk up a storm about playing the drums. I wondered how different the drums and the saxophone really were. Even to this day, I have an inexpressible amount of admiration for anyone who can pick up an instrument, or any object, and make it make music. Especially the Bucket Boys.

"Oh really. You should come play with me and my dad. We could have a jam session." He tossed his bangs back with his hand and smiled. I thought it was peculiar that he didn't want his sister to play, but immediately invited me. The concept of a family band like the Jackson 5 or even Hanson would be cool. Right? Even Hanson.

Our conversation about music continued until the end of lunch. When we were about to go back to class, Will invited me to eat lunch at his house the following day. I told him I would have to ask my mom but probably not. I did not want to be popular. I did not want to have friends. Friends meant obligations, feelings to protect, and all sorts of other requirements. I didn't want anything to do with the friend rush. I just wanted to grow up and be left alone. Plus, I was still getting over the whole white girl thing. What would they say if I had a white friend? What were the rules about dealing with white people? I was confused and didn't know how to feel. Emotionally stranded. I really wanted to go to Will's house but how could I? Wouldn't that lead to me meeting his sister? Wouldn't I meet his mom? What if they were cute? But Yvette was white. It doesn't make sense. I should've been able to have a white friend. Yvette was my mom's.

"I could have just one," I whispered to myself.

The day went on like every other, untouched. Mr. Bell, without fail, said some variation of my name every time I raised my hand. They did not even always start with a J. Jeremy. Jimmy. Jermaine. Kamal. I read aloud in English and the class giggled every time I got to a bad word and skipped it. I really didn't know what to do. We were reading fiction for the first time and there were some questionable words. So I skipped them. Others took this as their opportunity to curse in class. But I thought it was stupid. I didn't need to curse in class.

In Art, Krystal was my wheel partner. Her pottery made me look ridiculous for even trying. She was a master of the wheel. I couldn't understand it. Still can't to be honest. She knew how fast to turn the wheel or something. But at the time I was blown away. We were going through the exact same steps, but without fail, my wheel work came out looking like trash. Every piece was a vase of some sort. Cups became vases with handles. Ashtrays became short mouthed vases. I was terrible. It was always misshapen and the dimensions were off. If I tried to make a vase, it turned out looking like a troll cup. It was all bad.

But it was not until the end of the day that this day truly began to reveal itself for what it was—a chair in the doorway.

Right before we were dismissed, I was cleaning up the workstation, putting away the unused clay, washing off the wheel and tools, and dumping out the clay sponge water. It was really a difficult task. Clay was everywhere. Under my fingers, in my hair, my ears. It was bad. Krystal always acted like she was helping me clean our station, but her assistance was a front. It normally consisted of passing me the rag, picking up the tools, or asking if there was anything else she could do. Of course there was. She could've emptied` the water, rung out the sponge, cleaned the wheel, literally anything.

Her primary concern was making sure her work wasn't mixed up with the others in the class, and that she had thoroughly gotten every piece of clay off of her manicured fingernails. Her nails were always painted some fluorescent color. She was a really bright person. Constantly matching her blouses, shoes, and the rubber bands on her braces to her nails.

On this particular day however, Krystal chose to help me clean. Not only did she clean, she sang too. I couldn't make out the tune, probably didn't know the song anyway though it sounded pretty nice. She interrupted her singing to ask, "Why do you always clean up?"

"I don't know. I guess cause you don't," I said, not knowing if it was the answer she wanted. The comment felt mean so I looked back down at the tools covered in suds between my hands. They were sharp, and I had already poked myself twice that day. I remember because one of them managed to draw blood.

"Makes sense." She paused a second to read my face.

"You never ask for help either. I would've helped." She moved closer to reach for the water bucket. Reaching across me, she spilled a little on my lap. "Ohhhh, I'm so sorry."

I ignored it. In fact, I saw it coming. She reached aggressively and imbalanced the water. Water is always seeking level. I continued the conversation.

"To be honest, it just aint a big deal. We never talked about anything else, why would I talk about needing some help from you?"

"Maybe it would be better if we talked from now on. We do spend all art class right next to each other." She said it with a duh face. Like I should have known to talk.

"I don't know. What do you talk about?" Until this moment, I had not considered the possibility of her having thoughts, at least not original ones. To me, Krystal was a tall, slim, braces-having, Abercrombie-wearing, fad-breathing, teacher-schmoozing, white girl. But today we were talking. One conversation really can make a world of difference.

"Normal stuff. You know? Stuff people talk about. What kind of stuff do you talk bout?"

I wasn't pleased with her answer.

"Normal stuff too. Just not the same normal stuff." My mind raced searching for a subject that she might find interesting. All I could think of was her nails. In retrospect, I guess I didn't find her too interesting, at least not at first.

"Like what? I listen to you sometimes and you never say anything specific. What do you talk about?"

"What do you want to talk about?" I said naturally. "Why are you listening to me?" This too, I said naturally and somewhat jokingly. "I talk about a lot of stuff, I guess."

"Liiiiike?"

"Like . . ." Thinking of something you like to talk about at twelve years old can be pretty hard. "Like, art. I want to know why my pots don't look like yours." That was probably the most honest thing I said all day.

"A lot of reasons. You use too much water, you spin the wheel too fast, and your strips of clay are too thick." She delivered the list of all the things I did wrong with ease. She had been watching me.

"My parents are artists and own a gallery, so I know a lot about clay. Not that I want to. I just do." She said dismissively. I really didn't know what a gallery was at the time so I just nodded.

"Maybe you could show me how to do it next time. Sounds like I do every part of it wrong." I really wasn't prepared for the barrage of pottery critiques. My thoughts centered around her omission. How long had she been watching me and waiting to correct me? Why didn't she tell me before that I was so terrible? She could have saved so much clay that year.

"I will. It won't take much help I promise," she said with a smile.

At that moment, Krystal's best friend Monique, one of the three black girls in the class, called her over with a smile. I figured the conversation was over and with good timing because I had run out of things to say. The perfect distraction.

"Maybe it will make the class go by faster if we talk too," she said as she turned toward Monique. I hadn't expected that last comment. For a moment, Krystal wasn't white. It caught me sort of off balance. I was still wrestling with the conversation I had the week before with my mom and Yvette. Maybe I could have two white friends, I thought.

As she walked away, I thought about our conversation. I thought about Monique's smile. I thought a little bit. I was calculating and putting two and two together. The only conclusion I could get from two and two was that Monique had a crush on me. Mind you that two and two is the series of events. So let me break it down to you. Krystal does not talk to me for say two, three, maybe five months at this school. The first time she talks to me it's about nothing. Then her best friend comes over, cheesing at all this fineness, and breaks up the conversation. So you tell me. How else can the situation be seen?

I walked out of the classroom excited about (the possibility of) a new crush while at the same time questioning its validity. I didn't know what to do about it. I was nervous and I knew I was going to have to talk to Krystal again. She was my Wheel Partner after all. *She should have never said anything to me. I should have never said anything back to her. I shouldn't have to deal with this. Girls.* Twisted thoughts ran through my mind. I didn't know whether to be happy or not. Allusions kept throwing themselves at me. I never knew if they were worth following. I mean, I should have talked to Monique not Krystal. The time spent, well . . . it was time spent.

I made it to my locker drama free. Got my books. Put my scarf, coat, hat, and gloves on. It was freezing outside, the middle of December in Chicago. I went to the playground to wait for Chris. It always took him a really long time to get ready. The little kids had to wait for everyone to use the bathroom, go to the lockers, and then be walked outside in a single file line. I could have just gone to his class and gotten him, but I would get hot, sweaty, impatient, and still have to wait, so I chose to wait outside.

On my way out the door, someone grabbed my shoulder. It was Will. He said he had been looking for me but that I had "zipped off" after class. I knew he was lying because I was the last one at the lockers, but figured he just wanted someone to talk to. After school was the strongest example of social circles, next to the lunchroom, of course. When everyone was leaving, everyone was talking. If no one was talking to you, you weren't everyone. It's a pretty trying social experience. That is if you care. I was cool with no one talking to me. It was that sweet spot, right before Chris came out. I enjoyed it. Will wasn't so comfortable. I was cool with that too. Since he lived across the street, I knew he just didn't want to go home yet, and I had some time to waste so we walked to the playground.

The school had a pretty cool playground. A gazebo-type platform sat to the far left from which the rest of the structures stemmed. There were monkey bars attaching the gazebo to a taller landing from which sprouted a slide on the adjacent side and a rope bridge on the other. The slide lead to the wood-chipped floor of the playground while the bridge went directly to a zipline station. Across from the zipline were the balance bars, which stood next to a strip of swing sets. So many swings. There were so many swings. So many, that I never saw them all full at once. Decadence.

When we got to the playground, there was a huge crowd around the balance bars. The crowd formed a large and oblong circle. From far away it was hard to figure out which way they were facing. Will sprinted toward the crowd. I walked briskly behind him. I was in no rush to see any more spectacles. Besides, I assumed it was a fight with the cheering and jeering of the crowd. Will was really eager to know what was going on. He worked his way to the middle and I lost sight of him. Deciding to take a different path, I chose to climb up the zipline station. It had a ridged wall with a knotted rope leading from it. I climbed and watched from my perch up high. Surprisingly, I was the only one to assume a bird's eye view. Everyone else stood trying to look over the next person's shoulder, fussing, pushing, and trying their best to gain a better vantage point.

It turned out I was wrong about Monique. She was standing on the parallel bars, one foot on either bar, facing Nick, a tall, braces-wearing, acne-having, nose-picking, unappetizing, whine-about-everything type of white boy. She was facing him with obvious intentions of kissing. But it was stupid to be on the bars in the middle of winter trying to walk toward one another and touch lips.

The walk alone was treacherous. Each of them looked like a baby giraffe getting its footing. It was obvious that two steps into the idea, both realized how ridiculous it was, but they had to follow through because of the crowd. As the crowd pronounced so they did. It was probably one of those *A Christmas Story* style triple-dog-dares. They worked their ways closer and closer and closer, for what seemed to be five minutes. Inch by inch. Step by step. But I know it was much shorter. Both of them shaking on the balance bars. Their arms stretched out reaching for each other and their butts poked out searching for the ground, the gravity—counterbalance. It seemed like an eternity had passed. Waiting for a kiss, a kiss that you know will be disappointing, for any extended amount of time feels more ridiculous than the kiss itself.[8]

Suddenly, Will popped up out of the crowd. But in his rush to get through the herd of shoulders, he became part of the exhibit. Will was front and center. Somehow, he'd managed to work his way right between the parallel bars. He was standing directly in between Monique and Nick. Noticing the disturbance, someone in the crowd, Krystal, pulled Will's hair. Feeling the tug, Will swung around, knocking Nick over. He sent Nick rib-first into the steel bar. Nick's side hit the bar, causing him to go limp, hands flailing. His body ricocheted as his head hit the adjacent bar. His blood was shed immediately. Nick folded over in pain on the ground, holding his sides seemingly ignoring the gash on his head. Monique jumped off

---

[8] I mean even at a wedding, the ceremony is like 15 minutes. But the reception though. If it ain't open bar, you playing games.

of the bars and joined the crowd from what I could see. But Will, noticeably bewildered, and it wasn't just the long bangs hanging in front of his eyes, stumbled out from between the parallel bars. Someone tripped Will, sweeping his foot from behind, and he fell forward. I lost him as he became part of the crowd.

Now, just an aside, I did not expect what came next. I really didn't see him getting tripped coming, but I definitely didn't *not* see it coming either. It was in the realm of possibilities. I mean, something had to happen in response to Will knocking Nick off the stage. The crowd was waiting to see a spectacle. Will interrupted it. Now Will was the spectacle. But what happened next, I didn't think people did to one another. Now I know different.

Nick briefly recovered from his injury and after feebly getting to his feet, he jogged toward Will and jumped on his back. He held Will in a rear-naked choke. Blood poured from the gash into Will's hair, drenching his bangs. The top of Will's head turned a strange brownish-red. He blinked as blood rushed into his eyes. Will swiped up at Nick's arms. He tried to wipe the blood from his face but his attempts were useless. Nick dragged Will to the ground as Will's legs kicked in the air. He was riding an invisible bike. The elephant pants hung loosely and waved like flags in the wind.

Even this I was ready for. But it wasn't until the first anonymous foot came out of the crowd toward Will that they erupted. People started kicking wood chips in Will's face. Some of the feet came directly at Will's head. They came down on him with book bags, fists, boots, instrument cases, and whatever else could be weaponized. They didn't care who they hit. Nick even took some (non)friendly fire. Nearly a hundred people flooded toward the center. It was like seeing a donut fill. The mood of the crowd had completely changed when Nick hit the ground. It was like they saw the blood and turned into savages. The event that had been intended to make them happy, blush, giggle, spread rumors, and gossip, made them violent. Their spirits had risen to a point of lustful rage. They acted as one now. All of their hands and feet became one weapon.

Nick managed to get up. Will hadn't been so lucky. Hundreds of feet came down on him. I began to feel the chill of winter. It was December and hadn't snowed yet. I wasn't too eager to see snow if it had to accompany Chicago's type of cold. But the chill ran through me, tasting my marrow. I watched them stomp Will. I watched them stomp him until the snow came down. I watched them stomp snow out of his life. I watched these "students" violate William Breckner. I watched these hundred children become murderers that day. How could I have seen that coming?

Their feet stopped moving in unison, they became quiet, motionless, as if the news of Will's death hit all of them at the same time. They were one in his blood. Like the Jews and Jesus. I say news like they weren't the actors in his death, but the way they responded, it seemed like news. It shocked them. Their own actions shocked them. They only wanted Will to pay for ruining their entertainment. They acted like someone else had done what they had just stopped doing. Like they weren't themselves three seconds earlier. Their spirits sank together.

With a collective conscience, the students closest to the body reached down. They elevated Will's lifeless body above their heads. Like a musician crowd surfing, Will's form was passed through the mob. They placed him, minus his spirit, atop of the monkey bars.

The communal denial of their misdeed began.

I waited on the playground until every student disbursed, save Will of course. Will was there. I was there. It didn't take long for them to leave. In the time it took them to collect their thoughts about what they had just done, they were gone. Not one stayed to help. All of them, gone. Thousands of footprints blotted the snow, trailing off in every direction. Nick even pushed Will's lifeless body off of him in disgust. He didn't want any part of the tragedy.

In their steps you could see mingled traces of Will and Nick's blood. I was afraid to come down. Afraid to know for real what I had known for fake. So I sat there and watched the snow slowly delineate his form. I sat there unmoving, too scared, too dumbfounded, too underprepared for what I had seen. I sat there and watched Will's lifeless body become buried in the snow. I wanted to tell someone. I wanted them to know why and how he died. Instead, I watched their sins be covered by the virgin snow, never to be mentioned. Never even to be reasonably addressed.

I didn't know what to think. Against my better judgment, I wanted to wait for him to move. He had to get up. I waited but nothing happened. I waited for nothing to happen. All it did was snow and snow and snow. The wind whistled, mocking me, daring me to move to find out the truth. But I was not going for it. I was too scared.

Finally, the chill became unbearable. I climbed down from the zipline station. I jumped down. My legs had fallen asleep after dangling off the edge of the zipline for who knows how long. I couldn't feel my feet from the cold. But neither ache had my attention. A dull sensation traveled from my feet to the back of my neck. I ignored it. I wanted to go check on this lump under the snow who I had briefly known, but I found myself unable to look in that direction. So I tucked my head deep into my coat searching for a kernel of warmth.

By this time, it had become dark. Streetlights lit my path. I was fairly sure that Chris, Ashlene, and Calvin had already gone home. But most of all, I hoped no one blamed this on me. A part of me wanted the snow to swallow Will's body. Not out of malice toward Will but to protect me. To make sure no one and nothing was able to be traced back to me. God owed me that. If not God, someone somewhere with some ability to govern others owes me that, and just possibly a little more.

I was granted that blessing. The murder never found its way to me. In fact, Reagan Elementary covered it up. Before class started in the morning, the body had been moved. I made sure to walk past it. Although I couldn't get myself to look at it the night before, curiosity made me peek this time. I didn't tell anyone that night. In fact, I had been almost a mute. But I needed to know, did it really happen? As far as everyone was concerned, it did not. But I saw it. I know.

I came to find out later that Will's family was notified of his death that night. The school district said his death was the result of faulty playground equipment. Their official incident report stated: *The deceased Will Breckner (13) received fatal head trauma as a result of a malfunctioning zipline mechanism.* In response to this allegation, the school district filed a lawsuit on behalf of the Breckner family against the manufacturer. The school got a complete overhaul of their playground area. If it was nice before, it became immaculate after the renovation. The Breckner family received a seventy-five-million-dollar settlement. But as for me, it was back to school as usual, minus one classmate. But for Reagan Elementary, it was a time of mourning. Several lectures, a number of revivals, and a seance or two were held in honor of William Breckner who, quoting the principal, "Met his demise far, far, far too soon."

I encountered a very similar situation later in my life. Except this time it was on the South Side of Chicago at Fenger High School. The case involved a kid named Derrion Albert. There were some students in an actual fight, maybe or maybe not gang related, and Derrion was killed. Knocked out and stomped. They stomped the life out of him too. They beat and stomped him relentlessly. However, the snow was not stomped out of him. His murder did not cause a meteorological event to occur. No, he was stomped until his killer was exhausted. He probably would have been stomped a little bit longer had they been further from the school.

He was stomped until Jesse Jackson spoke, until preachers gave witness, until Fenger was closed. Derrion got killed and it brought more police, more stereotypes, less education, incredible amounts of publicity, and did I mention, a dead kid. Oh yeah, and it put some kids in prison because some asshole decided to record the fight instead of using their smartphone to call the cops. Will was killed and his family became $75 million richer and the school got better facilities. Disparities.

CHAPTER 8

The New Covenant

"*We* do not negotiate with terrorists," the general stated. His posture had changed drastically from our first meeting. The very first time he reminded me of this country's understanding of negotiation. If you ask the United States for anything, you have just become a terrorist. You remember when MLK was a terrorist? Then they killed him.[9]

He was stating this as dogma now. He didn't believe it anymore. The plagues took all the fight out of him. This last one especially. Surprising enough, they didn't change when the sun was blotted out of the sky. They didn't concede when the Great Lakes dried up. No. He was still pushing. They were still sending the general to talk to me with the same jargon. They didn't get it.

They didn't believe me when I said they were acting against God. It was not my will or even my plan that was being disrespected. The signs were not enough for them. How did I tear down the police station? How had I manipulated the weather? I had no power over life

---

[9] Who's the terrorist?

or death. It was Them. It was God. But he was starting to see. Not believe—but see. God was behind New Africa. He was still far from believing though. He still thought it was a magic trick. The sun had not shined for five days now. Each time the government refused God's will, a new plague befell them.

"We just don't," he finally looked up at me.

The Melanoid Nation surrounded me on the fifty-yard line. Citizens were still migrating from all over the country. Every moment of every day we grew. I saw a face in the crowd. She followed my eyes and waited on my words. It was Simone. Her eagerness for the movement was shown on her face. Her energy glowed. I turned to Billy who was standing behind me. I wanted to introduce myself. I wanted to tell Billy to go get her. I was nervous. She made me want to be a gentleman. She made me want to come right.

"You do not understand," I stopped, witnessing pure rage covering his face. He hated when I said that. All of them do. He still maintained a level of arrogance, some intellectual superiority complex. This is why I'm a terrorist. I waited for him to interject, but he didn't.

I was no longer focused on the General. Simone had aroused my interest. I remembered her scent. I wanted to speak to her on the train. I couldn't let this opportunity go.

Raising his right hand to his brow, he wiped backward, removing that annoying hat with those repulsive colors of "freedom." So I continued.

"This is neither a negotiation nor are we terrorists." The Nation cheered. I was not hooked to a mic, but it was like my voice echoed through the entire stadium. Everyone under my voice cheered. The general even smirked a bit. I searched for Simone's voice in the crowd. *Wait. I don't know what she sounds like.* My soul longed to find out.

"What would you call this gang that has killed thousands of innocent children? You are the worst kind of terrorist!" His anger came out. I saw it boiling. His face was flush red now. He had no facial hair. His entire face was shown. I had never seen his hair. He had that standard military fade—black, with white sideburns. He was graying. Before he could speak, I was overwhelmed by how unnecessary his presence was. There was no person to talk to at this point. The victory was ours. But I listened.

"You have murdered thousands and act smug..." I raised my hand, reminding him who We were. He understood. He stopped his allegations. We had been here before. But he was irritating me. I only wanted my Queen and she was yards away.

I stood up to find her. The General was confused. Pushing him aside, I walked into the crowd. They parted like corn rows. A clean part. I lost her among the Nation. I turned back to find everyone watching me. The General was frustrated. The Nation waited for each step with anticipation. She was lost. I wanted to yell for her. *I don't even know her name.*

I walked back to my seat at the fifty-yard line. As I ascended, the crowd filled the gap. I took a mental image of Simone. I imprinted everything about her, from toe to head, into my brain. Her legs walked from one mental hemisphere to the other. She wore a pencil skirt with African prints of women carrying dishes atop their heads. Her breasts perched in her black top. *She is perfect.*

"If you are correct, General Nash, tell me, what do you have to negotiate? What collateral do you have to offer?" The nation wanted to cheer. As I heard a number of claps, I raised my hand as I had become uncomfortable with the praise I was receiving. Every chance that I got, I tried to remind the members that we were a nation. Melanoid empowerment was the creed. Therefore, all praise was due to the Most High. But they didn't get it either.

"We have commanded your presence be removed from New Africa. As you have seen, if you stay, unholy terror will befall. But I have killed no one General. I do not have the power to turn darkness to light or life into death. Only They do."

"Please . . ." again, his demeanor changed. He was everywhere. It was clear he was under a number of pressures. The first being simply wanting to survive and second being his newness to the notion of being powerless. "Please, Mr. Dale, please."

I laughed audibly. He was unamused. He humbly put a handle on my name. "I haven't slept in three days. My children are sick and you know that I lost my oldest boy last night. We cannot live this way." I was unaware of his loss though I warned him of the plague.

I listened. I waited. They answered.

"When you return home, your eldest son will be alive . . . He will be well . . . but do not take this as a miracle. It is not . . . this is your ticket to leave . . . if you return, your entire family will be damned."

My words came in one breath. It was not my voice this time. With a large inhale, I looked around the crowd. Everyone, all eight hundred thousand citizens, was captivated. We were growing fast. Maybe too fast. Too fast to communicate the message.

The General looked back up at me. "But they will only send

another. They tried to nuke you two days ago. Just wipe out the entire city. They'll never comply. You're a ter—," he thought of his son. "You're a terrorist. At least that's how you come off. They don't believe you or your god."

"You will. Your son speaks. Go home."

With that, the General and his two officers left. They were the only "negotiators" that the government had offered up to this point. New Africa was five days old. We hadn't left our bunker at Soldier Field yet. The Nation was becoming restless. They wanted to explore our new land, our birthright.

As the Nation moved to let our guests out, I caught the sensation of her energy. It was warm, orange. I jumped up and ran toward the sensation. It grew stronger. But I could not see her. She knew I was on the chase. *I will find my Queen.* The thoughts raced. My heart beat outside of my chest. My head was on a swivel. Then Keith grabbed me. *Maybe she was a phantom.* "We need to talk fam. What was that all about?" It felt good to be called fam even though I had no clue what he was talking about.

I started noticing several things about the new community. First, there was no trash accumulating. Even though people were eating and there were mounds of leftovers each night, every morning it would all be gone. After a few more days, I noticed that people weren't getting sick. I thought for sure with so many people in these confines, some sort of contagion might spread. Nope, not even a case of food poisoning. It was bizarre. New Africa was becoming our home. She nourished us and took care of her people. Manifest[10] Destiny.

On day seven, the General returned with his officers. I was astonished. He was returning to bring good news, or so he thought. His men were escorted to the Council and the General was handcuffed. The look of confusion on his face was priceless. I was growing fond of the guy. He held some pretty redeeming qualities. For the life of me, I really wished he hadn't returned. But he was human and so was I. Therefore, we suffer, right?

I looked at him quizzically. "Was your son awake?" I asked. I needed to know. Why else would he return? He should have left. I wish he wasn't human. A dog would have left. A turtle even. But Nash. Good old Nash.

"Yes. Yes he was, oh Prophet."

The media around the world started calling me "The Profit Prophet." There hadn't been any communication between the Nation and the outside world. They had no clue how the citizens referred to me. Either way, that was sort of my name now. As the new citizens arrived, they brought news from the outside. Mostly news of terror and famine. But they also brought with them the fanciful tales of the outside world. One filled with those wanting to slander the movement.[11] They targeted me, of course. In the fable that had

---

[10] From the hand....

[11] Marcus Garvey talks about this in his letter from an Atlanta prison in 1925. He had an awesome understanding of time. You should check it out: "After my enemies are satisfied, in life or death, I shall come back to you to serve even as I have served before. In life I shall be the same; in death I shall be a terror to the foes of Negro liberty. If death has power, then count on me in death to be the real Marcus Garvey I would like to be. If I may come in an earthquake, or a cyclone, or plague, or pestilence, or as God would have me, then be assured that I shall never

become most widely spread, I was Mussolini, Amin, and Hussein rolled into one. They thought it was a genocide. Because of the proliferation of the title "Profit Prophet," the Nation had begun to refer to me as "Prophet" for short or for long. I preferred Jamal.

"Of course. You knew that! That's why I'm back!" He managed to blurt out. "I needed to thank you for using your magic to heal my son. It was amazing." He paused and fell to his knees. "Prophet, thank you so much."

"There is but One with the power to give and take life. I'm sorry you came back. But since you did, let's at least have a drink," I said, gesturing to the General and his men.

One of the best things about taking over Soldier Field was that there was a ton of well liquor. We left the field and took an elevator to the box seats. As the doors of the elevator closed, I felt Simone again. Faintly. Her vanilla perfume struck me for the second time. Then I saw her. My heart dropped. I reached for the button with arrows pointing in opposite directions. *Open, open, open.*

I looked back at the other elevator passengers. The General tried to spark an awkward discussion on the way up. I simply shook my head. The message was received. Once we got into the sky box, we sat

---

desert you and make your enemies triumph over you… If I die in Atlanta, my work shall then only begin, but I shall live, in the physical or spiritual, to see the day of Africa's glory. When I am dead, wrap the mantle of the Red, Black, and Green around me, for in the new life I shall rise with God's grace and blessing to lead the millions up the heights of triumph with the colors that you well know. Look for me in the whirlwind or the storm, look for me all around you, for, with God's grace, I shall come and bring with me countless millions of black slaves who have died in America and the West Indies and the millions in Africa to aid you in the fight for Liberty, Freedom, and Life.

in huge leather seats and looked out onto the Nation. The General walked over to the window to enjoy the view. We were still growing. At this point, the Council took our third census and we were at 2.3 million citizens informally. There was never a lack of food, drink, or space. People were able to sleep and live comfortably in the confines of our bunker.

I let the General pour the drinks. It was his choice of course. He chose correctly—whiskey. He poured drinks for all the members in the room. I chose not to talk about the inevitable. Instead, I wanted to enjoy time with my former adversary. The little time we had.

"What did he say when you saw him?" I asked the General. "I have never met someone brought back from the dead. What was death like?" I really wanted to know.

He doesn't get it. He still thinks I saved his son. "He said uh, he said that he was really scared. That wherever he was, there was no light, and it was really noisy all the time." The General paused and looked at me with wonderment. "I am losing it, Prophet. I am losing it. Why would you ask me? You sent my son to hell and you brought him back. Why are you playing with me?"

The General looked at me quizzically. Tears formed in the corners of his eyes. He really was losing it. I wished I knew what he was thinking. I wished I was there when his son awoke.

"Noisy and dark. Wow! Did he know where he was? Did you tell him?" I sipped my whiskey, ignoring the allegations that I had power over life and death.

The woodiness bit my taste buds. I reached for two ice cubes. It was slightly warm. Dropping the cubes in my drink, I looked up at the General. Everyone was now looking at the General. Again his face turned red.

"He knew, Prophet. He was scared. Thank you for bringing him back. At least Jonathan is safe and you saved him." He thought before continuing, "Why'd you want to have a drink? Just to ask questions that you already knew the answer to? I don't get it. I'm not the only one losing my mind."

General Nash sipped his whiskey and likewise placed an ice cube in it. No one else drank with us. They simply filled the room babysitting their drinks and listening to our back and forth.

"So we could have a very real conversation. Up to now, I haven't been completely transparent with you or your men. But it is time. Especially considering what you've done." I knew it was time to tell them. The General had damned the world. He misunderstood me when I said do not come back. "Before I tell you what you've done, why don't you really tell me why you came back? What do you seek to negotiate for? Remember, the Melanoid Nation does not negotiate with terrorists." I had a smirk on my face.

The General looked so confused, as if thinking, "What is he talking about? Why is he asking me so many questions?"

"You know why I am here. It is for the lives you took." He was trying to appear calm but was obviously desperate.

"News got out quick that my son was brought back. I couldn't go anywhere. People think I have some sort of inside with the Nation." He held up his fingers in air quotes as he said it.

"They wouldn't let me leave. The President contacted me on a conference call with the Secretary General of the United Nations. They told me to come back. They both lost their oldest too. The President kept calling for his oldest. Your president. He should be here too. None of this makes sense. The Nation? Why is your Black President dying with us?!?! I just don't understand."

Nash had several episodes like this. He couldn't control himself. I understood. He saw his son die and come back to life. He thought I had the answers. Several tears fell down his cheeks. He was human like me.

I chuckled. I never chuckle. But he was humorous. I wondered why he put the word nation in air quotes. He was becoming too familiar with me. Maybe I had become too familiar with him. It is that way with rivals. Either way, he chose to come back. I told him not to. He had damned his entire family without knowing it. All of those who shared the burden of Melanoid bloodshed. I chose not to think about his questions. The President was an oppressor. This wasn't a racial thing. It concerned power. He didn't deserve that answer. His mind was too small.

"What do you think will happen now?" I said, knowing what was expected of me at this point.

He fumbled around, looked at his drink, then he took an assessment of the room.

"We just want the children back. The President and the Secretary General both lost children too. We want the sun to come back. We want to negotiate now." He looked humbled. But this was not magic. I told him not to return.

I listened again, waiting for the sign to reveal and He came right on time. My body felt warm on the inside. It was ready. It was coming to fruition. New Africa was bourgeoning. New Africa was glowing. All of the citizens were in one accord. They listened to our conversation in spirit and acted accordingly. They knew. They felt the power too. The warmth. "The sun hasn't shined in seven days General. When you leave, the sun will be out." I paused thinking of Nash's son. I briefly saw their reunion. It appeared to me. I was choked up. The joy on their faces. The whole family. His wife overwhelmed with excitement fell to the floor in disbelief, sobbing and clinching their youngest child with a death grip. The General lifted his son's upper body and hugged his still lifeless torso.

"I do not control life nor do I have power in death. Only the Creators grants life and beckons its return to Them." I hesitated to reveal too much. I knew the General's heart was hard. So I fell back. "Um, I apologize for what you have done. You should have never come back. I wish you had believed my warning. There is no more time to negotiate. This Nation will expand soon and those who remain on the outside will be scattered and their tongues tied like a fisherman's knot. They will have no language, no home, no resources, no identity."

I saw the rage come across his face as I spoke. He wanted to stop me but couldn't.

"But . . . I told the President. I told him. There is no negotiating . . . I should have listened. I should have listened!" General Nash repeated himself, as if attempting to repent. There was no time for repentance now, just weeping and wailing.

I turned my head, looking quizzically at the General. "Because you returned of course, I told you your family would be damned. You didn't understand. Your family are all who oppress. Your children died before they could kill ours."

I looked down now knowing he still did not understand. We were still terrorists to him. The terrorized terrorists. Funny.

Warmness spread throughout my body. My vocal cords tightened. God spoke again. "You held the fate of your people. Now they must suffer for the bloodshed. We will start anew with this beautiful Nation. Please return and tell your family to repent. Tell the oppressors that all will be forgiven. Endure the suffering and grow closer to Him."

I knew it was time. I knew the covenant was going to be sealed when Nash left. God keeps all of His promises. "But for now, let us drink and enjoy one another's company," I said, feeling anxious about what was next.

"So there's nothing to do? That can't be."

Those were Nash's last words on the subject. We talked for another hour or two about life before the glory of New Africa. Nash seemed to come to an understanding by the end. He apologized to me for slavery, Emmett Till, lynchings, and "the whole cops killing Blacks thing," as he put it. I think he was apologizing more because I was hurt than because he thought they were wrong. But his heart had softened. He was able to listen. Now, there would be nobody to listen to. Rough.

Moving the Invisible Hand (The Creators)

*W*e have done well. The Downpressers have destroyed so many of our messengers. They have lynched, crucified, beheaded, and ostracized our messengers, turning their faces away from Us, the Creators. But this feels right. We have chosen the appropriate generation and the perfect messenger. The last are now first.

We walked around Soldier Field unbeknownst to this young nation of just women and men. Our prophets spent time weighing the hearts of all of the citizens. We have sent a messenger to every nation in every era and they have turned their souls against our messengers. Each and every one of them. The Downpressers now know they have sinned against their own souls.[12] My Husband, God the Father, and I have done well preparing Our children, those who believe, for the Promised Land.

Touching the hearts and souls of the citizens, the prophets

---

[12] The Holy Qur'an.

moved about the arena. There were hundreds of spirits moving about the population. My Wife, God the Mother, and I stand behind Our newest messenger, Jamal. He was chosen for many reasons, but mostly because he decided to seize his destiny. So many of Our children shirk their purpose fearing death. Jamal embraced death and the challenge of liberation.

We watched as Harriet Tubman walked passed the General. "His soul smells like a pigpen. Make me not even want to be near such a man." She exclaimed to my Husband and I. She took two steps beyond the General. "May I?" Reaching out her hand, she wanted to know if she could interject for Jamal. My Husband nodded. She grabbed his vocal chords, increasing the strain. Jamal looked off to the sky and spoke the words that Harriet fed his soul. "If you are correct, General Nash, tell me, what do you have to negotiate? What collateral do you have to offer?"

She released her hold on his vocal chords. "This boy here is a dreamer…" Harriet said, slapping her knee. "I saw all them thoughts jus now. He's a born leader. I wish I had him with me to free our brothers and sisters from that dreadful condition of slavery." Moving to the right, she continued to weigh the hearts of this nation. Harriet reached through Billy's chest with her right hand and Keith's with her left.

"Don't get no prettier than those souls!!!" Muhammad Ali shouted from among the crowd. "I done seen a lot of warriors in my day. Went toe to toe with em. But them boys got some fire in em."

We continued to watch. Interjecting when needed. The prophets worked to message the souls of Our nation, revealing to each their purpose and destiny in the Promised Land. Nina Simone had a special mission. She was purposed with the goal of finding Jamal's wife. She moved through the crowd weighing each heart like she was solving a word search. She navigated the crowd eliminating prospects like those distracting vowels. We chose her for this mission because of her immense knowledge of Love and heartbreak. Even in the hereafter, she still refers to Jamal's wife as his "lover," stretching the E-R like a white person saying nigger.

"I like her, she's into classical music, my first loveeerrrr," Nina retracted her hand. "But she is not ready for that young king. He knows himself faaaarrrr too well for her."

The General's words began to noticeably irritate my Husband. He was a self-righteous non-believer. Harriet was nice in saying he smelled like a "pigpen." He smelled worse than swine. His soul was saturated with the blood of the innocent. The spiritual currency he wasted for his country cannot be undone. He fought for the United States, without discernment, following the most wretched orders.

Muhammad Ali hugged the General. His soul towered over the much smaller man. Ali's arms wrapped around the General's spirit making it temporarily leave the vessel. He was not yet ready for the fire. "How many Vietcong he done killed for America?"

"Too many," we responded in unison. My Wife and I speak with one voice. "He will experience the fire. But now is not his time. He has to betray himself once more."

Ali released his hold on the General's spirit. On cue the General spat out more sin. "I haven't slept in three days. My children are sick and you know I lost my oldest boy last night. We cannot live this way."

"Black equality has always represented a dissonance for the white

American," James Baldwin mentioned to Marcus Garvey.

"Give them dee rope and dey will lynch demselves," Garvey said in response to all of us. "The work of our spirits shall be manifest in dis Black Man. You cannot shackle the mind of the Black Man. What he tinks is his business."

Garvey's spirit was lively. The fire inside that man when he walked Our earth was phenomenal. He, like all of Our messengers, was flawed. But his dedication to the movement and Black liberation is unmatched. It was like he knew the fate of the world without Our intervention. He is truly made in Our image.

We grew tired of the presence of these sinners. They were begging for their lives after hundreds of years of murder and genocide on Our chosen people. People who were kidnapped from their mother country and never given a fair opportunity to be human. My Husband and I grabbed Jamal by the shoulders. I placed my left hand on his shoulder and used my right hand to support the nape of his neck, he was my baby. Jesus, Our only begotten, joined us. Kneeling and placing both hands on Jamal's back, Jesus began to recite the Lord's Prayer. The conversation was over. We fed the final words to Our messenger. "When you return home, your eldest son will be alive . . . He will be well . . . but do not take this as a miracle as it is not . . . this is your ticket to leave . . . if you return, your entire family will be damned."

The General's thoughts raced. He was insecure because he had absolutely no control. It was almost ready. My Wife has grown impatient. But as surely as the sun will rise, this fragile man will sin against his soul and return to this place.

As the two leaders wrapped up their conversation, Sojourner

Truth found herself in the middle of the citizenry. Sojourner was face to face with a tall slim woman. Instead of placing her hand on her chest, she put both hands on her temples. Sojourner Truth jumped back. "She is me. But how God? She will give birth to this nation and she won't have to see any of her babies sold into that abominable state of slavery." We chose her to reincarnate because of the immense pain that she suffered in her life. She is a phenomenal woman, much deserving of this post. Looking at Us, the Creators, Sojourner was filled with gratitude. "Thank you for this second chance. A mother's love cannot be hindered by time. I am a woman and she is me. I bore thirteen children in my life[13] and now I will have a chance to raise them." Sojourner placed her hands back on the woman's head.

"Cheater!" Nina Simone shouted out.

Realizing what Nina was talking about, Sojourner Truth shouted "His WIFE!?! I am his wife." She was overjoyed. So much so that her own spirit amplified the essence of its duplicate in the woman. Her energy exploded throughout the arena. I focused Jamal's spiritual retinas to be able to capture the frequency. The sweet vanilla caramel smell of her spirit covered the field and draped over Jamal.

"I need a cigarette. Y'all got me hot," Nina Simone said in jest.

"When a man finds a wife, he finds a good thing," Noah exclaimed.

Jamal chased after his wife.

"It is not time," we told Sojourner. She hid her spirit and its duplicate. Purloined[14] at the thirty-yard line.

---

[13] Ain't I a Woman
[14] Edgar Allen Poe

For days, We hid his wife from him. Jamal sent Billy, Shannon, Chris, and whoever else he trusted to find his love. He was a man possessed. All of his thoughts about the nation were deprioritized. He felt human again. He even tried a census to find his love. But we kept her away. He began to think that she was a phantom, maybe he was going crazy in the stadium.

On the seventh day, Chris and Billy came running toward Jamal, who was eating fried yams with butter at the concession stands. His lips covered in the grease. Jamal looked up overjoyed. He thought they found Simone. *Sweet Simone.* He dropped the yam onto his plate, making a clanking sound atop the metal stand.

"Where's she at?" he said before they could get in a word otherwise.

"That cock-sucking General is back Jack," Billy said from a distance. He was trailing Chris who had already reached Jamal and was pulling him in the direction of the field. Chris and Billy jogged ahead of Jamal as they made their way back to the field. Jamal was unenthused. He believed the General to be a smart man. Why would he come back? But smart men who do not have faith are simply clever fools.

The chosen were coming from every corner of Our earth. They were filling in this nation with free, just, and unified women and men. Our prophets moved throughout the crowd. They feverishly weighed the hearts and souls of the chosen.

"The time to build is upon us. We had this opportunity to change our conditions and we took it." Nelson Mandela welcomed all who entered the field. "These people are beautiful. There will be no racial tyranny. No gendered tyranny. Equality shall reign. The time for change is upon us." He rejoiced as he welcomed the chosen to their birthright.

Jamal felt a mix of rage and empathy for the General's return. My Wife too felt sorry for him. I do not understand. We told him to receive Our blessing and follow Our signs. His son awoke from the dead and he still didn't believe. We knew he was going to return but she still feels for the sinners. "They can still change," She tells me. The only question Jamal can think to ask is, "Why?"

The General stammers through his answer. Nathaniel Turner grabbed his tongue. "His sin is more than deserving of his fate. He's just a modern slave master. Least that's how he sees it. I see a coward." Nat released his hold on the General's tongue.

"News got out quick that my son was brought back. I couldn't go anywhere. People think I have some sort of inside with the Nation…" He continued on and on about his sin. Explaining it away. He doesn't deserve Our grace.

They went to the skybox. "It is time." My Wife looked at me. Her eyes deep and black. Her face sheen. I looked down at Her body. Her hips, the ones that pushed out creation, framed by an Isis dress. Her crown perfectly aligned. It was time. Intuitively, Sojourner Truth appeared outside as the men boarded the elevator to the skybox. She assumed the form of her spiritual duplicate. Her brown skin and big curly hair glowed for Jamal's eyes only.

Jamal hadn't lost sight of his new and more important mission—establishing his family. "Did you see that?" he turned to discuss with Billy.

"I see everything chief. Been that way for some time," Billy retorted. Billy didn't see a thing.

All of the souls in the room were weighed and judged. We sat with the men as they discussed their lives and their separate fates. Bob Marley, Zora Neal Hurston, and Nina Simone all found it humorous that the General and his men didn't know what their fate entailed.

"Jamal has made manifest the falsehood of the inferiority of the American negro," Elijah Muhammad explained. "Through the divine power of melanin, we can establish Truth. God has decided and who can make a decision after God?"

Jamal spoke as the General and his men sat hypnotized. They were unaware of their transgressions. All of their transgressions.

Bob Marley sat next to Jamal. He took a guitar pic out of his hair and began to strum an air guitar. It made the loveliest rhythm. He sang his tune into Jamal's ear. "Because you returned of course. I told you your family would be damned. You didn't understand. Your family are all who oppress. The Downpressers. Your children died before they could kill ours." The melodic tone reminiscent of "I Shot the Sheriff."

The honorable Elijah Muhammad sat on the opposite side of Jamal to interject. He opened the Holy Qur'an and read a surah. Jamal paused for a moment feeling overwhelmed by the presence of the prophets. The honorable Elijah spoke for him. "You held the fate of your people. Now they must suffer for the bloodshed. We will start anew with this beautiful Nation. Please return and tell your family to repent. Tell the oppressors that all will be forgiven. Endure the suffering and grow closer to Him."

The fate of the Downpressers is one of sincere intentionality. They believed they could use Creation to challenge the Creator. Much like the Jinns before them, they too will burn. They shall walk the earth as strangers to nature, removed from the cycles of life. Their fire will be the sun. Their skin will burn. Their vision will wither and the falsehood of their manifest destiny will be proven. They have turned their faces from Us, so shall We turn Our grace from them.

Downpresser
(General Nash)

I walked out of that stadium just like I'd done so many times before. That crummy place. "Bear down!" used to be my slogan. I loved the Bears. But now I despised Soldier Field. I had a different feeling this time. A cold spell washed over me. Then, a blazing heat. A wall of fire met my men and I on our way out of Soldier Field. The irony of the name hit me. My men were the only soldiers in Soldier Field. Even people on the outside were calling this "Nation" New Africa. The sun was out but we were not able to see beyond the fire. The stadium seemed to be withstanding the raging flames. My men tried to re-open the doors. We tried to go back inside but were unable. The entrance to the stadium disappeared. There was a force pushing us out. We were thrown, head first, into the blazes. The only soldiers in Soldier Field, removed like trash.

"What is this?" Mario called out. "It feels and looks like fire. But we aren't dying."

"Why does it still burn? It burns like we're dying," Steve let out. He began to cough uncontrollably. It was hard to breathe. I never spent so much energy trying to inhale.

"I . . ." I began to say, but at that moment the Prophet spoke to us. Like a telepath or something. It felt like he was in our heads.

"It will not kill you until you have given the world this message." I have no idea how a kid could be so direct and cryptic at the same time. He forced me to hate and love him equally. I have almost grown addicted to our sit-downs. I needed to talk to him. I needed to learn from him. Me, a Gulf War veteran, I had to learn from a seventeen-year-old.

The seven days of darkness killed a lot of the forests and animals, making the Earth one big match when the sun came back. Even the oceans were aflame. The Earth was torched. Everywhere except Soldier Field. Maybe it wasn't magic. But what else could it be?

Hail Mary Full of Grace

*T*he General left. I finished my drink. Billy was behind me. He spoke inaudibly at first. Then his emotion grew.

"What a disrespectful cunt. Just a cunt that General Nash is."

I let him continue, uninterrupted. He bellowed on and on about how blessed the general was. But in my heart, we all knew it, especially the general. Now he was feeling it more acutely.

"But you know who the real victim is?" Billy asked with authority.

I was interested. I turned toward Sergeant Belly. He was particularly dapper now. He wore the most spectacular snake-skinned cowboy boots. His pants, freshly creased blue slacks, so sharp they could cut glass. His hair was freshly lined and cut into a Steve Harvey high top, with a tuft of grey in the front. His transformation was iconic of our movement.

"Who is the real victim?" I turned my head slightly, enjoying the fertility of the pause. "Are there victims?" I had not thought of it this way. Not yet at least.

"Of course there are victims, child."

I appreciated Billy. He never called me Prophet. Instead, he would say, "You just doing what everyone already knows to be the right thing!" No one had called me, child, son, boy or the like in a week. It felt like forever. But Billy never let me down.

He continued, "There are always victims. In this world of FI-NITE resources, there are always winners and losers." He pronounced finite like it was two different words.

I turned back to the window as Billy continued talking about resources. I looked out of the skybox an onto the Melanoid Nation. An uneasiness grew. What next? Where do we go from here? I wanted to ask God, but He had gotten us to the Mecca. I needed to figure out the next step on my own.

Before I got lost in my thoughts, a pair of hands came under my arms. They gripped my chest, then rose to grab my shoulders. Startled, I looked down. No one had touched me for days, outside of a handshake or two with the general. I thought it could have been Billy, Keith, or Chris playing around since they knew me best and would probably feel most comfortable pulling a prank on me or even touching me. But upon inspection, the hands were feminine and soft. The grip was not aggressive but inviting. Looking down, the hands were well manicured. A deep purple polish covered the nail. I closed my eyes as a sweet-smelling perfume indulged my senses. I didn't care who it was. It felt good to be human for a moment, not to feel like the father of this glorious nation. That was not what I wanted. I only wanted to free my brother. To free all my brothers then live like men and women. Real men and women in this country: complementary.

"It was in your eyes . . . that thing."

A woman's voice filled my ears. It was unfamiliar. The cadence, tone, pitch—I didn't recognize her. I looked back at the hands. No. I couldn't place them either. Her perfume. They were familiar. Her voice, I had never heard before.

My heart skipped. "I saw you reach out for me. I saw you save us all. It was so damn sexy." Her right hand dropped to my semi-erect penis. My right hand overlapped, gripping firmly. Mary had arrived.

Turning, I found that it was only us in the skybox. Apparently, Sergeant Belly left some time before. Who knows how long I was surveying the people? I probably did get lost in my thoughts. It wasn't the first time. But that moment felt perfect. I turned around to see Simmone standing there, shorter than I'd remembered. Her hair tickled my nose and smelled like mangoes. Her hands moved across my body. She had done this before. A professional. She was ready. So was I.

"My name is Jay," I said with a kiss.

Biting her bottom lip, I caressed her slim frame, slipping down the nape of her neck to her back. She moaned and grabbed me tighter.

"Sojourner," she whispered letting out all the air in her lungs. "But you can call me Eve." She licked my neck and stood to her toes to reach my ear, biting and pulling on my lobe. It pinched so good.

I let out a chuckle. "Why Eve?" I searched for a bra under her tank top and found none. Her breasts were perfect. They just stood up like that. She laughed. I couldn't tell if it was from my question or the aimless fumbling of my fingers. "I like Sojourner, myself."

"You're Adam. I am Eve. It was in your eyes. We will create a new world. I will follow you in the world that you have already started."

She threw her head back. I bit her left nipple, then her right through her shirt. Her breasts were pierced. My teeth clinked against the metal. She moaned. I pulled her in close to me by the waist. Our hips connected. Her curly hair was in my face. Our breathing increased. Her Thai clinch grew tighter around my neck. Her nails gripped my skin. It was a good sting.

"Eve?" I waited for her reply. Her reply never came. She was too concerned with wrestling with my pants, trying to unfasten my button.

"Journey?" I had given her a nickname. A natural one. Much more natural than Simmone or Eve. Journey, I liked it. It represented the one word to describe how we met.

"My mom calls me that," she said with another chuckle. "You can too. You can call me whatever you please." She almost sang her response. Lust consumed me and for a moment, I was looking back at myself. A reflection almost. Then the moment faded, and I was back looking at Journey. It seemed as though we'd exchanged eyes.

"I like it better than Eve. I think I'll keep it."

I was trying to stay in the mood but wanted to say my piece. I cupped her ass and bit her earlobe. She exhaled in my ear.

"It was not my world to create nor destroy." Even in the throes of lovemaking, it was important to communicate the will of the Creator. For I know They willed her to be mine, and what a good thing They have placed in my protection.

"I'll be your world." She succeeded in unfastening my pants. I could feel the warmth radiating from her crescent. Nothing could keep me from taking it, from taking her. She was right. She was mine. All mine. My pants fell to the floor. I kicked the legs off. Her hand gripped my member.

"Ooooo . . ." Her face uncovered her thoughts. Impressive. We worked to take off our shirts. She attempted to shimmy out of her bottoms.

"Keep on your skirt," I said. I loved the way her skirt hugged her hips and made her look like my very own hula dancer. Our eyes connected for the second time. Waves of deep brown surrounded her pupils, imprinted on an almond background. Her eyes were like a brown ocean and I was drowning. I kissed her neck and felt faint lips on my own. I was kissing myself. As my lips walked down her neck and chest, the feeling on my own neck and chest grew, and her touch faded. She jumped on my waist. She was not wearing panties either. Her juices bathed my stomach. I could not feel my kisses. I was once again overwhelmed by my senses. Her thighs were warm. She tongued my neck and collar bone. I felt her weight.

Reaching down to grab her inner thighs, I lifted her weight above my head. Journey assisted by pushing off of my shoulders. She held her lips open for me. I found her pearl. I was consumed by the sweet smell of her vagina. My knees almost buckled on the first lick. I have never felt anything so intense. My penis was completely erect. She looked down with concern but said nothing.

I continued to lick, chasing that sensation. I found my rhythm and the feeling came back. The lick radiated through my body. I had the sensation of being on a roller coaster. My stomach was in my chest. I was going to orgasm. The skybox closed in on me. A tingle shot up my spine from my dick to my chest stopping at my chest, right behind my heart. My heart was going to explode. I wanted to stop but I couldn't. Then the feeling faded again. No longer was I going to orgasm. My muscles felt strained and my breathing heavy. My penis was semi-erect. Journey's screams filled the skybox. They echoed. She held the back of my head tighter and tighter. Her thighs tensed around my neck, framing my shoulders. Then she relaxed, letting out a deep breath.

I placed her on top of the bar. She was so wet. It was overwhelmingly sexy. I wanted to bust just seeing her on the countertop. Between my spit and her waterfall, her vagina was ready. I was rock solid again. I licked her vulva and passionately kissed her clitoris. She tasted like water.

"I need you inside of me. I'm throbbing for your stroke."

I obliged. I dropped my dick in slowly for one complete stroke. She jumped. I eased out. Leaving only the tip in. Her eyes rolled. I watched her, she consumed me. Building up to the next stroke, the sensation came back. But it was different. Deeper. Much deeper. I could feel it in my spine. It was in my hips. It was everywhere.

"Don't stop, Adam. Don't stop." I couldn't stop. Her pussy opened up. I went slow. She sat up to reach for me, then laid back down. She moaned. Her torso convulsed. I sped up the stroke. She was getting wetter. She rolled her eyes.

My vision went blurry. The sensation grew and grew. It was building up inside of me, behind my heart. I opened my eyes and saw myself. The countertop was cold on my ass. I was getting fucked and it felt good, really good.

"Please cum with me!"

I licked my hand and placed it on my crotch. There was no need, everything was wet. Everything. I had a vagina. The other sensation came back. A heat went from my pussy all the way to my heart. I was about to explode.

"Jamal, cum with me."

But I knew that he was not going to orgasm yet. I looked up at myself momentarily, eyes rolling back into my head. I reached for my chest with my other hand and felt soft breasts. Every part of my dick pulsated with pleasure. The tip grew thicker. The strokes got deeper. My heart was exploding. The warmth filled every inch of me.

A chasm opened between our bodies and I transcended myself. I could see both of our bodies. I felt both of our passions. Our love was manifest. We looked amazing. Someone should have recorded us but that would probably taint it. We made love. Our bodies were one. Literally. I felt for her. She felt for me.

"Cum with me, Adam. Come with me. I'm about to nut again." I exploded on myself. We were emotionally and physically intertwined. Her waves crashed on my midsection, warm and invited. I was wet from belly button to scrotum. I got harder inside. I exploded in myself. The tip of my dick stiffened then opened, and released deep inside. We came for five minutes. Her legs raced but she wasn't running. She pulled me into her and kissed me passionately. Legs shaking. I was still exploding in her. I wanted to empty myself between her walls. Our foreheads touched. She kissed my lips. Hers were moist and soft. She looked up admiringly, my organ still deep in her and consummated our prayer with a timely, "Amen. Amen. And amen." She smiled. We didn't move.

"Round two?" I asked.

CHAPTER 9

Sodom and Gomorrah

*A*fter two months of living with Yvette, we moved into our apartment in Kimball Valley, on the West Side of Chicago. Chris and I attended Kimball Valley Elementary. I transferred schools, and this time I was one of thirty-two black students in my class. To them, unlike at Reagan, my skin was normative. But my accent wasn't a thing of amusement. I talked white/country to them, and I sounded smart. I had a hard time making friends because to them I was lame. I didn't know anything about rap music. I was often lost in the slang they used, and it was easily discernible that my mother still dressed me. Needless to say, I lost a lot of cool points in their eyes.

But within a number of weeks, I found my way. I had developed a couple of good relationships and I adopted some of the other students' interests, especially trading basketball cards, a far reach from roller hockey. But there was nothing like having that card everyone wanted—the Dennis Rodman rookie card or the David Robinson All Star joint.

Three weeks after we moved, Keith came to live with us. He took my room, and I was forced to share with Chris. I guess normally there would be some resentment among siblings, but I really just wanted Keith to be home. The day he arrived, Chris had gotten into a fight at school. After school, a boy and his older cousin jumped Chris. I don't remember the specifics, but I do remember a number of the kids running to me after school screaming, "They jumpin yo brother!" By the time I got there, the fight had been broken up, and although he held his own, he was in bad shape. On the walk home, as Chris limped and I carried his book bag, all I could think about was Keith's reaction. Luckily, we were the first to get home. When Mom walked in with Keith, what was supposed to be a warm welcome turned into a novice lynch mob.

Looking at Chris, my mother blurted out, "What happened?" She asked in a much calmer tone than I expected. I think she was still really excited about Keith's arrival. Her hand was on her hip awaiting a response from Chris.

"This boy had tripped me in the lunch line. An I spilled my milk, so I threw it at im," Chris said with a confidence that set us all aback. "Then he hit me and I beat him up . . ."

Chris never talked so forcefully. He was more of a whiner when it came to matters like this. I think he was partly angry about the event and mostly angry about the move. He had made a lot of friends at Reagan. Not only had we moved physically four times in one year, we moved schools three of the four times.

Keith interrupted Chris, "If you won what he look like then?" He said with a smile. "He must be tore up!"

Chris didn't laugh. He was still in the moment. Feeling every event in the recent history he was telling. "After school he got his cousin an I fought em boff." I saw the anger rising up in Chris again. His nostrils flared and his forehead scrunched. He was upset about getting jumped on. I also knew right then that this was not the end of their feuding. I, of course, was going to get dragged into their bullshit. I was angry too, but not enough to fight. I didn't want anyone to fight. I saw what fighting could do. I wanted to forget the whole thing.

Then, out of nowhere but with a sharp tone of query, my mother turned to me.

"And where were you?" The question itself insinuated an obligation. Her look was even more piercing than her tone. She saw my soul. She always could look right through my flesh and penetrate my very being. I couldn't think fast enough to answer. I was always supposed to be somewhere. Somewhere I had no idea about. My responsibility evaded me like the horizon. I could never get it right.

Where was I? Minding my motherfucking business that's where I was. I didn't know whether or not to tell the truth. What answer did she want? I didn't know.

So I lied. "I was waitin for Chris at the back doh then Ms. Wilkins (Chris's teacher) came an tole me he was in the office all day fo fightin."

I was whining. I didn't want to get involved. On the way home, Chris told me that he was in the office all day, so I figured I'd use it in the story. That's the best way to lie, tell 80 percent of the truth.

"I went to the office an he wadn't there an when I went back outside some kids tole me he was gettin beat up."

I thought with this story I had successfully avoided any blame. Wrong. Everything was my responsibility. My mother felt impotent, so I had to feel the same.

"So when you got over there what did you do?" Keith asked. I wasn't happy that he was home anymore. He was fanning the flame. "I know you got em off my lil brother." For some reason, he was no longer my little brother. But Keith hadn't been there for months. He didn't have a right to say anything. I was the big brother. I was the only brother. Nothing was constant. I had to ride the wave.

I was caught off guard by both the question and his phrasing. Was I not his little brother too?

"Well the fight was already broke up when I got there," I stated reluctantly. "Everything was over and they had left."

I told the truth, but I knew that the truth wouldn't work unless I told them that I was in the middle of the fight, wailing on any and everybody, looking for the next kid to wreck. Anyone. But I wasn't there. How could I be blamed. Chris fought a kid over spilled milk, literally. That too was my fault. They were really good at defining and then redefining my role in the family.

Keith let out a little laugh. "Well you know what we gonna have to do, right? Chris you know where dis kid live? Cause this just became a family feud."

He clapped his palms together three times. They sounded rough and dry. He was smiling from ear to ear. Keith was eager to make the fight a family feud. I could hear it in his voice. He wanted to fight. But to be honest, the other kid already brought family into it. I was scared though. This was a new school and I didn't want to have a bad reputation. I knew being a coward would be an even worse rep. Nothing is worse than a bully, save a cur. So I went along with Keith, mimicking his enthusiasm for revenge. Fronting.

"Naw Keith. Wait til tomorrah at least. You jus got in," my mother said, trying to calm Keith. She wanted to have a nice night, considering Keith had just gotten to Chicago. "I got some groceries. Let's have dinner and handle it tomorrow." She placed her hand on Keith's shoulder attempting to settle his spirit.

"Naw Ma. We caint take no losses in this house. You boys is gonna fight them til yall win. We gotta fight as a team."

Keith paused and looked at mom.

"That's what you made me do."

My mom looked down in shame. Her highlighted bangs fell delicately over her forehead. She had Keith at seventeen. He was more of an ally than a son. Her Little Prince.

Either way, I really didn't want to fight. It must have shown in my expression because Keith hopped right on it. Was he feeling my stress?

"You aint scared is you? Yo lil' brother fought boff dem boys by his damndest. And where was you? You let him fight alone."

This was not the homecoming I had expected. I let him fight alone? Wow. Keith moved closer to me. We were supposed to catch up, and he was going to tell me about all the life lessons I missed out on in Memphis. But instead, I get blamed for my little brother's quarrels and thrown into a fight over literal spilled milk.

"Where they live at Chris?" Keith asked once more.

Momentarily, his gaze transferred from me. I was relieved. He can be relentless that way, real stubborn. He was looking at all of us with one glare. Rage was building in him. This was a scene I was used to. As you can see, he had just gotten back and was already trying to run things. I sometimes feel if he had been given a different lot, he'd be President and not a felon.

"Stop Keith! Please stop. They aint goin to fight dem boys tonight. We are goina sit down an eat dinner as a family and celebrate you comin home," her dedication to the moment solidified the joy she had in Keith's homecoming.

She was on the verge of tears. This wasn't what she had planned either. But even my mother didn't want to abandon this line of conversation as much as I did. I could sense that in her use of "tonight" instead of just ending the statement. I would have preferred an "ever" in the place of that "tonight." But I knew she meant we would fight tomorrow because quarrels are never just that with Black people. We have to indulge the stupidity sometimes.[15]

"Naw Ma, we gonna deal with this now. They gotta learn how to be men and aint no way you can teach em better than I can," Keith's voice quivered at the end. He noticeably didn't want an argument, but his masculinity was in question. His slender frame slouched, shoulders moving into his chest. He wanted to help in his own way. He thought he was helping.

Our masculinity is always in question. Although very confused at the time, I now understand the sensitivity of masculinity. His authority and will to fight were the manifestations of his contrived manhood, and a shot at these aspects meant complete emasculation. There is no in between with masculinity. It's either all the way man or not. The same rule does not apply for femininity. Keith's role had been, since I can remember, to supplement the women in our family.

---

[15] The Boondocks coined the phrase "Nigger Moments" and I would have to agree, sometimes we do play into the man. Sometimes.

His masculinity was an assortment of roles left vacant by our absentee fathers, roles that the women of the family had not yet found a way to fill. His manhood was contrived in a piecemeal fashion—just like mine and the rest of Black America. Systematic. His artificial masculinity was molded by the women's abilities or inabilities.

Every liberty and every limitation he had was based on their agency. Crazy to think about. Therefore, his masculinity was as fragile as a Jenga set. With any negligence in treatment, the structure of it could collapse instantly. With this conversation, we were taking one block away at a time. Piece by piece dismantling my brothers and I with words. Words that mean so much.

With no regard, my mother's response did just that. With her statement, she removed the cornerstone of his masculinity. The Bob Marley of his temple.

"How you goina teach them an I taught you? Plus you just got here you caint be callin shots like you pay some bills round here. Let's jus enjoy ourselves tonight, and I'll go up to the school with Yvette in the mornin."

Keith's face couldn't hide the embarrassment of being checkmated. Everything she said was correct. That wasn't enough. Keith couldn't be a man without paying bills. My mom hadn't paid bills for several years, but she was a woman. You see the masculine feminine paradox? Who was the source of Keith's authority on manhood? Was it God Himself? Everything he knew about manhood, he learned from a woman. Or was it? He was the only man in the house, right? His was the only true masculine experience, right? Somehow, someway, even his authority in the house was real, even though it was not based on tangible grounds. For this reason, he fought. He fought to preserve whatever territory as a man he had.

God, Himself, blessed him with manhood. Wherever his feet stepped, that was his land. While I can see it now, at the time all I saw was mixed messages. What did my mother expect of me as a black man, if not to be the leader of the household? Does she just want a man around? What did she and Yvette mean by "all the good ones"? Why is she taking Yvette, a white woman, and not Keith to deal with the principal? What is his role now? Keith's role, astonishingly enough, was whatever my mother decided it to be. She decided, and so it was. At least in her mind.

We ate and played cards after dinner. When Chris and I were sent to bed, my mother and Keith stayed in the living room playing Uno. They talked about his plans in Chicago and the specifics of his situation in Memphis. They kept me out of the loop, so I was eavesdropping. But I couldn't hear much. It was my first night sharing a bed with Chris. Almost immediately after he laid down, his breathing became very rhythmic and he was asleep before I was able to turn the lights off.

I got into the bed perched on the edge because that was all that was left, and after the day Chris had, I didn't want to disturb him anymore. I wanted to be there, to protect him. I didn't want him to feel danger again. We slept head to toe, which we did not repeat the following night because I quickly became the victim of multiple heels to the face. It felt like I was being assaulted by a broomstick with a Brillo pad glued to the end of it. After the third blow, I determined that it was going to be a long night and I started thinking about the fight. I really wished I had been there for him.

But if I had seen it, I still didn't know what I would've done. I was still scared of the Will Breckner thing. I didn't tell my family about Will. It was a secret between me and Regan. Every fight I saw, in the street or in school, really brought me back to that singular moment when it started snowing. My feet would get numb. My face would grow cold. I figured I would have done something though. I couldn't live with my brother taking Will's place. I thought about the fight tomorrow, which I knew would be inevitable. Scenes from the next day floated into my mind, haunting me. I didn't know the kids he got into it with. I imagined they were middle school monsters. Tossing Chris and I up and down the street. I visualized being stomped and beat. My brother alongside me.

Then, because our bedroom was adjacent to the living room and Chris' breathing had slowed significantly, my mother and Keith's voices crept in. The sounds became words. I overheard their conversation. They were talking about Chris and me. Why can't they just act like I'm not here? I thought. That'd be too much like right, huh?

"It's jus that I want them to be tough. The world aint gonna give em nothin Ma, an you know that waaaay betta than I do. Look round this apartment. We aint been givin nothin an cause of dat we aint got nothin to lose but respect. They caint be scared out here in dis world. How they just gonna bring losses into this home? Losses need to stay where they are."

"Yea but we go up here with dese white folks actin like da way you was earlier and we not gon get nothin done. An I'm not raisin my boys just to be tough, I'm raisin em not to get none na dese fast booty lil gurls out here pregnant an to stay dey butts outta jail."

My mother was referencing Keith's recent trouble with the law. I didn't know much at the time, but I knew that was his reason for coming north. She pronounced girls like gulls. That was her way of being funny.

Keith interrupted before she could continue.

"Come on Ma, don't throw dat in ma face. You know Maw Maw was fo monfs late on that mortgage. On top of that, she couldn't pay the taxes for years. What you spect me ta do? I wadn't gon let er lose dat house."

His voice changed. He was whining slightly. I had never heard Keith whine. In fact, he would always tease me about it.

"Boy dat wadnt yo place. Yo Granmaw is grown and she been dealin wit dat house since fo you was born. She been about to lose that house for over thirty years. It aint goin nowhere fo she does boy." What about after she's gone? Do we lose her and the house?

"Then what is my place?" he paused to curb his attitude. Anger was building. But not toward my mom. The anger was ambiguous.

"Sometimes you gotta sacrifice they right for yo right. 'Specially when it's affectin da people you love." He hesitated, before the next statement. It felt as if he were searching for redemption, something solid and sturdy to hold onto.

"All I can say is Maw Maw aint gotta worry about losing that house neva again." The passion in his voice rang between my ears. To this day it makes me tear up. He found his manhood without anyone's help. He saved my grandmother's house and he did it on his terms. So what if he goes to jail, right? He got his manhood. That means it was all worth it.

I stopped listening because I couldn't take anymore. I wondered what Keith was going to do. I had never seen him not in control. He seemed much calmer than before, and I didn't know which personality was truly him. Maybe both I guess. I wanted to be him, but I didn't know how. I did not want to be him really. That was imprecise, because there were definitely times when I hated him, the way brothers do. It was more like I wanted to have the strength to please him. I wanted to do as Keith did when it came to being a man. Show the bravery he showed. He would have found those boys as soon as he saw what they had done to Chris. Would fighting those kids tomorrow make me more like him? I decided that was exactly what I was going to do. As soon as I saw them on the playground before school, I would steal on either of them and live with the consequences. That's how Keith lived and that's how I was going to live. But what was that he was saying about losses? Why can't I lose? People lose right? That's not in my control. Is it?

Often while growing up, I wanted to ask Keith why he was so tough on me. Looking back, I realize the reason behind the logic at the roots of rationality in the canopy of his conviction. His callous is a means. My callous is a means. Chris' callous is a means. Every move we make either validates or discredits us as men. We are tough, and arrogant, and angry because that's how we survive. All we know is opposition and all we have is respect. However, our opposition isn't simply external. I've never been able to reconcile why my skin must antagonize me so. Our skin unloads like shrapnel within us, and the heat of each particle of blackness burrows through each and every aspect of us. Especially our manhood. To be a Black Man is almost an oxymoron.

At the same time, our skin is simultaneously empowering, liberating, encouraging, imprisoning, deafening, and confusing, muting, and cloaking. I can't move without feeling the burn of Blackness. Each hole that my Blackness burns gives way to the vulnerability of my manhood. From whole to hole. Knowing the brilliance of my nature with no platform for it to manifest.[16] The powerlessness of our skin challenges our masculinity. All authority is intangible. So we ascribe ourselves natural power, God-given resilience. Any hint at vulnerability only reinforces the powerlessness we feel daily. Can we be men and Black? Do these two characteristics exist in contention?

In the morning, I awoke to a note from my mom. It said she had to leave for work early and would meet Chris and me at the school on her lunch break to talk to the principal. Chris and I got ready. I made two bowls of oatmeal and checked to see if Chris had his uniform tucked in. I did not do this for the reason that a big brother should make sure the younger is prepared—then again, men never do things for the proper reason. We always have underlying egotism as a motivator, tainting any good deed. Man can only see through two eyes. Instead, I did it because I hated when he had to serve detention for dress code violations because then we both got a detention. I would have to wait forty-five extra minutes after school for something I could have prevented.

We said goodbye to Keith, who was still sleeping, and walked to school. Along the way, I shared with Chris my plans to fight the boys when we saw them and that, as the older brother, of course, I had to throw the first punch. It is always necessary as the older brother to enforce rules. They didn't have to make sense. Often the rules were

---

[16] Nipsey Hussle "Dedication"

made up on the spot but he had to follow them. Not because the rules are important, but because the position to enforce is. I was the older sibling by design, not accident. He was in full agreement with the plan and encouraged me to grab a brick because they might be ready for us this time.

Before I proceed, you should know that this story is not in exact chronological order. Chris and the other two boys might have gotten suspended for a day. I don't remember. But the only significance that would have is it would push the events below back a day. Or forward a day, depending on how you view time.

"Yea and when we was done fightin, they said they was gonna get they brother's gun. So we should get somethin just in case. Ya know?" he said in all earnestness. He wasn't scared at all. It relieved some of my nervousness. It was just a fight, right?

I decided against the bricks Chris picked up initially. However, as if I wasn't scared enough to fight them, we had the possibility of being shot. Mind you, I was twelve and Chris was nine.

"I wish them niggas had of shot me, it would have been on. Maybe not with me but at least with my ghost. Niggas is getting haunted if they pop me. Ya heard me?" Chris blurted out.

It was like someone else was talking. Maybe this one fight had truly changed Chris. Or better yet, maybe all of the moving had changed him. He was really upset. He felt like we never had a home, nowhere safe, and I agreed.

Before continuing, I must revisit the issue of Kimball Valley. Kill-Vill, as it is fondly called by its residents, is a section on the West Side of Chicago with Blacks comprising ninety-seven percent of the population. While at Kimball Valley Middle School, I saw girls bringing Vaseline and taking out their earrings in anticipation of fighting. I witnessed students slicing one another with razors, twenty-seven-year-old men fighting eighth graders, fights starting over who was the fattest person in our class, and a whole list of other exaggerated situations. Fighting was the response to almost every negative interaction. The most outrageous being a fight in my Social Studies class in which it was contested that Mya looked better than Lisa Ray. It is not the most offensive of fights because of the severity of injuries, but simply because these women are both fine TO THIS DAY* (Deontay Wilder voice). [17] Fine is fine. Therefore, the possibility of a child bringing a gun to school was not far-fetched. In fact, I'd already seen two guns in school.

Either way, because I shared the plan with Chris, I had to follow through or risk looking like a coward once more. His revelation made me even more nervous. I guess when folks do nothing, they are considered cowards. Although some stuff is none of my business. This was clearly my business. I had to do something but I was scared. Scared of losing and equally scared of winning. Scared of fighting. We weren't tussling in the house. These kids hated us. They wouldn't stop after the point was proven, after they had established their manhood. They had resolved to destroy us, and I was scared.

I was quiet until we got to the playground. Chris had been speaking of the pain he was going to inflict on the other boy, whose name I now knew was Marcus. I remember his excitement.

"I'm gonna head butt em, you remember how I used tuh do," he

---

[17] If you haven't seen pictures of Mya after she put on a little weight. Oooooooooooooo boi! Thighs. Google it.

said.

He lurched forward, head first. I did and do remember his head butts. That little dude was nuts, "certifiable," as mom would say. However, while he was mid-sentence, Marcus' older cousin Trae rushed towards us and connected with a side-armed swing that landed like a whip on my left arm. The feathers from my coat went flying, disorienting me. I wondered what was going on but didn't have enough time to think about it. A burn came and went away immediately.

Trae swung once more with his right arm and missed. He was swinging side-armed. I lowered my shoulder into his chest, and with all of my strength, I brought him to the ground. Apparently, they planned on a sneak attack as well. My arm burned again now. The wind blew, but I heard it more than felt it. After mounting him, I was so surprised to be winning that I forgot I was fighting. I looked around for Chris and saw him busy scrapping with Marcus. He held the collar of Marcus' coat with his left hand while delivering rhythmic blows with the right. He was winning too. I was temporarily proud of the family.

Trae hit me from below and I was brought back to the moment. I saw blood-covered feathers falling on Trae's face as he lay below me trying his best to get back to his feet. Both my hands were on the collar of his red First Down puff coat. Rage filled me as I gripped his collar tighter, slamming his head against the concrete. My mouth filled with blood. I could taste the metal. An upsurge of compassion was suddenly aroused in me. We fought for the same reason, I thought. We fought out of fear. Neither of us hated the other. We simply fought to save face. Well he might have fought because he likes to. But God knows that was not my reason. I continued to slam his head. Trae no longer fought back. He too gripped my coat. His grip was tight and strong at first. The grasp loosened. His arms fell. Lifeless.

Soon I forgot I was fighting again. I became unaware of the forming crowd. I became unaware of Trae. My frustrations had peaked, and my mind wandered.

Then I was snatched out of my reverie. Upon my return to reality, I adopted the deer's fear, only I didn't know who the rhinoceros was. Would it be my mother, Keith, Marcus' family, or my teachers? Mr. Lucas, the gym teacher, grabbed my coat. He pulled me off of Trae who was lying limp on the ground and took me directly to the principal's office. He hadn't said a word the entire way, but his grip on my arm declared his frustration. I looked up at his pale face trying to appeal to some sense of mercy, but found none. My arm burned, then stung, then ached.

When I got to the office, I was surprised that my mother was already standing at the secretary's desk. I thought she was supposed to be there later in the day. This was a welcomed surprise. We needed backup. As if on cue, she was in the midst of an argument involving the assistant principal and Ms. Taylor (my science teacher). At that moment, I was overcome with pride. My family was uniform. We all had the same cause, and that was to protect one another. If Keith had been there, the feeling might have concluded in my attainment of nirvana. However, with his absence, I would have to settle with standing on the boundaries of the Promised Land. The sentiment was shaken when I saw Ms. Yvette, who was Keith's proxy, sitting across from the secretary's desk. Why had my mother asked her to come? I asked myself. She really contributes nothing to anything, save whiteness. I answered myself.

Then my mother looked at me and with a thorough inspection noticed my bleeding arm.

"What happened?" she exclaimed while simultaneously running towards me.

This had become her anthem. She was always panicked and always trying to assess the severity of something.

I had no response. I was still breathing heavily. For the first time, I was aware of the situation. I understood where I was and what happened. The sting of the cut quickly moved to the forefront of my consciousness. No longer could my brain intentionally deny it, the pain became so pronounced that I had to bite my lip to restrain the tears. I felt for the arm with my free hand, but Mr. Lucas only strengthened his hold on me.

Mr. Lucas then chimed in smugly, "Miss, is this your son?"

"What difference do it make?" my mother responded with an equally attitudinal tone and with no real respect for the fragility of the circumstances. "He is a student here. Why is there blood all over his coat?"

Mr. Lucas said, "This has got to be your son with that attitude. You need to talk to your kids like that, not me, while these little hoodlums are coming to school carrying knives." That was his checkmate. Or so he thought.

My mother's face dropped. Her high cheekbones sank, and her vibrant almond eyes appeared to be hiding behind dilated pupils. Honest to God, her eyes became Black. Not normal Black either. My mother's eyes became the color of the topside of your deepest secret.

That particular and unforgiving Black that can only be outdone by the deepest sorrows. Her eyes died in front of me, realizing that I could have been killed that day. Her worst fear. We were face to face. There was no rage. There was no pain. There was only a sympathetic understanding and apologetic body language.

She put her head down. She was sorry I had to face these situations. She was sorry that I had to face death at twelve years old. She wanted a better life for me but was unable to provide it. Her eyes betrayed her despair. It was hard for her to see past the darkness because it had overwhelmed her. She was the deer. Overwhelmed to the point of ownership. Embracing her fate. Now even her sun was beginning to dim. Her hopes, one by one, appeared to be dying. First Keith, now Chris and I. Life had begun to taint us.

Out of her temporary mourning for my innocence was born a spirit of righteousness. After a brief inspection, she became defensive, saying, "My son would never bring a knife to school. Why is his arm bleedin? Don't you ever lie on my chile."

Her eyes aflame again. She really didn't know whether I had or hadn't brought a knife to school, but either way, our family was a team. All parents understand their children's best and worst. My mom says it often, "I know my child." My earlier pride reached its peak as Chris walked into the office while she was mid-sentence. He was huffing and puffing too. Trae was behind him, weeping. My mother paused.

Hearing mom from outside, Chris confirmed her claim. "Naw Ma, Jamal aint bring no knife to school. It was Trae! He cut Jamaw. And then . . ."

Cutting Chris off in a commanding voice, my mother yelled at

Mr. Lucas, "APOLOGIZE TO MY SON!" She was possessed with truth. Her eyes challenging all who questioned her motherly instincts. She was not going to back down. She walked toward Mr. Lucas. His tall frame engulfing her. Her finger pointed like a dagger into his sternum. Maybe Mr. Lucas was the deer.

"Do you teach your children to let people cut them with knives?" she asked threateningly. Pointing her finger at Mr. Lucas. Jabbing it in the air like a knife.

Before Mr. Lucas had time to respond and declare his wrongness, Ms. Aikens, the principal, entered the office. She attempted to gain control of the situation, which was on the verge of getting out of hand. Ms. Aikens' ability to assess the circumstances and properly deal with them was impeccable. They must've taught her that in principal school. What do they teach in principal school? Her first demand was that Chris and I go to the school nurse. Knowing we were being cared for put my mother at ease, and Mr. Lucas, who had been antagonizing my mother, was given the mission of escorting us.

Once more, Mr. Lucas was silent. Chris and I were recounting the fight for the length of the walk. When we arrived at the nurse's office, Chris walked in and Mr. Lucas shut the door. We stood outside the nurse's office looking at each other. I wasn't afraid anymore. I stared right back at him. All fear was gone. After a moment, he leaned his long muscular form down and placed his white face near mine, whispering, "I'm sorry for accusing you earlier. I was just doing my job. But if it were up to me, I'd let you boys kill each other."

With that, he walked off, leaving behind his cool hatred and coffee breath. He smelled white. White supremacists are often bullies.

As angry as this comment made me, all I hoped was that Chris wasn't in earshot of his words. There was no reason for both of us to lose our innocence. For all I know, he heard that ignorance and we were both lost. Lost to the original sin of America. Lost to the hate. I lost faith in white people. I knew Mr. Lucas was the enemy. I didn't know why, yet.

When we walked into the room, we found Marcus sitting next to Trae. Trae's head and shirt were almost maroon. They were so drenched in blood. I hadn't imagined I had done so much damage and when our eyes met, my heart sank. Well our eyes never really met. His right eye, still slightly opened, strained to stare me down. His posture was beast-like as he sat on the hospital bed. His dark skin glistened under the fluorescent lights, and his pink lips hung dumbfounded. His head, swollen to the point that it was unrecognizably human, throbbed visibly.

He looked like a beta male baboon at the zoo. Lost and wounded. Nothing to stand on. Neither of us knew what the appropriate step was. We were young and didn't want enemies. Besides, I was just introduced to my true enemy—Lucas and all who thought like him. But we were young men and didn't want to forsake our pride for the possibility of a truce, either. We'd rather fight daily than admit our fears, even though we were only twelve. So we said nothing to one another and kept our distance in the office. Without looking, I was totally aware of him. Each time he was taken back into the office, I watched him like a hawk—nervous he might do something, thinking he might cut me.

The cut turned out to need a couple of stitches, and the nurse sewed it up. When we were released, Chris and I went back to the office to find my mother and Yvette still there talking to the principal. After about fifteen minutes of waiting, they all came out laughing. Chris and I were told that we'd go home for the rest of the day and Chris would be suspended for two days. I wasn't suspended and I didn't understand why, but I figured it was best not to ask questions. Trae was expelled, but that didn't mean he was out of the picture. A lot of expelled kids often came back to the school looking to start fights. They came back specifically for the students they did not like, which has never made sense. Why come back for the part you hate? When I return to a place, it will always be because I had good memories there. Or else I am not going back. For the time being, the situation had been handled and that was all that mattered. I hoped his fear was equal to mine because if it was, nothing could make him fight again. Neither of us were the beasts we pretended to be. I often wonder if anyone is. Don't all men consider the benefits of retreat or does emasculation outweigh death itself?

When we got home, Chris gave an account of the story to Keith. It was the most grandiose tale. He had a way with stories. Chris would later become the family griot. If there was something that needed to be known about someone in the house or a story we all experienced that needed to be retold, Chris was the go-to man. He knew everyone's role and could even impersonate all of us. He was the best at reenacting, and was the one who was always willing. Everyone else had to be in the mood or have the reliving come naturally. But Chris, give him a chance to talk and it's a go. That is both advice and a warning. If you don't feel like hearing a long, eventful, exaggerated story, do not give him incentive to tell one.

Chris and Keith were both excited about the fight. The fear

stayed with me though. I honestly had no immediate recollection of much of what Chris said. "And then Jamal head butted him. And I had just been talking about doin that. I'm glad I wasn't Trae."

In fact, the only reason I smiled at Chris' rendition of the fight was because I didn't want Keith to know I had been afraid. That I still was afraid. But now I know he was afraid before his first fight, too. We all are. Like Mos Def says, "every man gets scared when prepared for confrontation . . ."[18]

Looking back, my mother showed me a lot. She taught me it wasn't just the men who were calloused. The coarse skin manifests itself in different ways with women. Like everything in life, biology influences purpose. Their jaded outlook, the coalitions, and the uniformity of thought that serves to protect their sanity are all responses to pain. Women develop a means to look tough too. To front. They create false securities. A napkin over a drink. The insecurities, the posturing, and the hypersensitivity are all related. Yvette was there to let my mother know she was in the right and that the school had a duty to my brother and me no matter what the administrators said about us. No matter what type of hoodlums we were.

Yvette being white also helped. Even if she was white trash with too many mulatto daughters to count. Despite any of their bias and condescension, Yvette's presence told my mother we were human. With this unity, my mother also taught me that Black men and women don't hear one another. Our shared Black plight expresses itself through the filter of gender. The scar tissue which masks our

---

[18] "when the slugs penetrate you'll feel a burning sensation."

pain, but only allows for the wounds to be accessed more easily, creates barriers between us. We are both searching for manhood: her as a complement—us as a continent (something to stand on). No longer do the Black man and Black woman complement one another. We hurt alone. We hurt with our enemy. We simply hurt.

Life in Exile
(General Nash)

*I*t wasn't until the Exile that I lost my mind. I don't know what anyone else calls it but it has been three winters since I've heard another human being speak. I have been encapsulated in silence. All I have are my thoughts. The entirety of humanity, save the Nation of course but they're not quite human, has been stricken mute. The world has become barren. I sow and I sow, but she does not produce life. I've learned that the Earth, she gives life discriminately. Producing only couscous and oats. It's torture. I have only eaten unseasoned couscous and oats. I have been unable to hear my wife's voice, answer my kids' questions, or bark orders to my troops.

The Profit was right, I should have never returned to that damned place. I should have taken my family and left. At the time, all I wanted to do was win the war. I wanted the Profit to feel the same loss I felt. Revenge. So instead of listening to wisdom, I fought. I did what I had been trained to do. I was stupid. I was a soldier. I'd rather be dead than yield. Being a soldier cost me everything.

"General, what's next? What do we do? All communication is

down." The question had come from my first lieutenant. He was unsettled by my conversation with the Profit. The gates to Soldier Field had closed behind us and slammed with a permanence I had yet to truly understand. There was no going back. Our mission was almost complete. Or so I thought.

I didn't know how any of this was happening and I didn't know what to do. I was confused. My only hope was that my family was still alive. I knew I couldn't go home. But that was my only desire at the time. I wanted to kiss my wife and apologize. Apologize for what I was doing. I wanted to say her name and hear her say mine. Each second, seemed like I was messing up, ruining the fate of the world. Even though I had no idea what I was doing.

How was this seventeen-year-old black bastard controlling the weather? Scientists were trying to figure it out. They thought he had a satellite system controlling light, carbon, sulfur, or something in the atmosphere. Wrong. Completely wrong. Atmospheric levels stayed the same. Then they said he built tunnels under our houses and strategized with the nation to kill every first born. Who is he, Santa? That would have taken an eternity. Did he stop time too? This is driving me crazy. He was fucking seventeen years old. Was he an engineer too?

The Earth was on fire. We asked for the sun, and it scorched the dry Earth. How could I not have returned? We needed to know what he was up to. I had all the intel. I was the only person he would talk to. I almost became his pet, like I was chosen. But for what? Why? I hated myself.

"We return to the base Steve. What else can we do. We're dying out here."

I called him by his first name. He wasn't shocked. There was no time for formalities. Whose general would I be in death? The earth was dying. We were burning. My flesh was in agony. It was so hot. I could barely see in front of me. My eyelids didn't want to expose my eyes to the torture. Waves of ash and flames crashed against my face. It felt ten times worse than the tear gas drill we perform in basic training. The fire wasn't normal. None of it was normal. It burned, but there was no smoke. My flesh was seared. But every inch that was removed by the fire grew back, just to be burned again.

"We return to the base and report what we know. That's all we can do."

My voice rose with uncertainty. I had no idea what we knew. We could only report what the Profit said. What did the Profit say?

"But general . . ." Steve stopped himself.

We were dying by the moment. My mouth became so dry, I could barely breathe. I wished my lips didn't exist. I dreamed of my own death. It was so close. Why couldn't I have just died? Death would have tasted so sweet. We got so comfortable. I didn't know life could get this tragic.

We knew it was unsafe to drive, so we walked to the base. The government constructed two sizable buildings two blocks north and south of Soldier Field. We tried to keep watch on the "Melanoid Nation." We built the building in the dark. There were so few resources. In the beginning, we operated as though it was all a game or another psycho like they had in Waco, Texas. All of this happened before we became terrified of our own shadows, and before we lost our innocents, our children. We had no idea who we were dealing with. We still don't. I think it's God Himself. Maybe. If He exists.

But God would have intervened on our behalf, on behalf of mankind.

It got so bad we tried to send spies in with the growing Zionist movement. Honestly, we got about one hundred spies in the stadium. Not one of the spies retuned. It seemed like the second they entered that damned Melanoid Nation, audiovisual broke down and they were all converted. Converted by that cult. All of them preaching something about "Melanoid Empowerment." They became citizens and cut off contact. We thought they would never be able to survive in Soldier Field. We calculated that at best they had a week. One week later, Soldier Field seemed to be the only place where people were thriving. Their population continued to grow. While we relied on our technology.

Europe, too, had collapsed. With the fall of neocolonialism, they could not sustain their opulence. I have even heard rumors of a disease worse than the bubonic plague spreading throughout western Europe. The symptoms are like rabies. A bunch of rabid Europeans. That's what they get. They've been riding American coattails since the First War. If it weren't for us, the Communists would be in power.

We tried to smoke the Nation out of Soldier Field, cut off their resources and even nuke them out. Nothing worked. The harder we worked to end the movement, the worse our existence got. The more we lost. The death toll was astronomical.

Arriving at the North S.F. Base, we thought there was going to be relief. We were more than surprised to find the building was demolished. My men were on the verge of death. The dehydration was unbearable. My bones ached and my flesh boiled. Blisters the size of softballs formed on my legs, arms, and chest. I lost all the hair on my body. But my uniform was completely intact. The fire was attracted to my flesh. Bizarre.

"General . . . I can't go any farther," my first lieutenant shouted as his knees hit the ground. I could barely see his silhouette through the flames.

"You have to Steve. You've got to."

I was telling myself more than him. The only option we had was to walk a mile to the South S.F. Base. The mission seemed next to impossible. We barely made it to the North S.F. Base. What if the South Base had been demolished too? I was desperate. I shouted the way I assume Jesus did on the cross. If he was real? These ordeals made me question all of my beliefs. I shouted with everything I had in me.

"Make a way! Please!!!"

Suddenly, a cloud appeared overhead. A dark and brooding cloud. It blocked out the sun once more. Lightning struck the ground in front of us. There was no time to react because a massive downpour started immediately. The storm was torrential, extinguishing the fire. My men looked up at me as if I created heaven and earth.

"We must move. Who knows how long we have."

Along with my second lieutenant, Mario, I picked up Steve from the ground instinctively. We had to move. We communicated without talking. We had to.

I couldn't help but think about the fate of humanity. Who was the Profit? How could he set the world on fire, literally? We needed to get to the Base. That was our only saving grace. If the South Base was destroyed, the war was lost—the war to save "human" civilization.

"Soldier!" I shouted at Steve. He was my best friend. We'd known one another since basic training. He was the best man in my wedding. If he had ever settled down, I would have been his. There was no time for such thoughts. We didn't have time for anything, even planning. But we had to follow through on our mission: win the war. That I knew.

"Soldier, our country is at war. We need you to buck up!!! Steve, I need you!"

It was true. I couldn't take any more loss. That was the hardest part of the entire battle, we lost so much. I lost so much. I couldn't take another loss. Not my best friend.

Steve attempted to straighten himself up. He tried his best to stand erect and look like a soldier. I got a little choked up as if to weep but no tears came. My tear ducts were dry at this point. We were all in so much pain. Blisters formed and burst on our skin. Our flesh was boiling. The rain hurt too. It wasn't soothing at all. It ate at our skin. The heavy downpour ripped the raised flesh off. Slabs of my skin peeled off of my face and arms.

Although I wanted to cry, I stayed strong for my men. I knew if the South Base had been destroyed, there would be no way to keep my poise. I would crack. We had seven city blocks to go, and I could barely see in front of my face. Each step was more laden than the last. The rain was coming down harder than hell. As I wiped my eyes, I accidentally removed my right eyelid. It stung slightly. But the effect of looking at your own eyelid in your hand is unimaginable, especially after simply wiping your face. The earth wasn't prepared for such a heavy drenching. There were floods all around us. The puddles made each step more difficult. Mud was sticking and weighing down each step. The more Steve leaned on us, the deeper I sank.

We eventually made it to the base. It seemed as if weeks had passed. I was in agony. Everything hurt. Steve's weight felt leaden. Somehow, the base was still standing. The rain never ceased. Our flesh was raw. Most of the skin had been ripped away. We were in such dire straits. The mission still needed to be completed. If the world was going to die, we had to try to save her. Mario and I were holding Steve as we walked through the handicap doors of the building. Both bases ran on their own generators for twenty-four hours a day. Coal was being imported from Montana to ensure that power was maintained for our efforts. Our efforts were to save this world.

Pressing the handicap button, Mario released his hold on Steve. Skin from the backside of Mario's hand stuck to the round button with the blue wheel chair and stick man. The rain rinsed the blood. Steve got dramatically heavier. I wasn't sure I could hold myself up at this point let alone another's weight. Steve was my best friend though, my first lieutenant. So I tried to support him. I leaned away to counter his weight. Taking the first step through the doors, I looked around and everything seemed normal at the base. Nobody was rushing, there was no concern. Communication was down and I had a feeling that the torment we experienced was divine. They had no clue of what was happening on the outside. In those days, we got used to just surviving.

I took the second step, but Steve wasn't in rhythm with me. His weight pulled me backwards and we both fell. The drop knocked the wind out of me. I could see stars as the fluorescent lights came into view. I landed facing the counter. The receptionist looked up. The clock above her head had to be off. The small hand was on the seven and the long hand was just about at the three. It read 7:14 p.m. The eternal flame that tortured us for what felt like years only lasted three hours. What would hell be like? I thought of my son. I failed the world.

"General Nash, stay with us. Stay with us," a man's voice came through.

"What do you think could've happened to them?" A woman's voice chimed in. I recognized it. It was Lia, the Secretary of State.

"Oh my God. They look like bacon." She was never one for subtlety.

"Let's hope we can save one of them," the man's voice stated. It was a harsh proposal. Save one of us. *Where's Steve? What about Mario?*

I instantly sat up. "Where are my men?" I realized the male voice was a military doctor. I had seen him before but he wasn't very familiar. I grabbed his shoulder aggressively. I needed to know about my men.

"Mario and Steve? My lieutenants, where are they? Did they survive?"

Lia put her hand on my chest. Her touch hurt. I winced. She was being empathetic. I didn't know this side of her existed. She was always a tough little something. She was barely over five feet tall. Her hair was always pinned back in a tight bun, with three or four bobby pins holding it down. Not a strand of hair escaped her updo. She was Italian although she looked Spanish, like Cuban or something. This was the first time I can remember that she had been even remotely pleasant. Absolutely the first time we touched beyond a firm handshake.

"What did they do to you? I knew it was a terrible idea to send you back."

She had, in fact, argued against sending me back in. But everyone thought I had been chosen by the Profit. Even I thought I could do something. It was all for naught. I had been given a blessing, and I shit on it. That's why we drank. He was my friend, I suddenly realized. If only I had listened. "If only I had listened," I whispered, shaking my head. I wanted to touch my face, but I was terrified of what else I would lose. A lip? My forehead skin?

"What was that general? We need you to talk. Please let us know what happened. What we need to do."

She was trying to be nice. It was funny. It was unnatural for her. We were all scared but it was appropriate, and I needed it. I told them the story. I told them everything that happened. How the north base was destroyed. Everything that we endured trying to get to the base. I told them what I felt. What I now knew. They had no choice but to believe me. They were horrified.

However, the revelations didn't come immediately. The rain had apparently stopped when my men and I arrived at the base. After surgery, Mario, Steve, and I all shared a room near the military doctor's office. I found out that he too was a general. General Matthews. He was a good guy, and he even managed to reattach my eyelid. Though it still doesn't work properly. I have to think to blink. But after three winters, and no communication, even that has become a subconscious gesture.

We recovered in no time. There was no need for skin grafts. All of our wounds healed within three days. It was a miracle. Lia and the others put out a warning the first day. The world was at Code Black. However, as the days wore on and the revelations refused to manifest, the alerts lost their urgency. The people thought the sun was shining. Although it was clearly closer to the Earth and it never set, people were less fearful. People simply stayed in the house and avoided being in the sun. They tried to move on. Forget about those lost. By the time General Matthews released us, the alert was at a Code Orange. I blame social media. People just lost patience somewhere along the way. I remember the Cold War. Remember the Cold War? Nothing happened, but the alert was constant. They were victims of technology.

Upon the release, things were different. Life was going to be drastically different. The first thing I did was go outside. I needed to see what was happening. The sun was directly over the Earth. It hurt my eyes. Everything was covered in light, draped in white. Hot as hell. I stayed in the sun as long as I could and was thankful to be alive. I had survived Hell Fire or so I thought. I was wrong. The irony of my condition is not lost on me. The sun, the granter of all life in the universe, stripped me of sight.

I ran back into the Base. The ground beneath us shook. I thought of my family. I couldn't imagine what was about to befall them. Us. I still have no clue where they are. Corinne.

I call it the Exile. I wish I knew how others termed it. The last voice I heard was the Big Voice in the Sky. Strangest thing, it sounded like the Profit does sometimes, after those long silences. Was he God? The voice wasn't particularly male or female. In fact, it sounded like a bunch of different people. The Big Voice spoke with authority. I knew then that this was who controlled the sun, this was who turned on the flames and made it rain. This was who healed me in three days. I am still unsure whether it was God. But I am sure this was who Exiled us.

For three winters I have wrestled with this thought. Did I speak to God? I'm not sure. I wish I could go back and ask about my family. I wish I could ask a million questions. At the time, I was scared and ashamed. My soul was too exposed, like every step I took in life had been revealed to me. As though it was written all by the same hand. I was not a good man. I was ashamed. My knees buckled. I was on all fours in front of the Big Voice. Prostrate.

"Rise and stand for judgment," The Big Voice called out.

I stood up slowly, feeling more ashamed as I ascended. I wished I could stay down. I wished that I could hide my face in the ground. Why had I been born a human? I begged to be a beast: an ostrich, mole, groundhog, or worm, anything to hide from judgment. Then I realized that it wasn't talking to me. It was addressing "my family," the oppressors, as the Profit so eloquently put it. We were all under judgment.

"Where are your brothers?"

The earth stood in silence. No one replied. "They are at war with us." I stammered. "We are at war with them."

I felt more ashamed after rewording the statement. I looked down. My voice, too, echoed across the surface of the Earth. Everyone heard my proclamation. They now knew who I was. I wanted to take it back. I recoiled at the sting of being white. I hated that feeling. Knowing I was white. Maybe I didn't deserve my status in this country. My skin was raw, exposed.

"We can't stop them. Our lives keep getting worse. First the sun wouldn't shine . . ." I began to whine. I stopped myself. The world couldn't hear me whine. The Profit couldn't hear me whine.

"I ask again, where are your brothers? Where is Trayvon Martin?"

"He is dead," I responded. "So is my son. So is Mariah the president's oldest." I needed to explain myself. I needed to explain to the world.

"Where is Bob Marley, Sandra Bland, Tupac Shakur, Nathaniel Turner, Eric Gardner, Sojourner Truth, Harold Washington, Harriet Tubman? Where are your brothers? Your neighbors?" The Big Voice commanded.

I had no answer though. They were all dead. So many names that I didn't even know. But I knew they were dead. All of them. But now the Big Voice was talking directly to me.

"You have shared my proclamation with the world. Tongues shall be tied. Families shall be scattered. You shall wander the Earth as a drifter. As Cain did. All who do you harm shall receive Our wrath tenfold. You will walk the Earth eternally. For the sins of your father's father's father, you will endure great sufferings. The Earth shall be made anew and you will suffer many things. Your bodies will be broken. But they will not die. You will receive the punishment for every lash of the whip, every prick of cotton, tobacco, and sugar cane on the fingers of the kidnapped Africans, every lynching of Native and African children. You will feel the weight of each and every sin committed against your own soul."

God was already intervening. He was not on our side of history. The world shifted. It became clear then. I forfeited my soul before I even knew I had one.

"We will give you grain for nourishment and the knowledge to grow it. Nothing else."

There was a brief moment of clarity. I rose to speak. I wanted to beg for my life. I wanted to beg for all of us. I heard the voices of millions. It was overwhelming. I grabbed my ears and fell back to the ground. The voice went away. We were alone and all was silent.

Since my encounter with the Big Voice, I have wandered the Earth feasting on couscous. I believe that I am in D.C. I started going crazy a little while ago. I remember thinking it was a dream through the first winter. I thought it was all a game—the frostbite and all. The day I kissed my sanity goodbye was during the spring after the second winter. I was trying to find my family. I couldn't forget them. I wanted to see my kids. My wife. Trying to track people down now was next to impossible. There was no one to talk to. There was no way to know if you were going in the right direction. The sun never set. It was always scorching hot. After two weeks I could no longer tell the difference between East, West, North, and South. There was no rhythm to life anymore.

The Earth was almost completely barren. No one spent time in the sun. No one was out longer than it took to plant and harvest couscous and oats. Even that was difficult with the sun raging. The Earth gave only what we needed. Nothing more. I was always hungry. Every part of me wanted to starve to death. But death was no longer an option. There was no Amber Alert that I could deploy. Everyone was a lost child. Even me.

On this fateful day, I was in Columbus. I know that for sure. I grew up in Columbus. I followed the highway to get here. Walked the entire way from Chicago searching for my family. I found methods to last longer in the heat. I held water in my mouth for hours to avoid dry mouth. I wore white everywhere. If I found a white sheet in my travels, it was mine. On my final sane day, I found myself in an abandoned discount store. It looked like an old Walmart. But I couldn't be sure. With each passing day, my vision grew worse. The sun was torturing me. Everything was white, making me snowblind. I had the hardest time sleeping because of the Sun. My dreams were bleached. Everything appeared as a silhouette.

I remember on that day, I went down the picked over aisles. I tripped over an object. Reaching down, I ran my hand across it. It was a bike frame. The aluminum of the bike felt cool on my hand. I touched every inch of the bike. The chain felt slick. I nicked my hand on the pedal. The sting aroused my frustration. I had already stubbed my toe on the contraption. I tossed the bike slightly, with the little strength I had. I heard a crunch. Following the sound, I searched near my feet. Under the bike tire I found two bottles. They felt like water. I opened the first and took the longest gulp of my existence. It was the source. The mission was worth it.

As I turned down the next aisle, I saw a human. It was a white woman. She was crying. Her hair was matted and her clothes tattered. I went over to touch her, to help her. It was my wife. She was completely blind now. We were all almost blind. Between the sun and the lack of nutrition, our bodies were falling apart. I was filled with joy. The mission was complete. I found her. She found me. My soul mate. My heart flooded with memories of our wedding day. Steve was there. My wife was gorgeous. She was a choreographer. She made me memorize a dance. Our song was "Can't Help Falling in

Love" by Elvis. We killed the dance that night. Her body was frail now. She was defenseless in this new world of ours. Corinne.

I saw her. I touched her. But she didn't recognize me. I couldn't speak to her. Let her know we were safe. All I wanted to do was kiss her, ask where the children were, hold her and shoulder her tears. Instead, she fought me. Understandably, she fought me. She was blind and vulnerable. She hit me with mighty blows. Blows that I deserved. Blows that I needed to take. I ran out of the store tripping and stumbling on every obstacle. I sobbed when I reached the light. My mouth was bleeding. The sun dried it up. It was hot but I didn't mind anymore. I wanted my wife, my family, my world. I couldn't even think of my children. It was too much.

After that first encounter, I followed my wife for three months but kept my distance. She was gorgeous. I watched her silhouette from afar. Dying slowly. I couldn't leave her. I was chasing a shadow. But she was mine. I made a vow. She is my wife. I am her husband. She just didn't know. Corinne had difficulty finding shelter in this new world. She wasn't threatening. She was a dancer. Completely blind and petite. Oppressors wandered everywhere. Life was a struggle for us all. The Earth was stingy. We were foreign. Nature tormented us. The Sun ate at our skin, vision, and health. I was almost blind at this point. Corinne stayed out, exposed to the sun, far more than I was used to or could bear. This is probably why she went totally blind before me. Blisters grew on my face, back, and hands in my effort to chase my wife. I had difficulty keeping up with her at times. My vision was failing me. She was quicker than I remembered. Survival brings out the best in us in many ways.

We made it to Pennsylvania. I am not quite sure how far into the state we were. In Pennsylvania, Corinne found her way to a junkyard. There were a lot of prime resources there during the Exile. It was also a scary place to be blind. At the beginning of the Exile, gangs started to form at stationary shelters like prisons, hospitals, and grocery stores. She would have no idea if she was being watched. She had no idea that I was following her for more than two months. My wife was precious and at risk.

She had been in the junkyard for the better part of what felt like an hour. I've lost all sense of time since the sun never sets. Like all of us, she was looking for food or water. She hadn't fully adapted to being blind yet. I attest, it was more than I was prepared to accept. My eyesight was fading by the day. At this point, Corinne was a shadow. I could only see her silhouette. But I knew it was her. She was my wife. She made it to an open field. I believed we were being watched. I stayed behind. I lost sight of her. It was the last time I saw her alive. It was the last time I . . .

I moved around a mound of earth. It could have been a pile of garbage as well. I caught sight of her again. She was meandering through the field. She tripped and fell behind what I assumed to be a car. Bodies, dark shapes rushed toward her. They looked like ravens. But I couldn't be sure. They could just as well be humans. I was too far out to tell.

"Aaaaahhhhhhhh!!!" My wife let out a bloodcurdling scream.

It was the first voice I'd heard in years. It hurt. I let this all happen. The world didn't have to come to this. I should have never gone back to Soldier Field. I hung my head temporarily. It was all my fault.

I couldn't let anything take my wife away from me again. I ran to her aid. I would die before anyone could take her from me. Even the little bit of her that I still had. I had to traverse a mound of earth. I crawled up the trash heap on all fours. Once I got to the top, I had to recalculate. Where was I? Where was my wife? I couldn't hear my wife anymore. My heart dropped. I found them. They were human, humans with dogs. They were attacking my wife. The barking came into range now. Maybe they were cannibals or thieves. Maybe both. I couldn't hear my wife. Rage built inside of me. My feet hit the ground. I rushed down the mound of trash, picking up speed and momentum. I bumped into what felt like the hood of a car. Everything was bright. All I saw were shadows, human and canine. They surrounded me. I fought every one of them. There was no fear left in my heart. God could take nothing more from me.

My hands and feet felt flesh and fur. I connected with lefts and rights on jaws and ribs. I didn't know who or what I was hitting. I just kept swinging. Then I felt the familiar burn of a dog bite on my right leg. The dog shook and took me to one knee. My wife was on the ground. She had turned over and was crawling slowly to her feet. She was still moving. I couldn't see her injuries. But I could only guess. I wanted to give myself as a sacrifice. The people circled me. I couldn't see their faces. Something connected with the back of my head. Everything went black . . .

I woke up. My mouth was dry. My head was throbbing. The sun was wearing on my face. Everything hurt. My wife was gone. I wasn't dead. But everything in me wished they had killed me. I awoke completely blind. The last thing I saw and heard was my wife screaming for her life. I wish they had killed me.

CHAPTER 10

The Disciples

I finished middle school in Kimball Valley. I became very familiar with its culture, the kids, the beasts. Though I spent two years in that environment, I remained on the periphery, never fully adopting the mentality. I sat and watched. I interacted but always with hesitation. As the constant observer, I learned an incredible amount about myself. My time in Kill-Vill has proven to be one of the most fruitful periods in my life. I became acquainted with my people. I saw us in a different light. My status on the periphery was my hazing. I got a taste of what life had to offer me, the Black me. These students were my kin through skin and subsequent struggle. But as you know, one cannot stay on the periphery forever.

The summer leading into my eighth-grade year, I decided I would merge with my peers or rather, I'd assimilate. I couldn't remain on the outskirts any longer, so I mimicked them. But I did so not as a follower. I was me, but with their intensity and passions. I adopted their narrative. We joked about our pain. We ached in the sight of beauty. We hated the lives of those we saw on television. They didn't reflect us. No one was there to save us from the hood.

We didn't have an Uncle Phil. There was no Mr. Drummond. Their absence only reminded us of our missing fathers.

In their absence, we watched music videos. We watched music videos and celebrated when we saw Krucial Konflict, R. Kelly, and Twista. Their montages of Chicago's sites filled us with joy. They made us feel important. These videos let us know that the world saw us. We were proud momentarily. The way Chief Keef does now, I guess: Dr. Illinois. At those times we thought, *They can't turn their heads forever.* Because somehow, at some point, we're going to get the microphone and when we got it, we would protect it with an unyielding grip and an instinct so keenly maternal that it seems both foreign and familiar.

But our jubilee was always passing, never consistent. Our season was always yet to come. So while watching these videos, we indulged. We interacted with an intensity that was borderline hostile. Our excitement crept up inside us and it manifested in such a strange manner. We were young. We had something to prove to ourselves and to each other. I sat back while they demonstrated dominance.

I was on the periphery partially because I was still young. Although we were the same age, I was the one still naive, still a child. They would test one another. Pull each other's "hoe cards" as they called it. They would posture, showing off for one another only in the hopes of receiving admiration for any number of talents. While watching music videos, their posturing came in the form of lyrical recitation, recognition of places in the videos, and the beloved name dropping.

"That's K-town, my brotha stay on dat block," Romeo would say.

Barely listening and ready to one up the previous statement, Ferris would have a story ready.

"On da folks, I saw that nigga Twista on Leamington and Madison pushin a candy apple Maybach!"

Shannon listening intently, as always, looking for inconsistencies in their stories, would respond comically with the usual, "On my mama you a lie. You aint neva seen Twista on no Leamington. Fam, you don't even be on Leamington." To be honest, what you say doesn't mean anything if you don't support it with something important to you. For Ferris, it was the Folks. For Shannon, it was his mom. For me, it was my soul. "On my soul," I would say.[19]

After the fallacy had been found, Ferris, embarrassed from being called out, would offer up the futile response, "How you know where I be at?" Barely making eye contact but maintaining the same intensity and passion as before. Ferris always wanted to be the leader. But he wasn't. It's that way sometimes. He was the Raphael of the group and Shannon was Leonardo. I suspect I was Donatello. Hopefully, I was Donatello.[20]

With the quick and clever response of "Nigga cause I be witchu," the conversation would be put to rest. Ferris would be disproven, and we would fall back into the videos.

The roles would change. The struggle for dominance remained, and from time to time, comments were left untouched. But most opportunities to debunk were taken. Every day there were disputes like this. Some ending in fights but most ended in laughs. We were a

---

[19] You gotta merch it.
[20] This is a reference to the Teenage Mutant Ninja Turtles.

makeshift family. Not drawn to one another because of mutual interest, rather mutual pain. Our link was situational therefore our bond was eternal. Brothers in plight are forever brothers. Our households were in disarray. Our fathers killed, brothers imprisoned, mothers drugged out, we slept on couches and floors, our electricity was in limbo, rent late, refrigerators empty AND our sisters starved for attention while we watched music videos because when we nodded to the beat we nodded affirmatively. We said *Yes*. Yes to ourselves. Never begging the question to what do I assent? All we knew was that we were saying yes to insurmountable no's.

We had to succeed but weren't given the tools to do so. Our clothes were dirty, pants sagged, hair uncombed, save Ferris (who always had his hair freshly braided), and our shoes were biscuits. But we were awake. We were conscious but untrained. Our mission dog-eared in the pages of history, creased at the edge, our journey, though of similar origins, had not yet been mapped. We were alive so we nodded. We were alive before we knew it. We were awake. While others napped, dozed, slumbered, we were aware. In this plight, there was a hidden advantage. We had a secret culture. A private culture. Subculture even.

We went to school because we had to get out of the house. We succeeded in school because we were failures everywhere else in life. Failures without effort. I know that sounds redundant, but we were failures before we tried, before our talent could be appropriately assessed. I was a thief without stealing. To the Talented Tenth we called, "Why doesn't Atlas have a say? If we shrug, does the world tumble?" There was something improper about this fraction. We carried the burden and navigated with ease. But they are the talented.

That tenth is crazy, and without knowing it, we were carrying the world. Whites and Blacks alike we carried.

Although we all felt the weight, there was one of us who embodied the spirit of the group, who called us to arms. Shannon was the unofficial leader of our clique. Everything we felt, he felt to a greater extent. It was in his eyes, his swagger. We all wanted part of it. Even the teachers. Though his even-keeled temperament was a bit unsettling, his charming demeanor made up for it. A part of his soul was unaffected by the world, a step beyond detached.

Everyone around found that intriguing. It was godly in a way. His turtle-like nature, his ability to retreat while present fascinated me. Why didn't he show off? Why didn't people make fun of him? It was because we all connected with him in some way. All of our sentiments were accentuated in him. His grace was the reason I was allowed in the clique in the first place. Shannon vouched for me for no personal gain. Because of his selflessness, we gave him the throne (well it was more of a bench than a throne, but it was definitely regal). It wasn't necessarily given. I think it was just natural for him to be the leader. He was our John the Baptist. The opener of hearts and minds.

During the summer, the crew would stay at Shannon's house for hours on end. It became our second home. I even had my own chair. Every day I would arrive, go to the kitchen, and bring my chair to the living room. Everyone knew that it was my chair too, even Shannon's siblings who actually lived there. While there, we were welcomed guests into the chaos of Shannon's life.

We experienced the introduction of his stepfather, violent disputes between Shannon and his mother, and the birth of his niece

Jamiah. But through it all, he maintained. He was our cornerstone. I think his consistency and resilience were the characteristics I admired most. His transparency. We knew so much about him, save his thoughts. Even though he had all that shit going on at the crib you could never tell from the way he carried it.

He wasn't like Atlas. More like Prometheus, although I think he is referenced far too often. But I think this is the Prometheus reference to salvage them all. He was akin to Prometheus because it felt like there was some smug, Godforsaken, hope-free liberation in his punishment. He loved his life because it was his, the only thing he truly owned. Not because of the way it was turning out. So what if the eagle was eating his liver now, he knew Hercules was coming. He knew somewhere, or at least hoped deeply, that the suffering was temporary.

Shannon's biggest fallout with his mother was on the Fourth of July. The day started off with a set of omens. For starters, I woke up and the lights had gone out in our building. Keith had to go down to the basement while I held the flashlight, always too shaky for his liking. I stood behind him very careful. He knew I didn't like going into basements and I hated this one most of all because of its smell. It smelled like burning weave and flesh, and to this day I have the image of capital punishment at a women's correctional facility burned into my head. I got the image of women being fried in massive metal chairs, weaves catching on fire, and throngs of sadistic people acting helpless even though they were the actors, even though they could stop the entire event.

So when we went down to the basement, I was a bit nervous. He flipped the switch, making the image even more real. The circuit breaker went out often in our building. Definitely a fire hazard, but I'm certain there were many other city ordinances that were being violated in that building.

On our way out the basement door, there they stood. The fattest, ugliest, meanest, hairiest, whitish greyest, red-eyedest family of possums I've ever seen. There were five of them. I'm assuming a mother, a father, and three kids. But they were all about twenty-five to thirty pounds. Monsters I tell you. I immediately let out a scream sending them into a frenzy. The scream might or might not have been the manliest thing I've done in my life. Three of them bolted, climbing on the fences, scaling the side of the wall, and leaving the other two hissing and hunchbacked with their tails in the air.

I assume the two remaining possums were the parents. That was of no consequence, however. I stood there, Keith behind me. He was probably using me as a shield. Word to the wise, possums don't play. I've seen possums give dogs some go. Big dogs. We stood there not knowing where to go. Keith talked to me slowly. He told me to back into the death chamber. He placed his hand on my shoulder and pulled slightly backwards. "Step back and close the door bro," he whispered with one exhale. I didn't know who to trust: him, my fear, or the possums. Something about their stance let me know that they were scared too, and something else about it let me know that they were willing to take this situation much further than I was.

"Come with me," I said. "They're scared too." Keith said nothing. He simply slid along the side of the building with me. One step at a time we separated from the hostile possums. As we moved, they turned, never growing weary or disinterested. They watched us until we made it back to the front door. From the way Keith exhaled when he got inside the doorway, it was clear that he hadn't taken a breath for the entirety of the ordeal. He said nothing about the issue once we got into the house. He just went to his room, lit a blunt, and walked the event off in his mind. I understood the angst. It was too early for such an experience.

The fuse had been lit from the beginning. From the possum scare onward, the day blossomed. It grew into something of legend. Every day at around eleven, the crew would meet at the basketball courts about three blocks from my apartment building. I was already late because of the ridiculous possums.

I debated taking a shower and figured because it was the Fourth of July, I might be out for a long time doing who knows what, and I didn't want to be the musty dude in the crew. Girls do not like the musty one. So I hopped in the shower, got dressed quickly, forgetting to lotion some areas, and I was off. On any other day, I might not have taken a shower. I didn't quite have the hygiene thing down yet. Admittedly, I think I was the musty one in the group.

The whole crew was there, Romeo, Shannon, and Ferris. There were a couple of honorary members to our crew, but we were the only official members, we held the power to admit or reject new applicants. This day was different. Instead of playing basketball, they were sitting on the bench near the fence alongside the long-abandoned baseball field. The baseball field was completely unsafe. There were no bases, the sand had somehow reverted back to rock and glass, and the outfield was full of potholes.

Needless to say, no one went to the MLB from Kimball Valley. I often wondered why they hadn't just made more basketball courts. The field was practically a virgin. At least for its intended purposes.

There were broken bottles, used condoms, and I'm sure a number of syringes floating around the infield. More people had urinated on the mound than pitched off of it. Ferris was perched on the back of the bench with his feet on the seat stooped over, his dark face slightly frowned intently listening to Romeo who, as usual, was delivering a monologue with the grandest of hand gestures. When I approached cheerfully it was apparent that my lightheartedness was unwelcome.

"What yall on? I know yall aint trying to spit? You know I'm the illest."

The scolds that immediately followed my comment told me this was another conversation that would require minimal input from me but a significant amount of attention. They often had conversations about topics I knew nothing about, and it was apparent when I was pretending to be well-versed on such issues. It is always apparent when people pretend.

Informed or not, I knew an obligation was approaching that I wouldn't be comfortable refusing. So I waited for the question to come naturally. I had grown weary of probing because at some point it made the action seem like an offer and not a request. Probing is not good for relationships. Probing is not good ever. Let things be and they will come out. That might have been lesson number one about the crew. Mind your own business. If something isn't offered, don't look for it. All of us respected that. I think this lesson went naturally with my detestation of questioning.

Ferris was the first to smile. He extended his hand and slightly raised his six-foot frame from the bench to shake up with me. His style never varying. He wore a baggy Girbaud shirt, his jeans cuffed into his socks showing the extended tongue of his unlaced Air Max.

"What down mane? Where you coming from all happy an shit?" He stood about six-two. When we shook up, his shoulder slightly hit my jaw. I acted normal though.

"Nowhere. But if yall wanna get some of this fire. I spit hot fire like Dylon." I said conceding the lack of humor in my intended joke. Then Shannon and Romeo followed suit by shaking up with me. They both had to step off of the bench. The process was pretty labored. But there are only two times in a conversation in which it is okay and required for men to touch, the greeting and the farewell.

Shannon still had not broken out his classic thirty-two teeth smile. I knew something was troubling him, but I wasn't going to ask. In fact, I didn't have much interest in finding out what they wanted me to do. Romeo saw me looking at Shannon for a period and quickly sparked another conversation up to distract all of us from the rising discomfort of potential emotion in the way that all men do.

"So, where the hoes at?" he said while pretending to dribble a basketball.

His hands were permanently cupped as if they were holding a ball. Romeo's dream was to play in the NBA and he talked about it all the time. Although Ferris had the size, Romeo's love of the game was unmatched. If he had the opportunity to talk about basketball all day without interruption, he would. From the players, to the sneakers, to the cards, he was a connoisseur of the game. He knew basketball if he didn't know nothing else. He could talk about most players' entire careers from high school (especially Kevin Garnett), like how tall they were in their sophomore and senior year of high school. It was insane.

"Man I aint tryin to hoop today. You know they gonna be

shoot . . ."

Before Shannon could finish his sentence, a group of kids came from across the basketball court aiming Roman Candles at us. The whistle of the projectiles startled all of us. The firecrackers were breezing past our heads. Ferris was the first to take off running, and I followed stride for stride. We all split up and ran in different directions. We had an established plan that whenever we ran, whether it be from the cops or otherwise, we would meet up at Shannon's house.

His house was goose so to speak. Whenever we would get in trouble and have to separate, and this did happen often, we'd come back to Shannon's house, primarily because it was the house with the least supervision. We never had to explain why we were out of breath, dirty, why we had so many bags, or where we were coming from because everyone was preoccupied with their own issues. On the chance occasion someone did ask, they were typically so engulfed in their doped-out stupors, it made no difference whether we responded or not.

Shannon lived about seven blocks from the park in the opposite direction from my house. No matter the distance, for some reason, I was always the first to make it there. Everyone else must stop running at some point. But I was always in full sprint. Once I started, I had to make it to goose. I had to make it to safety. About two minutes after I made it to Shannon's, Romeo showed up. I wanted to wait for one of them because I didn't like being in Shannon's house by myself. His family was loud, televisions blared over the bass of the radio, and Jamiah was always crying because Jasmin (Shannon's sister and Jamiah's mother) was never home. Shannon's mom, when she wasn't nodding off in another cracked-out stupor, spent most of her time yelling at us to do things around the house. "If yall gonna be moving in anyways, might as well earn your keep."

His stepfather never said a word. Not one word. I wouldn't even have been able to recognize his voice if he spoke.

I sat on the stairs leading up to Shannon's. When Romeo was in sight, I stood up and walked to the bottom. Clearly fatigued from the run, he offered a pitiful yell, "Wait up Joe!" When he got closer, he managed to tell me the reason for their discontent earlier.

"Shannon's mom kicked em outta the house this morning," he said between intermingled breaths. Well he didn't quite decide to tell me, as much as he had to because it was vital information to have given the circumstance. Seeing we were about to enter the house.

"What she kick 'em out for?" I said really wondering why a woman would do that to her child. I had never heard of such a claim. I often heard of children running away. But, putting your seed out, that was new. Romeo shrugged, unaware.

"She kicked him out?" I repeated once more to myself. "You think we should go in?" I said finally after partially digesting the comment and realizing it may be unsafe inside as well. I had so many questions at once. I decided to stop probing.

Before Romeo could get out a response, Ferris and Shannon jogged up together. *They're slow as hell.* They weren't out of breath.

Then Shannon asked in a mildly condescending tone, "Why didn't yall go in?"

He knew why we didn't go in. If he wasn't welcome, we sure as hell weren't welcome. However, Shannon was as prideful and ornery a person as I've ever met and with that question, he walked right past us. With three steps, he glided up the nine stairs leading to his house and walked inside.

When we got in, we found the house empty. Ferris was scratching his braids while Romeo went straight to the kitchen and got a drink of water. I grabbed my chair from the kitchen and brought it to the living room as I always did. I sat near the couch. It was a brown corduroy L-shaped couch that was noticeably too big for the room. Its back faced the main entrance to the house, and if one sat at the end of the other section of the L, watching the television was out of the question. The angle was almost impossible, and the TV was small. So small. The couch was too big and the TV was too small. Totally out of Feng shui.

Shortly after I sat down, Shannon entered the room with two juice pouches and threw one in my lap. Although he didn't seem as angry as before, there was an ominous feeling growing in the house, but the juice made me ignore it. I appreciated every effort Shannon made to reach out to me. His generosity and the sincerity of his kindness made me forget. It made me forget the immediacy of our eviction notice. He made me forget the drama of being thirteen in Kimball Valley, like having roman candles shot at you while sitting in the park. That's not a fun game to play. I definitely preferred Bombardment. Shout out to Will, peace and blessing be upon him.

When Romeo came in and sat, he simultaneously turned on the TV. He had apparently grabbed the remote before going into the kitchen to ensure we watched something he'd like (which meant either music videos or basketball). So we watched BET for a while since *106 and Park* was about to come on. Ferris sat at the kitchen table, which actually gave you a better view of the TV than the end of the couch. When *The Basement* came on, we all got excited because The Clipse were in the Basement with Big Tig.

I waited the entire show to watch them freestyle. I secretly wanted to rap but didn't know where to start or who to ask to teach me. It's such a personal art so can someone really teach you? I figured you either had it or not. But I found out about NWA, Will Smith, and Drake many years later.[21] Then Malice and Pusha got in the booth, their faces inches away from the hanging microphone. Big Tigger stood behind them making faces and the occasional comment to express his appreciation for a particular line. They spit to Lil Scrappy's *No Problems* beat, recycled a line from *Grindin* and used it as their chorus. The chorus stuck with me. Its prophetic tone was unmatched by any holy scripture. If I remember it right, they said, "My grind's about family never been about fame. Days I wasn't able there was always caine." The line sent a lyrical chill through me, rattling my bones. That line deserves to be analyzed and dissected until nothing remains of it, but clarity of conscience. Cain killed his brother. Cocaine kills nations. The Clipse are brilliant.

Just then, we heard keys at the door. Ferris, Romeo, and I all looked at Shannon who showed no fear. His mother stumbled in the house more clear-eyed than she had ever been, at least in the time I had known her. She was carrying three or four bright blue and orange Aldi bags. She had been grocery shopping.

When she entered the house and saw us, she smiled. For the first time, she was happy to see us and said, "You boys just gonna sit there

---

[21] Maybe it doesn't matter if you don't write your own lyrics; if people like to hear you that might be all that matters. Case in point, NWA and Drake.

while I'm struggling with these bags? Go get them otha bags from the cab." The kindness of her tone shocked us. I hadn't heard her speak in an octave lower than a shout since I'd known her. She was only buttering us up to get us to do chores. Maybe she got the groceries for free off of a lost EBT card. Whatever it was, she wasn't being nice just for the sake of it.

So we went down to help her get the groceries out of the taxi. There were about nine steps leading up to the house. Ferris was directly ahead of me. He decided to jump down the stairs. He landed dramatically. His knees buckled, and he stumbled awkwardly forward. When we got to the car, the driver had already brought many of the bags to the sidewalk and was bent over torso long in the trunk. Then he stood up. He was tall. His disheveled oxford shirt with sleeves rolled passed the elbows, salt and pepper facial hair, and the deep wrinkles surrounding his sunken eyes offered character while simultaneously showing the beating that life had in store for all of us. Man, he looks old, I thought.

A curiosity was sparked in me. I wanted to know future me. What could I be like? I approached future me intently, trying to get all of my secrets which have yet to come to pass. I mean, he was an old Black Man and I would be an old Black Man one day. Inshallah. When I got to where the taxi driver stood, he intoned a friendly but stern greeting.

"What's happenin young blood?" The way he emphasized "young blood" was loaded with intentionality. It connoted my youthfulness.

"Nothing much, sir," I said automatically. "How's the day treatin you?" I asked out of kindness, knowing the potential responses.

"Same mess, different toilet."

His eyes betrayed his true sentiments. He wanted to say shit. The connection was mutual. He wanted to preach. He wanted to give a testimonial but was in no position to lecture. Instead he gave me a riddle in hopes that I would eventually crack the code. His words were a warning, but at the time I saw them as clever. I wanted that to be my response to people one day. With no more inquiry, he passed me two bags and a gallon of milk and offered only a nod in the direction of the house.

The others had stopped at the doorstep to pick up the bags that were at the bottom of the stairs. On the way towards the house, I debated whether I should drop the bags at the bottom of the steps or take them into the house. I was intrigued by the taxi driver and decided to place the bags in front of the house. I wanted to know my future. I wanted to know what being old and Black was like.

When I returned to the cab, the taxi driver was putting the last of the bags on the curb. He let out a nearly inaudible grunt and looked up at me.

"I see you got the right idea, chief," he said with a smile, "get a little chain gang action goin and the work'll do itself. Work smart not hard is the philosophy to live by."

I couldn't find an appropriate response to his barrage of clichés, so I smiled. There was something more to what he was saying. The pride in his tone gave his intentions away. I was trying to think of something cool to say in response and then it hit me.

"I'm just tryin not to break too much of a sweat over some groceries I'm not gonna eat, sir."

My timing was a little delayed and my words slightly beyond my years, but the point was clear, and the taxi driver chuckled anyway.

"Sounds like you know something I don't. All my work feeds other people. Don't take Independence Day to know you not free."

With that, the taxi driver let out a profound grunt then looked at the bags and nodded once more in the direction of the house casually dismissing me.

As I picked up the last three bags, I looked up at my elder.

"Have a good one," I said, wishing him a good day and life.

"Be easy," he responded, wishing me a peaceful existence. With those two words he told me that circumstance is just that: circumstance. In that moment, I felt transparent and as unnerving as it was, there was something soothing about it. The taxi driver got back in the car, and I hurried into the house carrying the bags.

After bringing the groceries inside, Shannon stayed in the kitchen and helped his mother put everything away. When he emerged from the corridor holding a ten-dollar bill in his hands, we were all confused. The joy in his eyes was only accented by the rhythm with which he spoke, he was almost singing.

"Yall wanna go to the store?" he said waving the ten dollar bill in the air.

Of course we did. All of us jumped up from our seats and hit the door simultaneously. Going to a corner store with half a twenty was a big deal in those days. You could nearly buy the whole store. Or so it felt.

On our way, Shannon and I walked in front. Ferris and Romeo fell slightly behind immersed in a conversation about which of them could jump higher. Ferris said that he could because he could touch rim, while Romeo argued that it was who got higher off the ground not who could reach higher, the winner in that case would be Romeo. I agreed with Romeo but decided to stay out of their conversation. I was more interested in talking to Shannon now. Besides, Ferris wouldn't back down from the argument simply because he was wrong and outnumbered. It would take a lot more to convince him he was incorrect. He was just that way. While they were distracted, I took the opportunity to ask Shannon about what happened. I didn't know quite how to do it. He never talked about his family outside of his sister and his niece. So I tried to lead him to it.

"Yo what happened this morning man?" I asked hoping he'd give me more than I already knew. A part of me was reluctant though. I knew there was a reason he hadn't told me yet. What would I do if he didn't want me to know?

"Moms kicked me out, and I was gonna ask you could you see if I could stay... stay with yall for a little bit . . . uh."

His directness was no surprise but I was happy I had found out what my role in the plan was going to be. It wasn't nearly as bad as I thought. I had a niche in the crew and I was starting to understand friendship. I hadn't had friends, and the transition was a bit jarring. Will and I could've been friends. But he was gone. I did not know how to need people, and it was different when they needed me. Regardless, he needed me.

"Why she kick you out and give you ten dollars just now?" I was confused by the sudden change of heart. "My mom's liable to get mad an not talk to me fo two days til she lookin for the remote but she aint never goin to kick me . . ." I paused.

"It aint that way wit my mom, Joe. I needed to know if I could stay wit yall just in case," he interjected.

Shannon's shortness let me know that he didn't want to talk about it. But my curiosity had to be fed.

"What you mean it aint like that? All moms is the same."

"Not mine Jay. She just go nuts sometimes. Jasmin said she bipolar or something." He shrugged.

"Jasmin say she's what?"

"Man I don't know. All I know is sometimes my mom just need to be left alone. And that's real. Like for days bro. Maybe weeks. She sometimes will hide in her room reading for days at a time. Not eating or drinking a thing."

After that comment, my mind was racing. I didn't know what bipolar meant, but I knew Shannon was catching the raw end of it. All I could think to say was "I know what you mean," even though I had no clue what he meant or how he felt. I never knew how to deal with others' emotions, so I let them be.

"I'll ask my mom just in case it happens again. She won't have no problems wit it as long as you clean up after yoself." I thought this would offer some sort of comfort for him, but with his silent reaction, I couldn't tell whether it did or not.

Then suddenly, after about a block and a half, he said, "I appreciate it mane. We gotta get to this store tho. It's hot as hell out and folks been playing games with them fireworks all day. Besides, I'm thirsty as hell. You know them juices don't quench nothing…"

When we left the store, we went back to the park. As usual, Romeo called next, shouting to a boy on the sidelines who responded with an underwhelmed "aight." Romeo had four of the five teammates already picked, and we would wait to see who lost before we chose our fifth teammate. While we waited for the game to finish,

Ferris, Shannon and I sat on the edge of the wooden frame that outlined the jungle gym. We talked and every now and again, kids running past would inadvertently sprinkle us with woodchips.

"What's score?" Romeo called out impatiently while shooting around at the vacant end of the court before the stampede of players came back on a fast break. No one answered.

"What's score?" he repeated.

"12-18," one of the guys called down the court.

"What's game?" Romeo asked while he still had the players' attention.

"32," the man responded more out of annoyance than assistance.

Turning back to us, Romeo said "Yall not gonna shoot around? We're about to play."

"Aint nobody shooting around. You see how hot it is? I don't really want to play," I said before I realized I was talking.

"Well don't play," Romeo said sharply. "You're not the prince no more," he said jokingly after realizing the irritation in his response.

"Naw neither of yall are the princes. I denounce both of yall. Shannon's the prince since he's my only son," Ferris said before I had a chance to usurp the throne.

"How you gonna be the King and I'm fucking the Queen?" Shannon responded with impeccable timing.

"Who you talking about Jasmin? Man everybody done fucked her. Jasmin fucks dicks," Ferris managed to weasel out. The gloves came off and anything was up for grabs when family was involved.

Romeo held back his laugh long enough to say, "You crazy, Jasmin dykin." Then he broke out hysterically bending in the middle like a paperclip, eyes closed, mouth wide open, and hands keeping his sides from rupturing.

With no response I changed the subject, as always, saying, "I think we're up." I was never quick witted enough. I would always find something witty to say after the joke was over. No more than three minutes into the game I came up with "How are you going to be King and you're my shadow. Shadows can't be Kings. You gotta kill me first." That would have been perfect to say to Romeo, I thought. He's jet black plus he hates being called a follower. But I was late. Next time I'd say it, and next time it'd be perfect.

We played for a while. Romeo had picked up Ronald. They played in AAU together. Ronald was never too fond of me. Even though we were on the same team, he wouldn't pass and on a number of defensive rebounds, he wrestled the ball away from me. The tension was obvious and on a couple of plays, Ferris actually told Ronald to calm down.

"What you doin? Yall are on the same team."

Is he trying to make a point of how little he cares for me? If he really cared so little about me, he would just not pay me any attention. Maybe he's gay. I hadn't held too many feelings towards him before, but as the game went on, I grew to hate that nigger. I'm not a basketball player. I'm trying to have fun and he's making it his mission to ensure that I see him, and that all are aware of his distaste. Why does he want to make me look bad? I can't take it too much longer. I don't care how good of friends he and Romeo are. This doesn't have anything to do with Romeo. In fact, it's Romeo's fault for choosing him. I'm going to do something. My mind was racing. I had to do something. If I didn't, everyone'll think it's alright to do this kind of shit to me. It has got to stop somewhere. How about with the first person to try me? Ronald. I had decided the next time he picked on me, I was going to rip him a new one.

The next time down the court we had a fast break. I was three or four steps ahead of Ronald when Shannon threw the ball down the court. I lost the ball for a second in the sunlight. The orb of yellow-orange brilliance engulfed the reddish orange ball. For a moment, they became one. One black shadow in the pit of the sky. I was running full sprint towards the other end of the court when the Spaulding emblem reappeared out of the glow. First, it was merely a shadow in the pit of the flame. Then it became more distinct. I put my hands out to catch it in stride. I readjusted because I had overcommitted and was too far ahead of the ball when I felt the unforgiving smack of the court. My weight was off balance. Head and shoulders were in front of my hips. I found myself flying suddenly, then landing on the blacktop. The hot sun-soaked surface of the asphalt shredded, almost melted, any part of my body that made contact. First my arms, the skin from my left palm, all the way to the elbow, had been torn off. Ripped from the meat in a leapfrog manner.

As I slid, burn move to my left shoulder. It was adjusting to my rotation. My feet still in the air, and as they landed, my jeans ripped at the knees and my left knee collided with the ground. My leg felt like it was broken in three parts, each throbbing with a different rhythm. Then I stopped sliding. I rolled over to my back and lay for a while resting my head among the scattered and empty weed sacks and blunt wrappers. What had happened? All I knew was that I was on the ground and, to be honest, when most people wind up on the ground, not intending to be there, they are surprised.

It wasn't until I looked up that I realized what happened. Ronald tripped me. *This nigger tripped me!* By the time the damage fully registered, I had already gotten to my feet. My left knee felt a little funny, slightly disjointed. Slipping in and out under my torn skin. I knew I couldn't run. I was already fatigued from the game not to mention my recently acquired and uninvestigated injuries. I didn't know what was hurting or how badly it was hurt. But I did know that I was left with only one option and that was fight. Fight until every ache became Ronald's. Fight until Ronald became the physical embodiment of every hardship I had ever known. Every lump on his head, each bruise on his face, and every miscellaneous scratch attained through tussling would be a testament to my undying joy. I would take out all my rage on him and be left with nothing but scabs and happiness. At least that was my intent.

Fighting no longer frightened me. Blood coagulated, scabs dried and fell off, and scars faded. But the lesson of *don't put your motherfucking hands on me again,* didn't. Who knows how this beating would make me feel? How do hands feel after they destroy? Is that what they are made for? But I do know how the beating will make Ronald feel. I guess loss comes with a lesson. Victory comes with indifference. There is no necessity known by the victor. No need to change or grow. Ronald would carry my pain. It would be nice, maybe even make us brothers. But the one thing I do know is that his lesson is going to be learned. If not this round then next, but that lesson would be learned. If I had to fight him every time I saw him, that lesson would be learned.

I rushed towards Ronald. He had backed up slightly and was on the other side of the free-throw line. I came from under the basket. I think a couple of cigarette butts and a little dirt fell off my shirt, can't be too sure, possibly a used condom. I was too angry to notice the falling debris. By the time I reached my feet, I was mid march. With every step toward him, my anger rose. I was puffing my cheeks out and breathing with the intensity of a wounded bull, but he was not my matador. I saw Ronald's lanky frame, soaked in sweat, his face covered in fear as he began to back step. He recognized his over-action. I would say reaction, but I hadn't done anything to deserve his contempt.

His shirt hung loose around the collar, and I knew I would grab it and beat him relentlessly. Oh that collar had my name on it. All the plans I had for that stupid, dirty, wet, smelly, hate-drenched shirt. Ronald's eyes grew into white disks, almost flag-like. I saw his pupils die into the milky white background. He wanted to surrender, but I felt Hulkish. His regret was palpable. Ronald was all that I saw, and he was all that I wanted to destroy. I wanted to set his soul free. Give it wings. Even if he haunted me eternally, my rage was justified. For that one moment I had the opportunity to overreact and I wanted to.

On my fourth or fifth step toward Ronald, I found that I couldn't put much pressure on my left leg. I stalked him with a slight limp. A lame leg was the least of my worries though. My intent was not to win but to bless him with my pain. If I didn't win, we would have just been some fighting niggers until one of our families moved. That was until my knee gave out and I collapsed about four steps into my march. But, oh was it a wondrous stampede. So magnificent even that the tumble, as my knee slid to and fro under my skin, possessed a grace befitting royalty. Befitting a god. As I fell, my glare went from his nervous eyes to his chest, which expanded and contracted in rapid succession.

My body was not in unison. My knee wanted to back down while the rest of me, especially my eyes, wanted to erase him from existence. After his chest, I saw his craven knees bent in a runner's stride, then I was looking at the soles of his Air Force Ones as he stood on the tips of his toes making small leather hills on the tops of his shoes. The most dastardly creases known to sneakers. I even hated his shoes. Fuck them off white ass Forces.

When I looked up from my second encounter with the pavement, I saw Ferris come from behind Ronald and put him in a full nelson, knocking the ball out of his hand. Oh, did I mention this nigger had the ball. (This asshole dislocated my knee because he wanted the fast break. It was a pickup game. I didn't give a damn about the points, even then. Who keeps stats in pickup games? NOBODY! Fuck that nigga.) The ball rolled towards me and in disgust, I swatted at it sending it flying toward the sideline. Shannon and Romeo ran over to assist Ferris, not me. They delivered punches like the tough guys I had seen in so many mobster movies, except their coordination was so much more fluid. They weren't trying to bury their hands into the sides of their opponents like the mobsters. No. Their hands were their own, they struck and pulled back, struck and pulled back. Their arms were like whips. The fist was the popper. It was more like a knife fight than a beating. Each jab a stab.

I was witnessing Ronald's crucifixion, Ferris serving as his cross, holding his hands high above his head. Ferris dwarfed Ronald, exaggerating his frame. Stretching his body out. Midsection fully exposed. Ronald struggled at first but, realizing there was no use, he began to rock with the most vicious blows taking some of the steam off of them. His body even slumped, imitating the affixation Christ.

The Passion of Ronald. Romeo, Ferris, and Shannon's faces held no mercy. Romeo, in particular, sent shots from the hip like a professional boxer. He ducked and dodged, slipping Shannon's loopy Wanderlei Silva type blows, and after each bob, issued devastating and rhythmic hooks that made a pendulum out of Ronald's head.

Ferris wanted some of the action. He was tired of simply being the torture mechanism. He wanted to be the executioner. I saw his frustration growing as Shannon and Romeo's hostile expression gradually transformed into sinister smirks. They were enjoying it. What started as a lesson turned into fun, and Ferris wanted some of the amusement. Suddenly Ferris released the clench that he held behind Ronald's head. To my surprise, Ronald looked alive. His eyes opened as wide as they could, although his cheeks and brow had nearly engulfed his left eye (both Romeo and Shannon were right handed), and it was obvious that he saw this lapse in offense as his way out.

When Ferris released the hold, it became clear that he was the only reason Ronald was standing. Ronald's mind became alert, but his body had shut down. His movements didn't have the same response time as before. As soon as Ferris released his grip, Ronald's knees gave way (much like mine), and before he could fall, Ferris dropped his hands to Ronald's waist, reestablished his grip, knees bent and back arched, and scooped Ronald off his feet. Ferris momentarily brought Ronald above his six-foot-three frame, angled him towards the ground, and brought him back to the earth just as quickly as he had picked him up, maybe faster, like the Giant Drop at Six Flags. Ronald put his hand out to ease the fall, but the momentum of the impact nullified his defense. His arm bent awkwardly under the weight.

In unison they looked at me still lying on the court. I was in awe, but I knew I was going to have to participate. It was my fight after all. "Nigga what is you waiting for?" Romeo yelled. I got to my feet with ease, relying primarily on my right leg. My left still dangled a little. The leg hung with an unfamiliarity. I didn't know whose leg it was. But it was going to have to work now. I knew I was going to have to put some pressure on it to get over to them. As good of friends as they are, they still would not have carried me over to the body.

I looked up and for the first time I became aware of the park, everyone was watching us. Some were yelling, but most were quiet. *How long have they been watching? Why haven't any of the adults broken this up? Why didn't the grown men we were playing with break this up? Maybe they felt it was a justified ass whooping. Maybe they saw it coming. Whatever the case, I have to do something.*

So I limped towards my brothers. They were my brothers now, no longer distant cousins. I had every intention of cementing our brotherhood. We grounded our blood bond by shedding the blood of another and it was my turn to take the mortal oath of friendship. Walking toward them, I heard a loud pop, it was my knee snapping back into place. The twinge and discomfort of the knee were not enough to distract. In fact, the knee immediately felt better after it was back in place.

Feeling healed, I hurried toward them with a slight uneasiness, and as I stood over Ronald who I thought had been knocked out, I began to second guess my decision. That was my decision to kill him. Not the decision to fuck him up. Naw, that had remained a pretty sure choice. I stared at him as he stared back. His eyes pleaded with mine. Almost as if he was asking me to forgive him. Maybe not forgive. He didn't want me to react. That's how physics works though. He lay there silent.

The very thought of him asking me to leave him alone sent me back into a spiral of hate. I balled my hand up and felt a twinge of pain surge from the palm through my forearm clear to the back of my neck. The burn of the pavement had ripped the skin off of my arm. I was reminded why he suffered once more. He crucified himself, and with no more thought, I brought my right knee to my chest, stared him directly in the eyes, and brought my foot down on his mouth as hard and swiftly as I could muster. At the last second, he broke eye contact with me, cringing right before I made contact. Blood shot out of his mouth and his front teeth lay on the court. His blood landed on my jeans mingling with my own. There was a tenuous bond between Ronald and I too.

Finally, after the fight was over as was custom, the Candy Lady came from across the park. She sold snow cones, Fruities, Flaming Hots, and other snacks each summer. She had a traditional post by the fence and really consistent prices, but most importantly, everyone respected her. Her thighs overlapping one another, as she walked hurriedly with her pigeon-toed strut. Her weave, golden with the black roots showing, waved in the wind, dramatizing her walk.

"Okay, Okay yall, I think he's had enough! Leave em alone!" she yelled over the noise of the crowd, which I became aware of only after she spoke, as if her voice opened a cavity through which the rest of theirs could enter.

I heard the noises of the street, of the crowd. They had been mute to me. When the Candy Lady got close enough, she pushed

Ferris and me out of the way gently but assertively.

"Well somebody call the ambulance!" she said to the crowd. No one moved. She was respected but a well-deserved ass whooping was just that to the crowd. She bent over to check Ronald's pulse. His body was limp now. However, my eyes were glued to her enormous butt, wrapped in purple spandex, with the crack peeking out just above the waist of the stretch pants. That was my gift.

She turned to us, we had spread out slightly now, and said, "You boys gone now, he aint coming to no time soon but he'll be alright." There was no panic or surprise in her voice. She had seen many situations like this before and many worse than this.

To my surprise Romeo spat back, "We aint worried about him coming to or from. He could be dead all we care. What we worried about is what he's gone say when he come to."

I honestly hadn't even thought about that, but it was important, maybe. I don't know what he'd say. How would he explain this lesson learned? I figure to this day, if he still talks about this incident, and I'm sure he does, he probably tells the story like all other folks tell the story of their losses. "Man them niggas was wilin." The end.

Although he had other, perhaps, more real and genuine sentiments about the incident, whenever he tells the story he likely makes his loss all our fault. He got caught off guard and jumped by us according to his tale. Maybe we jumped him for his throwback jersey or shoes. Or maybe we did it for no reason at all. But you and I both know that's not true. Right? Truth be told though, most ass whoopings that are handed out are justified. People might say they're not. But I don't get into fights every day. Do you? So when I am in a fight, chances are it is because I think the other person deserves to get punched in the face, repeatedly. I'm talking about over and over and over again.

Shannon tugged on Romeo's shirt and said, "She don't have nothing to do with what he say. Come on. We gotta do something about Jay anyway."

That was the second time that I'd been called a nickname and I didn't know whether it was because he didn't want the Candy Lady to know my name or out of affection. Probably just an abbreviation. He was right though, after delivering an ass whooping like that it was best for us to get out of there, at least until tomorrow. If we could wait that long. Ronald will probably come back around next week and if he never comes back that'd be too soon.

A lot of people came back after bad losses. It's kind of impressive and pitiful at the same time. You know what I mean? The resilience and strength of character it must take to face the same people who not more than three days ago saw you take an L like no other. But to have to face these people because you don't have anywhere else to go, because this is where people hang, is pretty sad. I don't know how to feel about it. People get beat up sometimes. Then there are those other times when a cat just gets the brakes beat off them, and the only thought is "how is he [or she] going to respond to that? If I was dude . . ." There are those times. The person's character, as perceived by others of course, is based on what they do when they show back up. Everyone knows loss. But there are differences. Important differences.

I wish I didn't have to do that. Why'd he make us do it? Why didn't someone stop us? Did they hate him too? I didn't hate him but for a split second, and that was enough to shed his blood. The truth is, looking back on it, I wanted to cement my relationship with the fellas, but I wound up sharing blood with Ronald. It was our blood that touched. Yes Shannon, Ferris, Romeo, and I were closer after the altercation, but Ronald was an undeniable part of that newly found bond. Well, it had already been found. He was unofficially part of our relationship now. His blood strengthened us. He was our support beam. We would tell and retell the story constantly, each time something would be added or taken away, but his suffering was our story, we owned it. The Passion of Ronald.

After the beating, we didn't go far. We walked two blocks to the corner store and stayed there until we heard the ambulance leave. I could tell we all felt differently about what happened. We didn't share too many words until we returned to the park. I guess we were all digesting what happened. After doing something potentially illegal or wrong, one is always left with the weight of the possible consequences, eternally. You remain wary of anyone finding out about your misdeeds. They are never truly in the past.

We came back, each of us holding a fifty cent juice, and sat on the throne, our bench. All of us feeling the elevation of victory. Our sentiments about the event were shown on our faces. The variations of remorse, pride, regret, hate, self-righteousness, fear, and joy swelling within and evidenced through the medium of personality. We were ourselves, therefore our responses were our own. As for myself, I was still confused about why it happened but felt it was an unnecessary question to ask because it did happen.

Ferris looked less impressed by the event than any of us. He held his head down while he sat in his traditional position on top of the bench, elbows on his knees and fingers clasped forming a cage. Ferris was almost ashamed it had to be taken that far. In fact, to some extent we all were. We would have much rather had Ronald as a friend. One more in the crew. That means one more personality, more jokes, more ideas, and more fun. The more the merrier. Right? We would have all been happy had he just been cool.

I hadn't really seen myself yet. So I couldn't properly assess my injuries. I knew they felt bad though. That too was a reason I had less regret for the fight, because I still felt it. Romeo, of course, wanted to relive the experience. He was jumping around and pacing back and forth tearing the pitch of grass left on the field, already wanting to tell us this recent history.

"What the fuck was that nigga on, Joe?" Romeo finally beckoned. "He got to be crazy to fuck with us like that. We had picked him up? This niggas got to be a fool."

"Fuck with us? He was trying to fight me the whole game," I said knowing the response, but realizing that it had to be stated that his beef was with me. "And for what? He aint get nothing but teeth knocked out his head," I barked, stretching my hand out, palm up, holding Ronald's whitish yellowish beigeish front teeth. They were long, one still had the root attached. They all cringed.

"What you keep them for? They still bleedin man," Shannon asked. The blood still on most of the tooth. Some transferred to my open palm. I didn't care.

"He don't deserve these teeth, or else he'd still have them. I still have all of mine. On top of that, he did it for no reason. We were on the same team." That response satisfied the masses.

"We know he was bogus, Jay. That aint no question. But either way it goes we put in good work. I bet he's gonna think again before he tries any of us. On my mama that make me wanna go handle some more niggas, just cause. You know what I mean? It's just in me now. I promise aint nothin like putting yo hands on a motherfucker."

We let Romeo continue to talk about it partially because we didn't know what to say and partly because we agreed. Hearing his voice took the pressure off of us to fill the silence. We had put him in his place and therefore affirmed ourselves. The Rebel baby. From that moment on, Ronald and all who witnessed the ass whooping knew where we stood and what we were willing to do to protect ourselves and our own.

"Shit, I know yall saw me get my highlight reel on," Romeo continued.

"Man you wasn't on nothing?" I said jokingly. It was the first natural laugh I'd had after the fight. It felt nice, and I thank Romeo for giving it to me.

"You lyin to me, Joe. How you see and you was on the ground. Twice nigga. But since you stuntin on me, let's recap for the viewers at home." Romeo made a box with his hands and placed it in front of his face, as if he was on television.

"Left, right, left, right, head, body, head, head, body, BOOOM, BOOOM, BOOOM, BITCH! Take this one home to your cousin nigga. How dare you eeevver, eevver, evvveeerrr think about touchin my mans." He was animated. His hands were flying, mimicking the attack. His voice grew louder and louder as he reenacted the fight. "Well since you don't know how to keep your hands to yourself, let me lay my hands on ya. Pastor Ro, they call me . . ."

"Nigga shut yo ass up. You act like you worked him yoself. Like I aint have no parts of it," Ferris stated indignantly. "If I had let the nigga loose, he might of whooped that ass. Then you'd be cryin, 'You supposed to be my mans Ferris, why you let him whoop me?' Man get yo ass on." Ferris was frustrated and mocked Romeo's voice. Romeo had the highest voice of all of us. Puberty was on its way I assumed.

"Wait for it you sensitive motherfucker. We gotta do Shannon's highlight reel first. Chronological order nigga." Romeo raised his hand toward Ferris, indicating slow down. His face was mischievous though. "Cool your jets my brother, we can all be the heroes."

"That mean me wrapping his ass up go first. Fuck is you talkin bout? Yall aint get them highlight reels by accident. I had been folded the nigga." Ferris stood up to explain the full nelson technique.

"Well then I meant order of importance. Niggas don't get highlights from sneaking up behind people. That don't make you tough, cousin."

I couldn't help but notice the familial references that Romeo was dropping. *How is he your brother and cousin?*

"Since when that make a nigga tough?" Ferris, now annoyed and amused at the same time, allowed Romeo to continue.

"Well aight. The story continues. So then my big homie clenched his ass. You happy, Joe? You got in the story." Ferris shook his head. Romeo continued.

"Fuck you too. So then I was sending shots, hitting every possible opening I could. Worked that boys ribs out. Tapped his jaw a couple of times. Den, my mans Shannon sent blows. I aint talking drugs neither. Although I'm sure that nigga felt high. Booom, Booom, Booom, Baaaannnnng Bitch! Bang Bang Siegel Street Gang nigga. I hope somebody's at home to hear this shit. And then big homie put the fufops on his ass. Slammed the shit outta that boy. I was so impressed by the sheer strength. It was like I was watching the WWF or something. Crazy I tell you."

Romeo paused to make sure he still had our attention. He looked at Ferris for recognition of his role in the fight. I was waiting on him to get to my highlight, so of course I was still listening. Selfish as it is, I like hearing how people view what I do. Maybe like is too strong, but I do find it interesting. I like comparing how I felt about it to how they saw it. Shannon and Ferris both took swigs of their juices but were still following the story. They appeared to be feeling the same relief of conversation.

"And then after we had officially fucked Ronald Atkins Jr. up, my crippled homie came over, all scarred up and shit, and left the niggas dentures all on the court. Excuse me sur, is thems yo adult teef? Sorry to tell ya thems was yo adult teef, theys Jay's now nigga. Sorry Boss didn't tell you about the gun-line before you crossed it, but uh, betta luck next time homie," he stopped to think of the next joke and it came. "Well, he picked them up. Kinda nasty if you ask me, drinking yo juice and shit with that man's teeth in your hand. Nasty."

We all laughed. Every time the story was told after that with different adlibs and renditions, we laughed just the same.

We talked for a little while longer on the bench, just shooting the breeze. Acting like the crazy day we'd all experienced was behind us, knowing the night was sure to bring us a new tomorrow. What we had done was never to be lived again so we didn't. We just kept living. What a crazy Fourth of July.

When the street lights came on, I had to get home because if I stayed out for too much longer, I'd be in trouble. Something about time and me. I think I only recognize day and night. There is no variation. A minute could be an hour and an hour could be a day. All I know is when the sun is up and when it goes down. Plus, Keith was barbecuing for the Fourth and I wanted to get home when the food was still hot. There was no real time schedule for the barbecue. It is not like I was missing a family function or good free food.

Thinking about going home made me want to tell Chris the story. Chris was on punishment for stealing a bike a couple of weeks back (he never returned the bike, so I think it was worth it), but I wish he had been there with us. I missed hanging out with him. I never realized how much time we spent together until we weren't together. He was my best friend. It is fun to have a brother. Even better to have two.

Before I went home though, I figured I would walk Shannon back just to make sure his home situation was okay. Besides, I felt like walking. You know how some people love to drive and just be on the road cruising. That's how I am with walking. I just cruise. I also wanted to talk to him about what I should tell my mother in regards to my recently acquired battle wounds. I hadn't come up with a good enough lie yet, and I wanted to make sure she would at least be willing to believe whatever I said. I don't think it is ever really about the validity of the lie sometimes. It just has to make sense. Sometimes that is all I think parents want. For you to give them something they can eat. Something that tastes good. I still had to deal with the pain of the scars. There was no real reason to whoop me. Any further physical harm would just be inhumane.

On the walk to Shannon's house, we hadn't gotten a chance to discuss what I should tell my mom about the game. Instead, we talked about what I should tell her about Shannon's situation. Too much information would be just as bad as too little. She didn't need to know everything about Shannon's home life. In fact, the less she knew and the more vague the information given, the better for both her and Shannon. Besides, I didn't know what Shannon was comfortable with her knowing. It was his business after all. My mother simply needed to know enough to temporarily shelter him and no more.

If I tell her too much, she's going to be worried about the baby too (Shannon's niece), and besides it might make Shannon uncomfortable around her. If I don't tell her enough, she won't think the situation's bad enough for him to move in with us. It was a difficult balance and even more difficult for a thirteen-year-old to manage. The agility of tongue needed to navigate a situation like the one I had on my hands—a difficult skill to master.

Shannon and I hadn't been able to come up with an appropriate way to propose he stay with us for a while if things got too out of hand for him at home, so by the time we got to his house, he politely asked me to wait for him on the porch and he'd be out to continue the discussion. As if I had time to wait for him. But I did it anyway. You know that whole time thing. I sat on the stairs refusing to take a seat on the wraparound front porch even though it offered more comfort. It's ironic the features of Shannon's house that were intended to be comfortable made me the most uneasy. Nothing and no one in his house reminded me of home.

The more relaxed I was physically, the less unhinged I was mentally. I was always aware that something was wrong. There was something unwelcoming. So I had no plans of becoming too familiar with a seat. On top of that, spending too much time on that porch spelled compounded trouble. If I got into a fight at 11 PM, it was much worse than a fight at 3 PM and me coming home at 7 PM. The 11 PM might warrant a whooping. I wanted to avoid making my day any rougher than it was. That is one method of navigating a delicate situation. You've got to make sure that every other aspect, facet, and molecule is in line. There cannot, I mean cannot, be other problematic areas of life when a delicate issue is raised.

Sitting on the steps, I heard Shannon's mother. Her voice was fading in and out. I was only able to pick out the curse words at first. Well the curse-phrases. Then, they rushed to the front. I heard heavy footsteps come from inside. They were fighting over something. What could he have done already? Maybe it was that bipolar thing he was talking about.

Then, I heard the sound of flesh on flesh echo in the doorway. Something in me wanted to leave, but I didn't have the heart to abandon him. I was scared though. I didn't know what else a mother who would kick her child out was capable of. I knew what was going on even if I didn't know why. Whys aren't for me. Whys were reserved for the kids in Kimball Valley—the people who could see past the present. For me there were only hows. How were we going to get out of this? How would this end? How often had this happened to him? How can I help? I didn't and don't have the luxury to examine the whys, although if I did, there'd be a lot more answers than we currently have.

Suddenly, falling in between the rhythm of slaps and yelling came the syncopated and unique sound of metal hitting bone. I jumped in shock, wondering who hit who, not with what they were hit. I knew what it was, and after I became fully conscious of the object used, I knew who had done it. I got off the step at once and turned toward the street. I wanted to leave but found myself unable. I stayed and even more than that, I went to the door and peeked in.

To no surprise, but with a fair amount of shock, I saw Shannon standing over his mother sweating, scratches showing on his face and neck, mouth slightly *agape,* breathing with deep exhales, and holding a shovel in his left hand. The shovel stood at the very entrance of the house next to the coat rack and on top of a bag of salt used in winter.

He looked like a statue standing there. Only the breaths he took were much deeper. In fact, he looked more like the stereotypical image of a lumberjack after chopping down a redwood with an axe. Only he wasn't wearing a tight plaid shirt with the sleeves tackily rolled up just below the elbow. There was no tree or axe. Just the woman who birthed him and a shovel.

I didn't know what to do. I knew what I wanted to do and what I had to do. They weren't necessarily in conflict, but they were opposites. Just a choice I had to make, quickly. Leave or stay, mind my business or interfere, play blind or participate. Obey my desire or my obligation. The choice was there, and I don't regret my decision one bit. I ran. What would you have done? Stayed? You're crazy. There wasn't anything about that situation that was of interest to me. In fact, I was running so fast, I don't even remember hitting the front steps as I exited the house.

I ran and ran until my feet got tired. Actually, I ran harder when my feet got tired. That was my cue that I might not be able to run much longer. I had to get to the house as fast as possible while my body still worked. I was in full sprint the entire way home. It was dark and I assumed everyone who saw me running had the same comment for their neighbor, "That's gotta be the fastest kid alive . . ." or something to that effect. But I didn't see them that night. All I saw was street. Street was the only thing between me and home. Street and block. Streets to be crossed and blocks to be traversed. That's all city is, that and a bunch of people, and that's all that lay between me and my new goose.

Getting home was my only goal. I needed it. I needed something to be constant. At that moment the only thing constant in my life was my family. My world had been shaken. Nothing was the way it was supposed to be. From the very start of the day I had been crossing lines, experiencing firsts, and making decisions that were foreign to me, but this was too much. Was she dead? How hard did he hit her? How can they live like that? How could Shannon do that? He can't live with us. What would stop him from doing that to my mom? That nigga's crazy. He's got to get out of there. Maybe she's the problem. Maybe they're all crazy. I just gotta get home.

Terrible thoughts raced through my head. I hadn't been built for this type of drama. Family was all I knew and family bleeds for one another from one another with one another. But Shannon was my brother now. I can't abandon him, I won't. But how could I stand up for him? Where should I stand and against who? Who were we fighting? I know he had fought his mother but she for sure was not who we were fighting against. That is for certain, but the who was not clear.

When I entered 18th Avenue at Pleasant, only four blocks from my house, I saw nothing but lights overhead. The yellow glow of the street lights, one of which was always flickering and the flashing of neon lights to advertise the Chinese-owned chicken slash fried rice joint, illuminated the intersection. I had two shadows from the lights. They lay opposite, one in front, the other behind. But both were slightly angled, one continually shrinking while the other grew. Shrink and grow, shrink and grow. The former became the latter as I moved forward. The front gradually shifting to the back, instantly supplanted by the next. Growing then shrinking.

My lungs were heaving, legs pumping, and the rhythm of my feet on the street ensured the steady flow of thoughts. The thoughts enjoying the brief silences between the pat, pat, pat of my feet. A silence which made the pats quieter and itself louder. My feet played the background noise while my mind raced. I couldn't get home fast enough. Lights and street, lights and street were all I saw. Feet and breath, feet and breath was all I heard.

Then came the skid of rubber on pavement as I had almost successfully cleared 18th Ave. The skid was followed by the blinding headlights of a Chevy Cavalier. An obnoxious horn and the voice of an outraged driver and several passengers caught my attention, but only briefly. I smelled the weed emanating from their open windows. This night could have been so much worse, I thought. But I was almost home and paid them little attention. The current events were enormous even in the sight of what could have been a death experience. My stride was slightly stuttered by the brief hesitation of almost being hit by a car. I slipped right back into full sprint though, just as careless as I had been before. Two more blocks, two more blocks, I thought. Nothing but street now, nothing but home and love waiting for me. Maybe this is what Shannon needs, I told myself. He needs LOVE.

I walked into the house still shocked and decided to wait in the vestibule to collect my thoughts and figure out what, if anything, I was going to say. Well I knew I had to provide some sort of explanation. But what do I say? Tell them about the whole day or just what they needed to know. I wanted to tell Keith. He could keep a secret, and he could help me figure out what to tell Mom. He was a master at hiding what's in plain sight. Or he could just tell her for me. That would also help. I needed time. I needed more time than I had. Who is upstairs? Please let it be just Keith and Chris. I could talk it over with them before mom gets home and have my story straight. She doesn't need to know everything. *They'll help me get it together.*

These were high hopes considering the time. I didn't have a watch, but judging from how dark it was in July it had to be at least eight-thirty. Everyone is probably home. So, I stealthily inspected the stairwell leading up to our apartment before I headed up, after successfully catching my breath and gathering my thoughts as much as I possibly could. The recollection process only allowed me space to remember. Space to feel my injuries, new and old. Mostly new though. My knee had stiffened post mile and a half sprint. My skin felt different everywhere—it burned, felt cool, uncomfortable, and dirty.

I walked up the stairs, just wanting to sit down, shower, go to my room, eat, or anything else that was normal. As soon as I was in the stairwell, I was overwhelmed by the smell of meat, barbecue sauce, macaroni and cheese, greens, cornbread, and spaghetti, smells that were normally more than inviting. Saliva collected in my mouth. But today they were anything but welcoming. They stood as a warning. "Get your shit together!" they shouted.

I tensed up and knew my mother was home. The door was

already opened to let the heat out of the kitchen, the old-fashioned way. Now kitchens have all those gadgets and stuff, like fans over the oven and all sorts of other jazzy features. That is neither here nor there. I was overjoyed at the thought of not having to knock. My super-secret and stealth movements would not be interrupted by the annoyance of people's habit of locking doors. There are those times when you get to a portal and just want to be able to walk through. Right?

Our front door entered into the kitchen, and I was even more excited to see unattended food cooking on the stove. There was no one in sight. Which really meant I was in no one's sight, at least for now. But I still hadn't heard anyone or anything. It was eerily quiet not even the sound of the television echoed. All that echoed were my thoughts. But they needn't echo. I heard them. What needed to be echoing at the time were the answers to all those questions I had placed in the universe of my mind, or which had been placed there in the universe of my mind, or which I transferred from the universe of my mind into our mutual universe. Maybe you could help me if the last option is the most accurate. But I really don't know where the questions are in total, but I hope the last option makes the most sense because then we can help each other.

One room down. Directly ahead of me leading down a hall was my mother's room. I hurried to the bathroom, which was on the left of the hall after the kitchen. Looking in the mirror, I didn't recognize myself. My face was filthy, eyes red, and sweat residue formed leading from my temples to my cheeks, overlapping the white salt stains and accenting the dinginess of the dirt. *Take a shower.* All I really wanted was to wash the day off of me. The water would take whatever happened down the drain with it, to keep the countless wedding rings and goldfish company. And that's what I did.

Turning the knobs proved to be a bigger feat than I remembered. I'd never realized how loud they were. Their squeaking alarmed me, and hopefully only me. I had to jump in the shower, and quick. The water was still cold and shocked my legs and chest. I turned slightly to the right, covering my chest with my scabbed over arms, readjusting the temperature until the water scorched my exposed flesh. I had to burn myself, that was the only way this day would leave me. The heat of the shower enveloped me. Relief covered me as if a weight was being lifted. Suffocated by the steam, I almost didn't want to breathe. All I felt was heat, and heat was all I needed to feel. I bent down and completely cut the cold water off; the heat was everything: solitude, joy, love, relaxation. The heat was a prayer.

Knock, knock, knock

"Jamal, that you? When you get in, Jack? Mom was looking for you," Keith's voice came through muffled by the door.

The knocks startled me, and I dropped the thinning bar of soap. I almost fell over myself, balancing on my swollen left leg while trying to wash my right heel while also trying to maintain my composure after being scared halfway to death. But Keith's voice put me at ease. After the knock I was expecting an authoritative voice—one demanding immediate answers and possibly commanding me to exit my prayer. It was Keith. Thank God.

"Yea, it's me. Where's ma at?" I asked trying to gauge how suspicious my shower would be considering that I had not told anyone I was home before jumping directly into the shower. Not to mention that in any normal circumstance, I almost had to be forced to take showers. Not that I did not appreciate being clean, it's just that I considered them a hassle. My mom's favorite lines before I was made to shower were, "Boy you smell like all outdoors" or the more creative and much more frequently used, "You smell like a billy goat." For some reason I suspected that my mother had no clue what a billy goat specifically smelled like. I am sure she knew what the outdoors smelled like, but I really and truly doubt that she can point a billy goat's smell out of a lineup of olfactory stimulants. However familiar my mother is with billy goat odors, the fact still remained that both comments were usually followed by a "go take a bath" with a repulsed expression. Which was then followed by me complaining for the next half hour about showering later.

Keith thinking nothing of my uncharacteristic shower responded casually, "Her and Chris went to the store to get stuff for spaghetti. They was lookin for you, better get an excuse ready bro." He called me bro when I was in trouble, I never knew whether it was intentional or not, but I always liked it. Also when he was mad at mom he would call her "your mom." She belonged to me when he was mad at her. Most sentences starting with "Man, why yo mom . . ."

"Aight!" I shouted through the door. I needed help. Maybe the shower would do the trick.

I hurried out of the shower, grabbed the towel and dried myself rapidly. In my rush, I rubbed my legs too aggressively with the towel and tore at the scabs. Wincing at the irritation, I dabbed at the moisture and wrapped the towel around my waist.

Keith was sitting on the couch as I passed through the living room on the way to my bedroom. I looked at him and then at the girl readjusting her bra and shirt as she walked out of his room. I might have had a chance to be an awkward preteen if I could have moved faster, hadn't been in all that bullshit, and wasn't used to girls walking out of Keith's room by now. But the fact remained that I was a thirteen-year-old half-naked boy with the thoughts of a girl who I know was very recently completely naked. Probably at the same time I was completely naked. In the same house. Meaning that everyone in the house was simultaneously naked at one point. Or at least I like to think so. It makes me feel like I was almost having sex before I lost my virginity. Funny, right?

"Food's almost done mane. Soon as mom and Chris get back we can . . ."

Keith paused and looked at my collection of scabs. I did not know what to make of his face. It looked like he had a lot of thoughts at the time, like he traded places with me and adopted all of my fears. Maybe the thoughts were in our mutual universe.

"You better get yo ass in that room and put on a shirt with some sleeves, nigga. Hurry up! What you lookin at me for? They gonna be here soon!"

He spoke without inquiry, without acknowledging the third presence now standing in the living room with us, without caring about the whys, whos, and wheres. All that mattered was avoiding the ole lady's wrath.

If it had been anyone but him, I would have been shocked at the near indifference in his voice. Not indifference, it was much more like a simple concern. His concern was simply for my well-being, in the hopes that I would not get into any more trouble than I was probably, to his knowledge, already in. I guess he knew if he needed to know I would tell him.

Without a word I went into the room, lotioned the necessary areas so that the scrapes wouldn't get too dry and rushed to put my clothes on. Jeans and a t-shirt, like normal. I didn't really like lotion at the time, so it was a little bit of a stretch. It was just too creamy.

Getting dressed was a combination of scabs stretching as I bent my limbs, itching caused by my clothes rubbing against my skin, and a numb throbbing of my left leg. My leg ached as if I was unthawing from a frigid day, like I was regaining the feeling in my extremities after standing outside for too long in winter, but I couldn't shake the throbbing. It reminded me of the dead feeling I had in my legs when Will was killed. From my foot to my knee the numbness ebbed. With a little intentionality, all of my other injuries could be kept a secret. That still left the issue of the leg though. How would I hide it? Should I hide it? I was scared of what might happen if I let it get too bad. Would the Candy Lady tell anyone?

To answer the questions left open, Shannon eventually winded up moving in with our family. He moved in with us later, when we got into high school, after much more turmoil in his house. My mother never found out about the incident, and to this day I still have not explained the scabs to Keith, or the scars to anyone for that matter. Also, ever since that day, I can feel the impending rain in my leg. I developed a terrible case of arthritis in my left knee. I kind of like it though. It makes me feel old. Like I'm in tune with the Earth.

That Shannon stayed with his family, at the time, was no surprise. But his home situation never really got better. It was always in flux. In fact, there were times where it seemed like it couldn't get worse. It got to the point that I don't know how you called what he had a family anymore. After that unforgettable and possibly unforgivable night, many more insalubrious events occurred in their house. These events include but are not limited to, the birth of Jasmin's triplets, the hospitalization of Shannon's mother at the hands of a needle, which resulted in the doctors discovering an advanced case of lymphoma and the first stages of AIDS, not to mention hypertension and high blood pressure, and the institutionalization of Shannon's stepfather in prison and the crazy house, although he spent significantly more time in the latter.

But Shannon is and was resilient or inured whichever works, one is probably just a form of the other. A part of me feels he was the only constant in his house. A constant that I am sure every single person in that home needed. Part of me feels like he liked being that constant. Although it wore on him, I still think he liked it.

Shannon grew in those days. Although his home situation never got better, he began to recognize it as his own, his property. But I think he also found his voice in those days. He saw what he deserved and a drug addicted mother, insane stepfather, and a baby-making sister were not it. He was worth way more. We all were.

There aren't too many things in this life that are yours. It might have been the only thing that belonged to him in this world—his voice, his plight. To be honest, I never really believed he wanted to live with us. But he eventually gave in. He liked his family, every dysfunctional aspect of them. Family is family even after getting knocked out with a shovel. There was no love lost. Even if there was some love lost, it doesn't work like that with family. When a little love secretes through the pores of familial relationships, like sweat off a pig's back,[22] bonds are surprisingly reinforced.

That night, I did not gain another brother. I gained experience. The thing about experience is that you don't have to experience it again. I'm glad for that. I don't know if I could do it over.

Shannon and I grew closer after our Fourth of July celebration. I believe our bond grew because I had been exposed to his fears and hesitations. I experienced in him the kind of brief but lasting fears that force irrational responses out of weaker men and make people ask others for divine favors, while at the same time making the person—the one suffering from the unexpected misfortune—behave ungodly. In that moment, I simultaneously saw desperation, trust, concern, loyalty, and anger. I was not astonished, maybe a little surprised. More than anything, I was impressed. I was impressed by his composure. He was a veteran down to the shrapnel in his soul. I saw Shannon that day. I was impressed by his heart, his Faith.

---

[22] Pigs don't sweat. Love never leaves. That's not how love works.

CHAPTER 11

The <u>Beam</u> in Thine Eye

Of the crew, I was the only one who was still forced to go to Church. In fact, Ferris and his family had never attended a service together. They were heathens of the highest degree. Not really, it just wasn't a part of their lives, I guess. He never gave a reason for their religious delinquency, and I honestly don't think he ever had one. Church was just not a part of his life. As a kid, I found that weird. But that might have been because in a lot of ways I was still from Memphis. Church is what was done on Sunday, Tuesday, and Friday in Tennessee.

If you didn't go, it wasn't out of lack of people inviting you. It was because you had developed either indifference, resentment, or shame. As for Shannon and Romeo, their families stopped going to Church at some point in their lives, probably when their parents got into other situations. Drugs primarily. However, there wasn't, and there never has been, any doubt in my mind that these three had God. They carried Him with them. God was the fifth member of the crew. We kicked it in his grace often. That is why they would become my council. I knew I could trust them.

I say I was forced to go to Church, but the truth is, I loved God and I loved hearing about Him even more. It didn't matter where I was. I had no problem sharing Him. Every Sunday after Church I would get home, change my clothes, and go hang out at the park or at Shannon's. I gave synopses of the service just because I found the services more fun once they were over. I found the stories of the Bible and their obvious connections to this life to be very thought provoking.

Some things in life are just that way. Like roller coasters, they're always more fun once you get off the ride. I'd tell them what the pastor talked about, the songs they sang, and anything else that went on that I found funny in the service. They typically nodded and feigned interest in my renditions and reenactments. But they never told me to stop. They never broke eye contact. For some reason, I had never invited them to come with me. I was so interested in their lives and the interesting stuff that came with being their friend that I never thought they might be interested in mine.

But one Sunday after Church in the middle of me talking about Jeremiah, the (quite) possibly gay deacon who should have been the choir director as loud as his singing was, Ferris looked up with piqued interest and said, "They got gay folks in church?" The question caught me off guard.

"I don't know if he's really gay. But I think so and other people think so. I don't know. We never asked him," I responded.

The conversation continued without reference to Church and became about gay people. But Ferris brought it back to his original question. Apparently, my answer wasn't satisfactory. I hadn't realized the purpose of his question at the time. He was really asking me was he welcome too. Not that he was gay, no, but that all types of people went to Church.

Maybe I hadn't realized that he was actually listening to all of my stories about Church. Maybe I hadn't noticed that I made it sound cool, but I genuinely thought it was cool. Especially the stories. My favorite, of course, was John the Baptist. Even though my mother had to drag me every Sunday, I knew why, and I knew Him. I also think if Church (and school too) had a later start time, it would be a much easier enterprise. Because they are both really cool and interesting places with very particular sets of experiences.

Church is a glorious institution if you go there for the right reasons. They told stories. Most of all they had singing, interesting speakers, and they talked about God, the coolest thing ever, for free. (Well they had those collections called tithes but who counts that as paying for an experience, you don't even have to put anything in the plate.) They talked about God I tell you, this thing that we have named and proscribe as the reason for everything. God. This thing, people try to relate to themselves. God, the unequivocal source. I liked the speakers and how they would try to relay the message of God in a way that doesn't diminish His greatness.

"I can't believe they got gay folks in Church. So who aint in Church?" Romeo said with a slight lilt at the end.

I wanted to say "you" but felt that would be unfair. With an issue like Church, that was too judgmental. It was his decision to go but all were welcomed. If we were talking about anything else, that would have been a beautifully spicy comeback. I had to save that comeback for a better time. Building a house out of comebacks baby. Instead I said, "Everyone's at Church. Crackheads, preachers, gays, straight folk, pimps, and I don't know what other kind of people there are. Even white folks be at Church sometimes. And you know bout white folks." I paused to think who else might be at Church. "They all act like they don't be in the streets though," I said. Which was true. There were gang leaders, pimps, drug dealers, and fiends in the Church, right next to the nurses, teachers, doctors, and lawyers. Everybody's money was accepted.

"You crazy Jay. Why you always talking bout white folks like that," Romeo responded. He didn't know what I did. I had seen them up close. They were different. At that point, I hadn't totally put my finger on it.

"Cause they the crazy ones," I said. I never told them about my last school. That was honestly when I realized they were crazy. Well, I never told anyone until this story.

"Naw nigga you crazy. But I like it though. Where yo Church at? You say everything but where you go. That's crazy too," Shannon said with emphasis on all the crazies.

"Yea, that is weird. Make me think you don't be going to Church. Man this niggas been lying the whole entire time," Ferris said laughing. "Aint no gays in Church. Yo lying ass."

The time was perfect now to make a joke. I had been waiting with anticipation for a time to jump on someone's comment, anyone, it didn't matter. He was way too into the fact that there were gay people in Church for my liking. Why did it concern him so much? And I had the joke. "That's cause you're not there, homo."

His feelings were clearly hurt and unaffected at the same time. I think the fact that I was calling him a heathen hurt while the homo softened the blow.

Of the crew, I was the only virgin, and they were very proud about making that distinction. But the comment was important for me and the conversation. I was really done talking about gay people. Church is not about the people in it. Well at least it's not about the particular lifestyles of the people in it because everyone's lifestyle in one way or another is in conflict with the teachings of the Church. That is the very reason we go to Church. We want to be reminded of the teachings. For "we all fall short of the glory."

"You keep playing with me and I'll show you who's gay," Ferris said confusingly.

"Enough about them homos, man. Yall are really making me uncomfortable. But where do you go to Church?" Shannon said, protesting our tangent. I was still wondering how Ferris was going to show me I was gay. Weird comment.

"We go to Church in the city. Divine Grace Baptist Church on North Avenue and Leclaire." I had memorized the spiel a little when talking to people. So they didn't ask where after the name, I just put the where there.

At the end of the conversation, it was made clear that they were coming to Church with me. We planned to go two Sundays from that date because my mother had to borrow a car to take all of us. We normally got picked up by a Church member. Me, mom, and Chris got picked up every Sunday. Keith never came along. Chris and I had reached the point where we stopped asking if we could stay behind too. It became clear that my mom was irritated to no end that Keith didn't come with us. I think she felt like she raised him better than that. Or at least that she should have raised him better, and perhaps she had, but it was his choice, as it is all of our choices who we listen to. One thing is for sure though, he got God wherever he went.

On that revelatory Sunday, my mom was rushing Chris and me

as usual.

"Get dressed!" "Stop looking at that TV!" "Put some lotion on your face and hands." "Where are your shoes at?"

Eventually, per usual, she would come in the living room and turn the television off and make us get ready. She did all of this, worrying about us being prepared to go even though we always, and I mean always, had to wait on her for nearly an hour once we were ready. As I got older, I would state this observation to her as she rushed me to get to school, to pack for vacation, to do anything. But it always fell on deaf ears. Maybe not deaf just unconcerned. I had to eat the fact that we worked on her time not vice versa. Perks of being a parent.

Chris and I sat on the couch next to one another probably in two different worlds, dressed to the Tee, slightly annoyed by our ties, and constantly readjusting. I was sure he was looking forward to the day he could stay home like Keith and avoid these futile and vain expressions of faith. But I enjoyed them a lot. They reminded me of God. The process of getting dressed for Church was like a prayer, an annoying, tedious, and loving act of my devotion to Him. On top of that, my friends were coming. I was sure they wouldn't like it and think I was a lame, but they already thought that. I was just happy they were coming to share something special with me.

When we finally got in the car, we were an hour behind the planned schedule. But that was okay because we were normally late. However, we got up an hour early today so that we could pick Ferris, Shannon, and Romeo up. On the drive to their houses we bumped Gospel music. I liked that my mom played Hezekiah Walker, Shirley Caesar, and the Mississippi Mass Choir as loud as many people played Bone Thugs and Jay-Z.

There was a pride in it. We are Christian in the same way you are Gangster. We practice it, we speak it, and we listen to it. Now these are not two mutually exclusive terms. There are some Christian ass Gangsters. My mother is a prime example. So we were riding down the street listening to my all-time personal favorite gospel song, "Come On In the Room." I love that song. In this song, the narrator recounts a story of a grandmother who is praying in the home of a white family for her son's well-being after a car crash. While the grandmother is praying, a doctor shows up at the door on his rounds. The rest of the family had been trying to get a hold of him by telephone (the doctor, that is). But granny got a hold of Him (God, that is).

When she sees the doctor, she says my favorite line of the song in the old M-I-S-S-I-S-S-I-P-P-I manner. She drags it out and lets you know who her God really is. Granny says, "There is johoy in my room, mmmhhhhmmm, there is johoooy in my room. Jezus is my doctor an-hand He writes out all my scriptions. Uhuh, He gives me all my med'cine in my roohoom." And there was joy. Because that's what it means to have God. There was joy in the car. Granny sang about it and God brought it. Even for my uncomfortably dressed little brother. We were all smiling. Her voice, her joy, her expression of faith, and her love for the Father (granny that is), had to be felt. She makes you feel it. We all smiled and sang along. Amen.

We got to Ferris's house to find him standing at the front. He was dressed in his finest attire. Because his family didn't go to Church regularly, and they rarely if ever did anything formal, he was dressed to the Tee. He was in a baby-blue and white pin-striped, double-breasted, three-quarter-length Zoot suit. His tie, a solid baby-blue on his crisp white shirt. I hope to this day that it was not a clip-on. But he hopped in the car smelling like fragrance oils, the kind sold by the Black men with black Velcro straps with little bottles of oil attached. The black straps often cross the chest, making the bottles look like bullets, and it makes these black men look like smell-good superheroes. Rambos of fragrance. He plopped in the car, going to great lengths to protect his suit jacket from the puddle that my mother had parked over. He closed the door and my mother took off, on to the next house.

"Good morning Ms. Dale," Ferris said. "What up, Jay? What up, Chris?"

"What up?" Chris and I said in unison.

"What time does Church start?"

"Normally at like eleven," I said. I never really knew what time it started. My guess was always when we got there. That was the only time that was important to me. Plus people mosey in throughout the ceremony. So I just assumed it started before noon.

"The service starts at 10:45," my mother said more precisely. "We not going to be late if that's what you're worried about, baby."

"Oh naw I just wanted to know. I kind of like making a grand entrance anyway, Ms. Dale. Especially in Church." We all laughed. I don't know why it was so funny, but for some reason talking about Church like a party was funny.

"The real question aint 'What time it starts.' The real question is what time are we going to get out?" Chris said sarcastically. Chris was still salty about Keith being able to stay home.

"Boy shut up," my mom called back. She was looking in the

rearview mirror. Because she didn't drive often, it made that look all the more piercing. I saw Chris's mouth shut up for him. Out of self-preservation his mouth closed itself.

Ferris, not knowing my mom's real reason for telling Chris to shut up, continued the questioning. "So what time do we get out?" he asked. I wanted to tap him and let him know that question was off limits, but I was sitting in the front. After his question, I tensed because my mom could react one of two ways in this situation. I was hoping it would be the second.

"Why? You got somewhere to be?" she said sharply. I was not sure which response she had chosen yet. She could be joking or she could be snapping.

"Naw it's not that I got to be somewhere. I just don't want to be there until like five at night," Ferris said very honestly. Black churches like to kidnap the congregation from time to time.

"Five tonight? Hecky naw we aint gonna be at Church for no seeevvveeeen hours. That's like a job boy. I already got one of them. Damn near two," she said with a chuckle.

"Naw that's not in our plans for today, baby." She had chosen to joke. My mom was that way. She was always nicer to other people's children than she was to her own. I never thought of it, but I guess going to Church has a culture of its own too. Looking back, she probably expected us to understand the importance of what we were doing, and she treated this cultural nuance between us and Ferris delicately. That's just me thinking too hard, I guess. I always feel like my mom has a very intricate reason for everything she does—well maybe she makes me feel that way.

We drove a little farther. The plan was that we would meet

Shannon at Romeo's house for a number of reasons, but primarily because my mom didn't get along with Shannon's mom. The reason for the issues between our mothers has more to do with parenting styles than sincere dislike. They actually both love playing card games, and they hung out for a while after Shannon and I became friends. But my mother doesn't "like the way she runs her house," as she puts it. She thinks a mother "just shouldn't treat her kids like people on the street." I agree. I say parenting styles because I don't want to disrespect Shannon's mom.

But to be honest, I wouldn't call her style one of parenting, but of coexisting with her children, which is much different. The problem originated from one parent (mine) expecting the other parent (his) to be concerned for her child's well-being and whereabouts, and she (his mother) didn't. Now there are a number of particular incidents where this issue is stated more clearly but they just serve to highlight this basic disconnect between our two parents. Shannon's mom never did the things other mothers do to make sure their sons are safe and cared for, including communicating with their friends' parents. So instead of losing her religion on Sunday morning, my mother decided to have Shannon meet us at Romeo's house up the block.

We got to Romeo's apartment building, and no one was standing outside so I had to go ring the bell. His apartment building stood four stories and opened onto a courtyard. There were three entrances leading from the courtyard. Romeo's entrance was the middle. After walking across the courtyard, I rang his bell. It was the third from the bottom right above R. Miller and T Stanley. *Buuuuurrrrr*, the bell rang. A staticky voice came through the intercom, "Who is it?" "Jamal," I said trying to get the timing right. By this time Chris had joined me at the bell, "I just wanted to get out of the car," he said.

"Romeo . . ." the voice managed to get out before the static ate anything that was audible. So I rang the bell again.

"Who is it?"

I hate the type of conversations when the other person controls when you can talk, or what is considered valid in a conversation. That's what it feels like talking over an intercom. All I have to do is say two or three words to clear everything up, but I can't get them out because the person on the other end of the conversation has decided it's not my turn to be talking. "Jamal" I say out of frustration and impotence. With even more frustration, they called through the intercom "I said he's SLEEP!"

I wanted to ask them had Shannon stopped by, but one more bell ring would likely have me banned from their house. It doesn't take much more than that to be banned from a Black person's house. If your actions qualify as an irritation, you might get banned. Can't be disrupting the peace like that.

I walked back through the courtyard trying to take my time. I wanted to see if Shannon was going to walk up. I didn't know what time it was, and I knew that my mom, who is reluctant to blow the horn in most instances, would toot it with pride to make her sons run back to the car.

It was funny seeing her with a car. Because she didn't have one, when she got the chance to enjoy the luxurious life, she took every liberty she could. It was kind of fun riding around with her because her excitement was palpable. I finally got back to the car. I was disappointed. I wanted all of my friends to be there. We had planned it. My mom was driving and they should have been awake and there.

We borrowed the car. I was mad. Maybe it was an anger and a disappointment that needed to be hidden, it deserved to be stored. It was like I didn't feel justified in it. Something about me felt feminine or womanly for being upset in this way. I was upset in a way that I couldn't do anything about. So I just put it away. It's like because I couldn't do anything about it, I shouldn't have any feelings about it. So I didn't.

Chris and I got back into the car. We entered on the same side except I got in the front, and he got in the back. After I put the anger away, I became sad. I was sad we got stood up. It felt silly even at the time, but I was still sad. The despair must have been on my face because my mom leaned over to comfort me saying, "We can get the car again next week." But I didn't want them to be there next week if they weren't there for this week.

They missed their chance. I was mad for the most part. We pulled off and made it about half way up the block when Ferris, who was looking out the back window for whatever reason, saw Shannon running behind the car in his Sunday best. Ferris tapped me on the shoulder from the back seat.

"I think that's Shannon. Or someone who looks just like him running after the car."

Ferris always had a way of not being sure about what he was sure about. My mom pulled up to the curb to wait, and sure enough, it was him. I saw him in the sideview mirror. Shannon's suit jacket wide open, tie flailing, shoes clacking, and pants waving, he looked like a ceremonious flag placed on high for all to see. I was immediately relieved, and my sadness was washed clean. All it took was two of the three.

Shannon got to the car clearly excited that he had caught up with us and more than that, fatigued from the run. It is definitely a different beast running fully clad and in dress shoes. Without practice, it is almost dangerous. There is a different bounce and give to the dress up joints. But when he got to the car, he was hot, tired, and out of breath.

"Man it's a good thing I caught yall. I would have been salty if I had gotten all dressed up and been left behind."

"Why good morning to you too," my mom said indignantly.

"Oh I'm sorry. Good morning everyone."

"Hey," Chris, Ferris, and I said in unison.

"What up?" he said back even though it was unnecessary. You know how it is with greetings, sometimes you go one or two overboard. It does no harm to anyone. It can just be a little awkward.

"We stopped by Romeo's to get you but they said he was sleep. We didn't even get a chance to ask them where you was at," I said excited that he was in the backseat to say it to.

"Man, I had stopped by there earlier, and his sister said he was sleep. It was that bell. I tried to tell her I was there to get picked up, but they don't give you enough time to get nothing out."

"Exactly. I think they just don't like talking to people anyway," I speculated. "And I was going to ring the bell again, but that would have been too much in the morning." I never really got to know Romeo's family outside of his older brother who broke into a lot of houses. Like, a lot of houses. He even helped me break into my house once. I blame the fact that they are mean and don't like to talk to other people.

"Yea, they probably would have thought we were Jehovahs or

something ringing they bell four or five times like that in the morning," Chris said humorously. "You know how mom gets when them Jehovahs come around." I knew that his reenactment of mom's Jehovah's Witness full-proof hiding strategy was about to take place. "Lock the doors! Close the blinds! Turn off the TV. They can't know we're here." Yep. It never fails. Chris was hunched down in the back seat, hiding below the window line. Peering over it. Impersonating mom at the door.

We pulled up to the Church. It was weird. Parking, I mean. Because you have to drive all the way up to your destination just to find a space as close as possible to it. But you already know there won't be any spaces. So then you drive away from your destination looking for spaces. I know it makes sense but it's just weird. When we found a space, we were about three blocks from the Church. We bailed out of the car ready to sit permanently.

Walking toward the Church was fun and full of light conversation. I hoped my mom had brought snacks for us, but she probably hadn't. If she didn't have enough for everyone, we couldn't have any. She had rules like that about children. But I was overjoyed with my company that the rumbling in my stomach as a result of missing lunch shouldn't bother me. I don't know why Chris and I never ate cereal while waiting for mom.

Entering the Church doors was amazing. The heat had been beating on me the whole three blocks. I don't know how Ferris held up with that heavy ass suit on. The wind from the refrigerated air consumed me. I was wrapped in it. The beads of sweat stopped in their tracks and made me a little uncomfortable. Being chilly and wet is not a great combination. As we entered, the usher held the door open for us. He gave each of us a folded piece of paper with the order of the ceremony on it. Inside of the paper was an envelope. That envelope was never used. It was for money. I guess some people used it. The tithers. But I was there for the experience.

I walked on greeting everyone, some with a head nod and others with a hug or handshake. We always wanted to get in and sit down though. We were a little earlier than usual, meaning our favorite seat was open. Generally, we liked to sit on the left side of the aisle toward the middle rear. It was wide open. All of us had room on the same bench, which was nice. The older people tended to come to Church earlier, for Sunday school and the early service. While the younger people got there later when they came to Church, if at all. Like Keith.

I don't know if it has something to do with anticipation or not, but as you get older, the closer to the front of the Church you sit. We were near the middle rear because mom was old to me but not old in Church years, and she wouldn't let us sit with the bad kids in the *rear* rear. We were just close enough to hear their murmurings and several obnoxious statements.

Church was about to begin. The praise singers were upfront. There were seven of them and when they started singing, that was the cue for everyone to sit down and pay attention. The show was starting. Indeed, it was to the sound of celestial voices. There were five women and two men holding down the praise team. I don't know how they always chose the right songs for the day, but they did. Or did they or someone else make it the right day for the song? He does say the Son of Man is Lord of the Sabbath as well, whatever that means to Seventh Day Adventists.

To be honest, I don't remember the songs they sang on that

joyous day, but I do remember them setting the tone. After they sat down, there was a scripture reading. I remember it being a scripture with a simple moral: Philippians 4:10-20.

The deacons got up and went before the congregation. They were all men of different ages, temperaments, and beliefs to be honest, and it showed as they walked to the microphone that was stationed in the front of the pulpit. I think of them as the reverend's disciples. They rarely, if ever, reach the pulpit. I wonder why that is. I think they know.

"Everybody bow your heads," Deacon Lewis said, as he was generally the deacon who prayed. He would deliver the longest most unbearable prayers. He was old.

"Lord, Father, God, we come before you thanking you on this your holiest of days. We thank you God, and we praise your name for waking us up this morning and for just giving us the air in our lungs to say your son Jesus's name."

The congregation would shout and say "Well" and "Thank ya Gawd." They were still somewhat hyped by the praise team's leadership. Deacon Lewis would continue feeding off of the congregation's energy. He listed about twenty more blessings that he was thankful for. Then he continued.

"Lord God we open our mouths right now blessing your name. Knowing that you are the reason for all things. We come before you now with our arms outstretched, our voices raised, our heals stomping, and our hearts and minds focused on you and your mercies. We know you are a loving God. We know you are a caring God. We know you are an omniscient, omnipotent, and omnipresent Lord. But you are a forgiving God, and we thank you for looking down upon our sins and wiping us clean as snow." By the end, it felt like everyone was daydreaming. At least I was. Not necessarily disrespectful, still thinking of the grace of God, but my attention started to wane when he thanked God for giving him the strength to brush his teeth.

Where had He brought them from? Where was He taking them to? God that is.

Skipping a just amount of Deacon Lewis' prayer, he would always wind down in the same fashion. As if through his repetition of humility and sincerity he was acknowledging the example set by our Lord.

"And Lawd, we ask for your hand of protection as we traverse your lands. There is a lot that we don't know, and we leave our lives in your hands until the day we meet face to face. Until the day when your great plan is revealed, we shall wait and praise by our faith. For it is through love that we were created and by love that we are kept. Thank you, Father for your glory and your bounty. My cup runneth over because you have given me more than I could imagine. Thank you, Lord. Thank you, Lord. Amen." *What had God given him?*

The congregation responded with a grand "Amen!" This was how his prayer ended, each and every time. I might have gotten a word out of place or two, but the gist of it is right there. I loved the way he prayed, and I loved this wrap up to it the most. *We were created in love.* Why don't we live in it? A question I pondered much later.

Deacon Lewis then dug into the verse of the day. I wonder if he or the pastor chose the verse, maybe it was a collaboration. But for some reason, the verse always seemed to be related to the scripture selected for the sermon. Maybe the whole Bible is related, I guess. But I still think the pastor chose them. Either way, the liberty was taken in the passion of the deacon, their specific passion toward God was what made me think they had selected it. In fact, like Deacon Lewis, many of the deacons took this as their opportunity to get a little preaching off of their chests.

I think a number of them really wanted to be ministers but decided at some point that they didn't have enough for the job. Enough of what, was unclear. Maybe it was eloquence, intelligence, or something more like patience or compassion. I don't know, but I felt their aspirations at times, and it was realistic, to say the least. Maybe the disciples envied Jesus to a degree. Did they want to walk on water? Did they wish to be crucified?

"As Paul states to the people of Euodia and Syntyche his words of encouragement. In Philippians four verse one to eight, saying that they must put away their feud for they are God-fearing nations. He says 'Always be full of joy in the Lord. I say it again rejoice. Let everyone see that you are considerate in all you do.'"

He would pause. He spoke each word like it had a period after it. Pronouncing each syllable. I think he was deciding whether to read further or not. Because it was important, but was it more important than the previous line?

He decides to read on. I like that he gave us the option of discerning the meaning of the Word. He doesn't always. I'm not too sure he likes to read, he seems to get more satisfaction out of the prayer. He's old.

"And he goes on to say, 'Don't worry about anything; instead, pray about everything. Tell God what you need and thank Him for all He has done. Then you will experience God's peace which exceeds anything we can understand.'"

I liked having my Bible. I saw the part he skipped. It said "Remember, the Lord is coming soon." I like that he skipped that too. It seems very onerous and just like it's not a good reason to praise God. But that's what some people need, I guess. For them, God is the spook who sat by the door.

"Now looking down at verse ten we encounter Paul's reason for praising the Lord. What has God done for you today?" And the congregation shouts. Praises go up, and people acknowledge what the Lord has done. The organ gets flared up, the piano gets going, the drums take off to the usual rhythm, and people feel the same high. For thirty seconds or seven minutes they dance and shout and sing.

I stand up and wave my hands. I don't shout because it doesn't feel right, but I raise my hands. He made me. This I know. This goes on until the congregation settles down. The time is not an element. We rejoice in the time because it is God's gift.

But when people return to their seats and only one woman remains simultaneously shouting and sobbing, Deacon Lewis returns to the Word just as calm.

"And he goes on to say in verse ten, 'How I praised the Lord that you are concerned about me again. I know that you have always been concerned about me, but you didn't have the chance to help me... I have learned the secret of living in every situation, whether it is with a full stomach or empty, with plenty or little. For I can do everything through Christ, who gives me strength.' There we go! Now that is a reason for celebration! I can do, EVERYTHING, EVERYTHING, not some things, not most things, but EVERYTHING, through

Christ, who, what Congregation?"

"GIVES ME STRENGTH!" we all shouted back. The passion of the congregation filled me with love and motivation to do right.

With that, Deacon Lewis was done. In my opinion, per usual, he had done a great job. At least I got the message. I don't know how others took it but I took it very literally. I can do anything and everything because I know my maker. That sounds pretty reasonable. There was no need for a parable, not that I don't like those too, the message was just simple.

If the deacons did not come up in unison, they definitely returned to their seats with very similar expressions and senses of urgency. Their part was done. Now it was the choir's turn to lift our spirits in a different way. They sang with voices as big as cannons. All of them. It didn't matter whether they were talented or not. They sang big and full, and it sounded good. The good voices carried the bad and the bad voices underscored the good. There was indeed a harmony among the choir members.

I don't know why they say the Devil enters the Church through the choir, but who cares? God must have something to do with it. But they got up and they sang. They sang of His wonders and His strength. I remember they sang "Let it Rain." They gave such an enthusiasm to the song. Over and over the choir says "Open the floodgates of Heaven. Let it rain." They just keep repeating this anthem, this command. They command God to open the floodgates. The reason I remember this song is because there was a theme that day. The theme of rain (reign).

The choir's second song was "Drip Drop." It has a great repetition too. Over and over the choir states "RAAAAAINNN,

RAAAAAIIIIIN, Holy Ghost fall down on me. RAAAAAIIIIN, RAAAAIIIIN, Holy Ghost fall down on me." But just when you get the routine of the repetition they switch to a layered "Drip Drop." There is a point in the song when two women who are magnificent sopranos send out this piercing call that pours the spirit into you. The crazy thing about the women is that they are almost opposite one another in demeanor, size, and overall personality but their voices are of the same accord. The woman who stands on the left is named Tiffany. She is short, yellow, round, and a very open and pleasant person. The woman on the right of the choir stand, countering Tiffany's voice, is Lynne. She is short, slim, pretty as all get out, and browner than milk chocolate. They hold it down. With the layers of the "Drip, Drop, Drop, Drip, Drop, Drop, Holy Ghost rain down on me," the song just took you somewhere else spiritually. They were amazing.

After the choir's selections, we took offering. We didn't use the envelopes in the pamphlet. We didn't have enough money to make a note about it. My mom gave us each a dollar to put into the offering whether we had money or not. In my case it was not. I don't know about the others. Well in Chris's case it was not too. We got that over with. The choir had another selection and then came the main event of the hour, the pastor was up. He was a medium-height man, with strong features, light brown skin, and although he was thin, he seemed large, larger than other men, much bigger men. He seemed confident and well prepared always. Not in the sense that he knew something others didn't. More like he knew what they knew. Maybe that's the rhythm of the spirit?

Revelations
(Reverend Nelson)

I leaned over to the visiting minister, Reverend Jacobs, as he wanted to give me a word of encouragement before I took the pulpit. He's going to be delivering the sermon for the afternoon service. Man, am I excited to be able to sit that one out. No offense, God but Your servant is tired. Everyone thinks Sunday services are all I do. I go see people in the hospital. I had four funerals this past week, and three bible study classes. Not to mention pre-marital counseling. Lord, Your servant is tired. Not ungrateful or reluctant, just tired. So please forgive me for not listening to this man's prayer and for making one of my own. I ask that You might bless my tongue with Your Words. May You hold my thoughts and let me rely on Yours. You are a great God and I love You. Amen. Now please give me the strength to take this pulpit.

"Amen, amen, amen. Praise the Lord, church. How many of you are here to praise the Lord our Father on this Sunday the Lord has made?"

The congregation responded with shouts and praises.

"I said, who is here to praise God the Father today? Not now but right now. Give Him praise in the highest for He is more than deserving of the highest of our praises." The congregation was ecstatic. They had been shouting since the original question. They knew why they were here, and they knew it was almost over. At least until this afternoon's service. Fill your spirit. You have to wait seven more days to get this complete experience again. The climax was coming. Shout now.

With a sweep of the hand and a gentle command "Let us pray." I brought order to the congregation.

"As I come before Your people and deliver the word that You have placed on my heart, I ask that it might be pertinent. That the message might resonate among their souls. And that they might find some purpose and space for it in their lives."

I hope that my words will find a home among them and grow like seeds in their hearts.

"So now we place our faith in our works and we work for the benefit of Your kingdom. Putting You above all else we say, amen, amen, and amen."

"Church, I'm gonna let you know right now that a message bears heavy on my heart, a message about injustice and suffering. This message which God has given us, is about a world of pain, sin, and grief. I want to talk about a world of oppression and mistreatment. This world, this very world, where twelve-year-old Black boys get tried by a SUPREME Court as adults. Where millions of pregnancies are intentionally aborted every year. Where people who believe in something, in anything, are demoralized and humiliated. A world of lies, wickedness, and disbelief. We are facing a craaazy world, and as

Christians we must be prepared."

"Amen!" The congregation said in response. Sister Tyler could be heard over most of the voices. She was liable to catch the spirit at any time and hold up the service until she collapsed from exhaustion.

"I want to talk to you today. I want to let you know a thing or two about my God. I say my God because you're going to have to own that relationship. You're going to have to take hold, trust, and listen. God doesn't have to be loud to be shouting. But you're going to have to listen. God tells you when your partner is no good for you. Well?"

I knew that would get a reaction. An eruption of cheers came from the women in the congregation. So many of them had been hurt time and again.

"Are yall ready for the Word today?"

The congregation shouted back a barrage of amens, hallelujahs, and praise Gods.

"Now turn with me, if you will, to the book of Numbers, chapter thirty, verse one. We're gonna look at two books today that discuss wisdom. In our respective journeys in this life, we will find that one of our best friends will become the discernment that comes with wisdom. The situational understanding of right and wrong. As we learn what is best, we also learn what Christ would do. We gain a knowledge of personalities, of nature, and of God. Wisdom requires a certain (I)eye, a specific way of seeing the world, of calculating Life. The wise give life in their deeds. Now turn with me to, uh, uh, the book of Numbers, chapter thirty, verses one and two."

I turned to Numbers, the book I just called out, and the Words ran together. They swirled at the center of the page like coolant fluid traveling through a funnel. They bled and they changed colors, from red, to black, to green. Then they would repeat the cycle. Suddenly the Words returned to their rightful place and abandoned their regal multichromatic attitude.

"And we find in this, the book of Numbers, that Moses is addressing the leaders of the twelve tribes. He is letting them know the gravity of their words. And what it means in the Lord's eyes to make a vow. So we listen with our hearts to hear what God sees."

I paused to gather my thoughts. Looking at my notes, this was my point.

"Now what do we find in the book of Numbers as he has summoned the leaders of the tribes? It says, 'This is what the Lord has commanded: A man who makes a vow to the Lord or makes a pledge under oath must never break it. He must do exactly what he said he would do.' Now why should a man never break his vow to God? What has he vowed upon? What penance might he face? Who has he shamed by lying? These are questions we must ask."

"It goes on to tell us why in Proverbs chapter seventeen, if you might turn with me. 'Fools have no interest in understanding; they only want to air their own opinions...Wise words are like deep waters; wisdom flows from the wise like a bubbling brook...The mouths of fools are their ruin. They trap themselves with their lips.'"

"You betta preach preacher!" A voice of encouragement rang out.

"In this book of Proverbs and in Numbers, we find the importance of words, the significance of truth and upholding righteousness in speech. Are our words wise or foolish? Do they give way to conflict or the Peace of God? This is how we must see our words. Choose and select your words. Uh, uh, uh, believe and know the meaning and the power of the words we speak."

"Fools deny justice to the innocent. They speak wickedness because it is on their hearts. Their hearts are hardened and they, they, they are grieved. But, the, the, the wise. Now the wise, oh Lord, the wise give life water through their words. I'm trying to tell yall."

"But thirty seconds around fools can feel so draining. All of the arguments and buffoonery are offensive. They call for rash deeds to support them and lead to ridiculous fighting. Any of yall have that relative? I know I do. That relative that just keeps up mess? Always wanting to talk about how so and so are raising their kids? Or how so and so is cheating on their husband?" Most of the congregation laughed.

Speak to their hearts God. "Foolishness is weighed down with immorality and a rejection of the salvation offered by God's grace. But way too often, our culture and our society rejoices in and praises foolishness. Far, far, far too often our goal in life is to see how many people we can hurt, how many hearts we can break, how many wars we can rage. Because being tough and rude is more important than being forgiving and kind." Several members of the congregation seconded the notion in their own way.

"We all know those foolish folks as the Bible would call them. The type to sell the house to pay the light bill. Backwards folks." My voice felt raspy. I reached for my water.

"Preach, preacher," one woman shouted.

"Worst of all, you could be married to one of them people. Now don't go home and say pastor told you to get a divorce because I didn't say that. I just said recognize the foolishness. You should've seen it before you got married. Do you know this person, Church?"

Everyone let out a shout of affirmation. I heard members speaking in tongues and stomping in place. When I was younger, I was always told that the Devil didn't know this language. It was the way to get messages to God without the Devil's intervention.

"I figured as much. But it is our goal as Christians to be wise. To bring God's peace to this life. We are the body of Christ, and as His body we must transform this world and conquer any inclination to feed into conflicts of words, of the flesh, and most especially of the spirit. Guard your spirit with the full armor of God. Now this never means don't fight. Peace and nonviolence are not always synonymous. Always fight when it's called for. Fight for righteousness, for Truth, and for Love."

"For we know as Christians that the civilization of today is gone drunk with its power and by such, it seeks through injustice, fraud, and lies to crush the unfortunate. The system is fed by inequity. It was born of iniquity. It thrives off of oppression. But if Christ and His people were apparently crushed at the Crucifixion of our Savior, our cause rose again to plague the conscience of the enemy. Our day may be fifty, a hundred or two hundred years ahead, but let us watch, work, and pray, for the civilization of injustice is bound to crumble and bring destruction down upon the heads of the unjust. Because it is well published that the minutes of suffering are counted, and when God comes back to measure out retribution, these minutes may multiply by thousands for the sinners."

"Observe God's enemies and their children and their children's children, and one day you shall see retribution settling around them. Cheer up and be assured that if it takes a million years, the sins of our enemies shall visit the millionth generation of these that hinder and oppress us."

The congregation followed, hanging on every word. They were my people and in search of their purpose. That's why they showed up so religiously. All of them were looking for a way to lift the yolk of America off of their necks. Individuals and families stood. A few congregants danced in along the aisles, their spirits moving to the rhythm of the drums. I continued, now close to concluding.

"The reason for this sermon, well, is to look at our own action the way God the Father does. Now my Bible lists a prayer in which it is stated 'Forgive me my trespasses as I forgive those who trespass against me.' This is grace. This is what we should speak. For 'wise words are satisfying like a good meal.' Wise words anticipate future salvation. But the words of a fool destroy others. Their words kill relationships and create conflict."

"What is there left for us to do? We must 'repent and let every one of you be baptized in the name of Jesus Christ for the remission of sins; and you shall receive the gift of the Holy Spirit. For the promise is to you and to your children, and to ALL who are afar off, as many as the Lord our God will call.' The Promise of the blood. Christ bled out so that we can be saved from ourselves. Drink and be filled, eat and be filled. The gift of flesh and blood, let Christ not have died in vain. Let your flesh be redeemed and filled with the Spirit. If you do not have a Church home and you feel at home fellowshipping with us, the doors of the Church are open...Let all who are called come."

The choir stood as I opened the invitation to discipleship. They rose and sang, "Speak Lord, Speak to Me." Slowly people trickled to the front of the Church. They joined by way of baptism, letter, or simple conversion of the heart. But all I wanted everyone to consider was one commandment. For them to think of the world if all truly believed in HIM.

CHAPTER 12

The Big Bang

*B*y this time, the seeds of New Africa had rooted deep inside of my soul. I was starting to see the world for what it was, what man had made it. Something was unfair. The worlds I'd seen were too different, divergent even. But I still couldn't identify what or why yet. I simply knew that something was off about the way that Blacks were forced to live. Circumscribed to live.

My family moved to the Southside of Chicago after my freshman year of high school. I went to Kimball Valley High School freshman year. It was a reckless place, just like Kimball Valley Elementary, save there were more drugs. Way more drugs. The transition from eighth grade to high school was one of the largest leaps I had been asked to take to this point. There really is no buffer. More accurately, there was a void. I was thirteen years old and everyone expected me to be different after three months of summer. I was asked to care about fashion, what others think, trends, music, reputations, etc. Or at least I was *expected* to care about those things. I had to compete with adults: the seniors. They were eighteen years old, had cars, mustaches, and muscles, and they were trying to sleep with people's fourteen-year-old daughters. Which is why the drugs were such an issue.

The move to the Southside was nice. As I alluded to earlier, Shannon moved with us. Chris, Shannon and I all shared a room. I had no problem with the arrangement. Sure, things were tight and someone was always wearing my clothes, but I had another brother. A true brother. It was like we were from the same womb.

New Africa broke through the soil one fateful day in October. One glorious Halloween she sprouted her roots, ready to bear fruit. My mother asked Keith to walk to the grocery store around the corner. It was a nice distance from the house, and Keith hated pushing the buggy all the way to the store. I understood the sentiment. It did possess the essence of a feeble old lady. Besides, Keith never missed an opportunity to shoot his shot at women on the street and pushing a buggy isn't the look he was going for. So, obviously, he asked Shannon and me to tag along. One of us to push it there and one of us to push it back. In exchange, we got to be seen with Keith. He was our idol. We secretly practiced acting and talking like him. Memorizing his walk, the cadence of his voice, his gestures. So of course we took the trip.

It was also helpful having us around on Halloween, in particular. People in Chicago used to be crazy on Halloween like it was a full moon or a Purge or something. The kids on the southside took advantage of any excuse to wear masks and hide in anonymity. I remember being on the CTA, on many a Halloween, and getting pelted with eggs or snowballs as I got off. Groups of boys in masks, waiting behind the bus shelter to bombard you with eggs. At least they were typically not frozen. If they happened to be frozen, the eggs felt like bullets. Each one landing with a burning sensation.

"Ma, just called and said we gotta go to the store."

Keith made the statement like there was no choice for us. But we knew better. Mom hadn't enlisted us to go. It was a Sunday. My mom was working a new job and had to take all the overtime she could get. We had stopped attending Church regularly. There was a mild relief from the break with Church. We all felt it. It felt like dating the same person for seventeen years and realizing that you carried the relationship everyday of that seventeen years. We were annoyed with Church. Church was the girlfriend. She kept talking about all the stuff she was going to do. All of her plans that never became manifest. For seventeen years. Keith was working too. I don't remember where though. I just remember he used to ride his bike everywhere. Everywhere. Needless to say he was in excellent shape.

Shannon and I had started to catch up to Keith in height. He seemed more human. He was still densely muscled, brown, and shiny like polished wood. He started cutting his own hair at the time. The blades of the clippers were too sharp, and his lining held the reddish scab marks of a novice barber. He was already dressed and ready to go grocery shopping.

"Where's Chris?"

"He's knocked out," Shannon responded. "I've been trying to wake him up for an hour. He fell asleep on my pillow. I don't want him drooling on it. You know he goes into hibernation like a bear or something."

Keith and I both laughed. It was true. Chris was an abnormally hard sleeper. I peeked into the bedroom. He was laying awkwardly, half of his body was off the bed. Shannon definitely needed to wash his pillow case. So we left Chris behind with a note saying that we'd be back. We didn't have cell phones. We had notes.

I decided to push the buggy to the store. It was a lot easier than pushing it once it was completely full. With some limitations. Pushing an empty cart is like riding a wave. Every crack in the concrete felt like holding a jackhammer. The wheels were shaky and made it difficult walking down the pothole ridden sidewalks of Chicago. We didn't talk much on the way. It was a nice fall day. A bit cloudy with a slight breeze. A bit of tension stirred in my stomach. I always feel like something crazy is going to happen on Halloween, and normally I'm wrong. Halloween is such a weird day. I don't like when people have an excuse to wear masks. People really like any reason to wear masks. Anonymity is a powerful thing.

We got to the store without issue. I love shopping with Keith. We split and we all went down different aisles with our own missions. We met back at aisle seven when it was time to check out. We had almost everything we needed.

"Oh snap, we forgot the ground beef. One of yall go grab some while we wait in line. Who's the fastest?" Keith asked looking at Shannon. It was clear that he thought Shannon was faster. It was our Sophomore year of high school. Shannon was a star football prospect while I was a star debate prospect, if there is such a thing. We were different. He was lifting weights, I wasn't. I preferred to argue. I wanted to be a lawyer at the time. Still do in a way. There's just no room for law in New Africa, meaning no room for lawyers. No arguments here. Zero conflicts. All Faith. All God. All Love.

"You already know!" Shannon said with a smirk.

I let him take that one. I didn't feel like going back through the store to find the ground beef. Keith was a master of reverse psychology. Shannon was happy to run back and grab the ground beef. Shannon shot off toward the frozen foods aisle. He darted, looking like a track star. His back erect, knees coming high. *I could dust him,* I said to myself as I watched his stride. We have the competitive spirit of brothers. It makes us better.

When we got outside, Shannon pushed the cart. The groceries were nearly toppling over. We always got too much for the cart. I think that's why the wheels were in such bad shape.

I wasn't going to say anything, but the competitive spirit got to me. I had to make my argument clear. Shannon could not beat me in a fight, a hot dog eating competition, a nose-picking contest, or a foot race. He couldn't beat me in the cricket spitting Olympics. I will not lose to Shannon.

"I saw you running back there. You aint as fast as you think. You aint on no Mike Vick shit."

Shannon let out a sarcastic laugh. "Stick to Madden. That's the only way you can beat me." I definitely mopped him on the game system. I knew I had to dust him in real life. I had to let him know all the practice in the world couldn't make him stronger than me. I will always have the mental victory.

"What you trying to do?" I responded, knowing what he was trying to do. It was a challenge. There could only be one. We would have to run until somebody lost the race. Until someone gave in. Even then, we would have to run again to prove the point.

"I got that Michael Johnson shit, boy."

"You mean Magic Johnson." Shannon said quicker than expected. Keith and Shannon both laughed. It was an AIDS joke. Who laughs at AIDS jokes?

"Next block then. Race to the end of the block, Joe," Keith orchestrated.

We were crossing the street. I started to take deep breaths and try to stretch as much as I could. Circling my arms, like that would help. Shannon did none of this. He continued to push the cart. He got it over the curb with some effort and passed it off to Keith. He was ready. He looked at the end of the block, eyes set, fixated. He knew a lot about sports psychology. Shannon always had a way of turning it on when he needed to. I admired that. It's hard to stay calm when you really want to perform well.

"Matter of fact, we going to do this the right way," Keith stated with authority and a slight laugh. "I'm going to go to the end of the block. Wait for me to tell yall when to go." He paused, thinking. "Matter of fact, wait til my hand drops to go." Keith rushed down the block with the cart. He found our feud funny. He knew Shannon really wanted to impress him. So did I to some extent.

The competition brought us all closer. But to Keith it was hilarious. When he got to the end of the block, he turned to face us. Raising his right hand, he shouted out, with three fingers extended, "Three . . . Two . . ." then he dropped his hand after signaling one. Shannon was in a three-point stance. He took off like a Corvette. I wasn't prepared for the track-like start. My feet were delayed. My legs were heavy. It was though I was running on sand. They couldn't catch up with my eyes. He had a reasonable head start. I saw him looking back at me.

My eyes were on Keith the entire time. Like a hooper looking at the net, I had a goal. Shannon looked back again. I was on his tail. My chest was pounding. My breathing was becoming more and more strained. Our strides were very different. My strides were short and choppy. My posture poor. He stood erect like a giraffe, taking giant leaps with each step. His knees were in his chest. Arms stiff and tucked tight to his ribs. Mine were loose, flailing. My feet almost hitting his. I moved slightly to the right to pass. He moved to the right to block. He stuck his arm out to hold me back. Like race cars hitting a rough turn. I feinted left with a slight jab step, and he fell for it. I moved ahead. We weren't just racing. The competition was deep-seated. My lungs were hurting. A city block is further than you might think. It felt like I hadn't taken one breath the entire race. I was winning though. I was going to win. I could pass out at the end. It would still be all worth it.

Then . . . *Bwwwooooop Bwwwooooop.*

A police siren went off somewhere near us. I looked to my left, but it was too late. A police car pulled up on the curb in front of me. I was running full speed and didn't have any time to pivot and get out of the way.

BA-DOOM!

I ran right into the hood of the car. The bumper chopped me down at the shins. The collision stung a lot. I braced myself with my forearms. Shannon was able to slow down, but only managed to slow down enough to piss off the officers. Shannon was to my left. He ran into the door as the officer on the passenger side was getting out. His palms hit the window. The momentum forced the car door to shut on the cop's face. Her head was caught between the door and the roof. She wasn't too excited about that. We soon found out.

I tried to regain my composure, but I was out of breath. Exhausted. My heart was racing. Lungs were burning. Hitting the car full speed didn't help. My leg hurt somewhere around my ankle. The cop on the driver's side got out screaming. His hand was on his pistol, and he was pointing at the ground. I couldn't even hear him he was yelling so loud at such close range. All I heard was body language and bass. I couldn't read his lips. He was pointing at the ground. The sirens were still blaring. It was Mr. Lucas. He didn't recognize me. I didn't care either. This job was a much better fit for a racist, I guess. Better than teaching anyway. At least he could only kill my body as a cop. Much better than killing my mind as a teacher. Or my spirit? If that was even possible.

"Get down, now!"

He shouted, still pointing at the ground. How long does it take to become a cop? He had put on some muscle and some stomach since he left Kimball Valley Elementary. His partner managed to finally get out of the car. I looked back at her and then at Shannon who was back-stepping away from the police car. She was a short Latina-looking officer. She was busty. The uniform and vest fit loosely making her appear just as wide as she was tall. There was a noticeable gash on the bridge of her nose.

Two streams of blood were coming down. It didn't bother her much. She was aggressive. She reached for Shannon's hand. He snatched back instinctively. I turned back to Mr. Lucas. I heard a scuffle now. Behind me. I was focused on Mr. Lucas. I didn't want to do what he said so I refused. I stood there. I didn't get down. I was running and wasn't doing anything wrong. But his hand was on his gun and I was a little nervous. I couldn't do it. I wouldn't. He would have to shoot me. That's when she broke free: New Africa. That's when I knew the vision.

Mr. Lucas came around the hood of the car and got in my face. He was completely unaware of Keith. I couldn't tell if he recognized me. Pushing me to the ground, Mr. Lucas stood over me. We had been here before. His hand now on his taser. Before I could post my hand to get back up, Lucas crouched over me and disengaged the taser. I had no time to respond. Within seconds I lost control of my limbs. My heart froze and my stomach tightened. Every muscle in my body jerked. My head hit the ground. I was in agony. Then it stopped. Suddenly it stopped. Everything was silent. I lay there until I no longer hurt. Officer Lucas was no longer over me. Then I jumped up. The siren was still ringing in my ear. Time slowed down. I turned to my right. Shannon was wrestling with the female officer. They were on the hood of the car.

Wommb Wommb

I got up off the ground. Officer Lucas was laying there. He wasn't moving. There was shouting now, all around.

"Put it down! Put down the weapon!" the female officer shouted at the top of her lungs.

I located her again. Shannon must have let her up. He was getting the best of her. I found her voice. She could barely hold the gun up she was so fatigued from the tussle. Her gun was pointed passed me. She was shouting behind me. But who was she talking to? Who had a weapon?

"Move Jamal. Move. They crazy."

It was Keith. He wasn't excited. He spoke in a very clear tone. It was surreal.

"Get down Jamal," Shannon whispered. I didn't turn to face them. I simply shrunk down. I listened to the orders. I was scared.

Like the melting Wicked Witch of the West, I tried to disappear. I became one with the ground. I couldn't watch. I felt ill. Something was wrong. What was going on? Why were guns being drawn? Why had the cops pulled up on the curb? Why was Mr. Lucas a cop? Why was he on the ground? Everything was happening so fast. Too fast. The officer's voice revealed her fear. She wanted to go home tonight. I didn't think that was going to happen and neither did she.

Wommb Wommbb Wommbb Wommb

Sound filled my ears. Four shots were fired. I didn't know the direction. I didn't know what was happening. I needed to know who fired the rounds. Friend or foe? That was most important.

I finally mustered the courage to look up. But I could only roll over onto my back. My head felt heavy with fear. I was scared to lift my eyes. Terrified. Laying on my back, I saw that the female officer, too, was on the ground. She lay there lifeless. There was no pain on her face. Just blood and hair. She was at peace. I looked to Mr. Lucas. There was agony on his face, blood too, but mostly agony. Though he lay lifeless, he died by a Black man's hands. He was eternally pissed. They were both dead. They shared one fate.

I looked up to find Shannon and Keith most importantly. I found them. Home. I wasn't scared anymore. Shannon was in pushup position, getting to one knee. Keith was stoic. The gun hung at his side. It wasn't smoking or anything like you see in the movies. It hung loosely like a dumbbell. He wasn't lifting weights though. But he was exercising freedom.

We took off for the house. All of us running neck and neck. We couldn't make it home fast enough. The groceries were a non-issue. We were out of breath. We ran up the stairs barely hitting each step.

Gliding. I took long strides up, grabbing the railing as I hit the corners. We made it to the house, banging on the door. Chris was up at this point. He had heard the shots. We were out of breath. No one talked. Keith was still holding the gun. No one talked. Not even about the groceries. Chris overstood.

We waited and nothing happened. It seemed like a day had passed. But it was probably twenty minutes. We waited. The phone didn't ring. The doors were not kicked in. We felt like the world had already forgotten about us. About our deed.

My stomach growled as my own humanness returned. The weight of the deaths hit me. They were cops.

"You know they're coming for us? It's just a matter of time." I managed to sneak between my teeth. It seemed unnecessary. I wanted to know what we were planning on doing. Were we just going to sit and wait, silently?

"Yall didn't do shit. We need to figure out what we gonna tell 'em. If they haven't come yet, we got some time," Keith mumbled.

Clearly, he didn't know what to say. He was as confused as me about us still being alive. In America, the roles were always reversed. The cops would be manufacturing a story about the last hours of our lives, pulling up incriminating social media photos, explaining how we were suspicious and resisting arrest with furtive movements. This time, we got to tell the story of their final moments. Why we felt justified in pulling the trigger.

Chris sat on the couch. Still silent. He knew the gravity of the situation and could infer that the shots he heard came from us. He sat intensely silent.

"We gotta do them like they do us," Shannon was thinking hard.

He hadn't looked up yet. His thoughts were wandering. All of our thoughts were wandering. What was about to happen?

"Let's make this story epic."

"Let's hope they didn't have a camera on the squad in that case." I advised thinking of ways that the system could engulf us. Prove us to be liars.

The living room lit up. Blue and red strobe lights filled our room. There were no sirens. Like lions in the tall grass, they were hunting for the cop killers in silence. They were not looking to make an arrest. I was prepared to die. I was glad Chris didn't share the burden of blood with us. We tried to send Chris into the room. But he refused.

"I'm not scared of the po-po. I wish we all had guns."

His youth and ambition was usually a relief. Now it intimidated me. I didn't want my little brother to witness what I had. Death isn't fickle. I'm sure those cops thought they were in control of their lives until they weren't. With us in this pinch, Chris was all mom had. I had to protect him, even if it made me look weak.

The cops patrolled the block. One squad after another. They even turned their lights off. They were trying to flush us out. We stayed away from the windows out of fear of being seen from the ground.

Radio voices snuck through the apartment. The crackling of the radio echoed. We became even more silent. Keith pointed to the bedroom. His face was like mom's in Church. Chris went to the room without resistance. This was more serious than he could grasp. We killed actual Americans, not just Black ones—the Americans who are worth more than three-fifths in a census—the Americans in blue.

Moments later, booming voices filled the kitchen.

"Get down! Get down!"

Police have a thing about making people lay down. When we saw them approaching, they filled the doorway. It was difficult to tell how many were in the squad. We all sat there waiting. Shannon was the closest to them. A Black officer hit him with the butt of his assault rifle. He cracked him behind the ear. A deep gash opened instantly. Shannon fell. The officer kept the rifle leveled at me while putting his knee in my brother's back. Shannon remained silent.

Almost immediately, I was staring down the barrel of three rifles. There was a cacophony of voices.

"Hands in the air!"

"Get down!"

"Don't move!"

They all wanted me to do something different. I just looked down the barrels wondering which one would fire first. Which weapon would snatch my soul?

Keith dropped his gun. The officers grabbed me and wrestled me to the floor with several punches and kicks being thrown. I covered up to protect my face. Most of the blows landed with no issue. I took a shot to the liver from an AK that hurt like hell. The blow made me gag and throw up air for the next ten minutes. I couldn't catch my breath.

We were all in the paddy-wagon. None of us was dead yet. All of us were prepared to meet God that day. We were ready for the investigation. Shannon's blood began to coagulate. It was drying. He was covered in brownish red from the back of his ear to the left sleeve on his royal blue shirt. He hid the discomfort and pain well. We were all too tired and frustrated to care. It was too late to hide.

Before we pulled off, the police raided the apartment. They came out holding a gun and Chris's unconscious body. My heart dropped. Was this their payback?

CHAPTER 13

Closing Arguments

"*I* couldn't reveal this information earlier, but I knew Officer Lucas. I knew him well." The jury looked suspiciously at me. I was a seventeen-year-old child, defending his brother, the Cop Killer. I was dropping my final bomb on the jury. I hadn't revealed my relationship with Mr. Lucas until this point in the trial for a reason. "Mr. Lucas was a race soldier."

To this point in the trial I had simply alluded to it. I had referenced his relative inexperience when it came to the enforcement of the law. Repeatedly. But I saved the best information for the closing arguments. I wanted to drop this bomb last, with no opportunity for a cross examination.

"Yes, in fact . . ." a shiver came over me. Something over my shoulder. I ignored it. "I have known Mr. Lucas for the better part of five years." I held up an open hand representing the number five. Everyone in the courtroom gasped.

This was the reaction I was looking for. I told them about being stabbed and having the then Mr. Lucas, now Officer Lucas, manhandle me and call me a "hoodlum" to my mom. I then went into detail about how he'd pulled me away from all of the adults, just to let me know I was better off dead. I saved this bit of character destruction for the closing arguments. I simply wanted the jury to think about it. Think about the absent Mr. Lucas. Think about what type of man would whisper such things to a thirteen-year-old child. I wanted them to know that he was a White Supremacist. That he was something worse. He was a destroyer of innocence. I also wanted them to know that he became an officer of the law with a purpose—to terrorize and destroy Black bodies.

"Objection! Objection! Objection!" Neal Jefferson, the prosecutor, spouted off.

He didn't seem like a bad guy. But he was a staunch attorney. He was determined not to lose to me. So much so that he avoided even looking at me or referring to me by name.

"Defense is making a mockery of the court, your honor. Please do something?" He ended with a slight inflection. He was tired. More than anything, Jefferson wanted Keith to spend life in jail. More than once during the trial, he explained that his father was a cop for more than two decades. "During the good ole days," he would reminisce. He wanted Keith to pay for slaying Lucas and his partner. He was the appropriate man to put my brother away. But I couldn't afford that. We couldn't afford that.

Before the judge could weigh on the relevance, "Your honor, the prosecution had an opportunity to question my relationship with mister, um, Officer Lucas when I took the stand."

I paused, letting Jefferson think about his error. "He must not have done his research. He worked at my school. Kimball Valley Elementary. I did not have an opportunity to cross-examine myself."

"Kill them both!" A voice from the back of the courtroom shouted.

"Fucking COP KILLER!" Another voice rang from the opposite side of the room.

The court began to rumble. Nobody cares about race soldiers infiltrating law enforcement. The public hated my brother and me. The media only played up the conclusion of the event. Two police officers were dead, not that all three of our lives were in direct danger. The police officers had a legal right to murder us that day and based on American politics, they had a duty to exercise that right. My body. At any point. Gone.

"Order! Order!" Judges Graves knocked with his gavel.

But the rumble had grown. There was a commotion behind me. Two men were yelling. Judge Graves stood up. His gown flowed like he was a choir member in a Baptist Church. There was a look of concern on his face. Keith sat across from me. I was in the bullpen, where all of the fighting took place. The gallery erupted. Voices everywhere. Keith and I made eye contact. All was overstood.

Keith was unamused. Everyone was excited to see how his life would be decided. Everyone except for Keith.

Then I saw the reason for the commotion. Hector, Officer Hernandez's husband, was fighting through the crowd, trying to make his way toward the bench. I was unsure what he was doing. But his gaze was set on Judge Graves. I leaned back onto the jury stand. I wanted to have a good view of it all in case I needed to duck. Keith and I held eye contact. He nodded at me. We had an understanding. Duck under the table if anything happens.

Hector was married to Officer Hernandez for the better part of twelve years. It was tragic how her partner got her killed. They have four children. They had all been in the courtroom for the duration of the case. The eldest daughter sitting next to Hector playing in her long jet-black hair throughout the case, sniffing it from time to time when the trial became contentious. The other three children sitting in descending order. The eldest daughter was fifteen. We were very similar in age and she was absolutely gorgeous. Her name was Naomi Hernandez. She looked like her mom without the stupid cop hat and bulletproof vest. I chose not to cross examine her when prosecution called her as a character witness. She made me nervous. Her stare. She never broke her stare. The death really affected her. I didn't think I could take her stare.

But today Hector showed up alone. He worked his way to the front of the courtroom. The aisles of the gallery were full of bodies. The court didn't recognize Hector Hernandez and couldn't identify his intent. He gazed at Judge Graves, his nostrils flaring, eyes wide. His brown skin showed a flush of red. As soon as he made it to the dividing bar, he reached into the right side of his khaki peacoat. But before he was able to pull his hand out, the bailiff and three courtroom police tackled him.

The courtroom fell quiet again. Everyone stopped to observe the tussling.

Poppp Poppp

Then everything stopped. My ears rang. Blood covered the courtroom floor. Hector shot himself. Judge Graves went directly to his chambers followed by the bailiff. It was understood that we were dismissed for the day. Everything had to settle down. Four children were fatherless.

This might lead to a mistrial. We can't afford that. I looked to the defense table. Keith was where he was supposed to be, perched under the table in a fetal position. The chains on his extremities hung loose now. All the tension was reserved for his eyes. His eyes were glued to the chaos. The blood created a crimson stream that flowed toward him. He did not move. Death had become commonplace. It was sad.

When the commotion cleared, Hector's body lay there, twitching and convulsing. He was not quite dead. He didn't seem alive either. He was somewhere in the middle. His chest heaved. Each breath seemed more difficult than the last. I was waiting for him to release the ghost like the movies, but I waited in vain. This was real life. He lay there for more than ten minutes, shaking. None of us moved. Keith sat watch. He was now sitting in a small deep red pond. His jumpsuit drenched to the hip. His arms wrapped around his legs. I know we were thinking the same thing. Or maybe not. When the paramedics finally arrived, they too moved in slow motion. They were not rushing. A suicide at a murder trial—how appropriate? Husband and wife together in the end.

Once the paramedic arrived, Keith finally got up. He moved towards me. He was two steps away. Nobody noticed us because of the commotion. The chains on his arms and legs sang a negro spiritual. He looked at me and said, "He was going for Graves. Not me." He took another step in my direction, reaching to shake my hand. But now the courtroom police were aware of the "Cop Killer." They would have none of it. Signaling with a glance, they rushed Keith to the floor, creating a three-man dog pile in the pond of blood at the center of the courtroom. They rolled around with no clear intention. The floor was slippery, and their momentum wasn't met with resistance from my brother. He had become inured. They just tumbled on the floor. Yelling for me to "Clear OUT!!!"

Of course Hector was gunning for Graves. From the point that I took my brother's defense, the case was a media spectacle. It went from being an in the park home run to a grand slam within the space of one conversation. But the case had been closer than many assumed. Way closer than anyone thought the trial of a cop killer could be. My brother killed a man and woman who threatened his family, and I had made that clear to the jury. My job was to humanize the police force in this case. I had.

It had become a very common opinion in the national media that Judge Graves and the prosecuting attorney, Mr. Jefferson, were throwing the case for some reason. The investigators couldn't believe that a 17-year-old kid in a baggy suit could call into question the outcome of the trial. The case was in the fifth round of a UFC championship match: Dan Henderson vs. Mauricio Shogun Rua. The fight would be determined by the closing arguments. The nation couldn't take it. Of course, Hector was trying to shoot Graves. He was probably trying to earn a mistrial by attacking the judge. We couldn't afford a mistrial. I needed my brother. My family needed him. My people were due a victory.

Keith was taken back to his cell. I watched, knowing he wouldn't be there for long.

How did I become Keith's counsel?

It was my senior year of high school. Keith had been in prison for two years. The trial had to be continued four or five times because of incompetent public defenders. Every two or three months, we'd get a new lawyer. They didn't care about my brother and many of them wanted to see him die. His own lawyers! Didn't they take an oath? They would make grand statements like "I wish that Illinois was still practicing capital punishment," or "Why didn't they kill you during the arrest?" Two of the bastards even told Keith they wanted to flip the switch themselves and watch him fry, like in those old Tom and Jerry cartoons.

They believed in the law and the enforcement thereof. We were acting outside of the law and must be handled accordingly. In fact, according to them, and the rest of public opinion, we should have been compliant. It doesn't matter that we were simply racing down the street in our neighborhood. So what if one of us gets tasered to death? The nuances of the case are unimportant. Law and order reigns supreme over Black lives.

The defense lawyers provided by the state were complicit. The entire time they were practicing incompetence, my brother was being tortured by the guards in jail. He was losing weight. Keith's body was always bruised. He was a cop killer, and they were cops. Keith had been beaten nearly to death twice. But after the Sandra Bland incident, the police couldn't afford another "suicide" on their hands. The next time would require a federal investigation. So they would send him to the infirmary claiming that inmates had abused him. How, when he was their hero? The Cop Killer, savior of the inmates. The other prisoners looked out for Keith. They made sure he lived after each assault. But the public defenders looked the other way each time my brother was beaten. They were part of the fraternal order too, I guess. We were eternal outsiders: poor and Black, the two things they hate. We all felt impotent. We couldn't reach Keith. Couldn't save him. Our brother was lost.

The next time the guards beat Keith, he was despondent. They made it look like inmates did it. The guards even implicated two of the inmates. They stabbed him in the ribs and stuck foreign objects in his mouth and anus. They tried to humiliate my brother like those Muslim "terrorists" in Abu Ghraib and it worked. Keith was humiliated. But it wasn't for the reasons the guards hoped. He was embarrassed by his helplessness. He was embarrassed by his apparent worthlessness. He asked me over and over, "Why didn't someone stop them?"

Keith stayed tough in those days but I remained concerned. He thought there was no choice for him. He was right. He was close to giving in. It was truly us or them. They could have murdered all three of us and eaten dinner at home that night. Keith discussed pleading guilty to manslaughter and getting it over with. He wanted nothing to do with the trial and verdict anymore. It had been sodomized out of him by the enforcers of the law. Why my brother?

It was my visit after that incident that really changed our relationship. Keith needed me and I owed him. He was here because he loved me. They beat him because he loved me. He was my John the Baptist. I was his Jesus. I started going to visit Keith daily after that. It was in his second year. Sometimes Shannon or Chris would go with me. Most days it was just me. They hated seeing the shell that used to be Keith. Mom never went with me to visit. That hurt him deeply. They all thought it was too sad. My mother was scared of prisons and had only been once to say bye. I was all Keith had. I had to be enough. But in a way, Keith was all I had too.

Upon entering the visitation room, I saw him sitting at our usual table, near the main guard, Officer Winslow. He was a short, round officer. His face was pale with bushy eyebrows and a thick mustache. His lips were nonexistent. They kept a close watch on us. In fact, I was being followed by two different squads, day and night shift. But that didn't stop us. We didn't have any secrets or hidden information about the case. We told detectives everything the first day. We had nothing to hide. Actually, up to this point, I had only seen the glory of New Africa in aspirations of my brother's freedom. But every camel's back has a straw limit.

"What up?" Keith asked. I wanted to hug him, but he looked fragile and that wasn't allowed anyway. It looked like he was gaining weight again. There were no noticeable bruises. He still favored his right side where they stabbed him. But that was to be assumed. After the first beating, the guards broke his jaw and he had to eat intravenously. He lost about thirty pounds. The skin on his face sagged around the eyes and mouth. That was why Shannon stopped coming. He couldn't take it. He thought Keith would die in prison before he got to trial. I didn't. I knew better. Keith always said the other inmates looked out for him. It was just the guards who beat, raped, and shit on my brother.

"You know. I read your letter on the way in," I replied.

I wasn't making eye contact. It was difficult. I wanted to cry. We couldn't discuss everything in our meetings with the guard standing over us. So we wrote letters and exchanged them when we saw each other. Sometimes he wrote sprawling journals about his newfound prison life. Reading them was difficult. He was my brother and I hated this new life.

"You said you needed a favor from me? What? What do you need?" I asked, willing to do anything. Willing to break the walls to the prison down and walk my brother out—by hand at that, brick by brick.

He hesitated and thought for a moment. He brought his hand to his face, then reached for me. His arm dropped. The guard behind Keith, pulled out his baton and cracked Keith across the forearm.

"No fucking touching, Cop Killer."

Keith didn't flinch. He simply continued to speak.

"Did you fucking hear me?" The guard waited for a response from Keith. He didn't get one. He was satisfied.

Keith waited a minute before he spoke. Gathering his thoughts and catching his breath. He rubbed his arm.

"That's gonna bruise." He laughed. But it wasn't real. A phony chuckle. He continued. "I need you to do something, bro. Something really really important." He leaned forward. I was waiting for him to say it. But he didn't.

"What?" I asked. I needed it. I needed to get him out of there. Nobody deserves to be there. Nobody. You cannot be both human and behind bars. I needed my brother's humanity more than I needed my own.

Keith leaned forward even more. I thought he was going to ask me to sneak something in for him, maybe even ask me to kill someone on the outside. Why? I don't know. But what came next was completely unexpected.

"These goddamned lawyers I got aint taking the case seriously. I been talking to the fellas in here. They say aint no lawyer gonna take the case seriously."

He fumbled around with his forearm. He inspected the contusion that was forming. It was probably fractured. It was swelling rapidly.

"I need you to be my lawyer. They say because I killed a cop that the lawyers are gonna lose on purpose. Cops can kill us, but you know how it go. And you see how they keep giving me new lawyers?"

Winslow made a sound. I looked at him with disgust. The anger was building in Keith. He was focused on getting out. I was focused on getting him out. But even I questioned this game plan.

I thought back to the baptismal pool. I had to jump in and save Keith. I had to save my brother. I was scared to death. But if he was asking me, I knew it was the only way.

"I'm going to need your help." Keith finally smiled. A real smile. I saw my brother. He was free for ten seconds. I saw the look he has when he thinks he's being clever. He was free for the first time in a year and five months. He was free for ten seconds. In his eyes. If only I could've stopped time.

I became his lawyer. I had one suit. It would have to do. I brought my brother his Church suit too. I knew we would have to be prepared. And we were. From that moment, we met every day. In between, I was doing my own research. So was Keith. Every day I made the two-hour trip to DeKalb State Penitentiary. Every day I was searched and harassed going in and out of the prison for being Keith's brother. In the research though, I discovered some pretty interesting loopholes in the law. Keith was working with the prison library to research similar cases. Precedent. We just wanted to see what there was. In every single case that we researched, we found that the "cop killer" was charged and found guilty. In fact, in most cases the accused had been killed while being taken into custody. Maybe we were lucky. Most of the lawyers were state appointed and encouraged plea agreements on men too poor to afford lawyers. We knew we needed a different approach.

Judge Graves suspended the case for two days after the attack on his life. I don't think Graves knew the attack was on him. Otherwise he might have decided to go directly for a mistrial. I was temporarily relieved.

During that time, I went to see Hector in the hospital. I wanted to talk about his choice. Soon, I would have to make a similar decision for a loved one. Maybe he had some advice. But when I arrived, he was in a medically induced coma. His vitals were low but stable. I was told that the bullet ruptured his spine, leaving him paralyzed from the waist down. His body lay there, chest rising and falling rhythmically. His arm was cuffed to the bed. Cops are funny. They'll find any reason to take out those handcuffs. Even a paralyzed man fighting for his life after surgery needed to be restrained.

The surgeon had his legs propped up to promote circulation. Tubes were coming out of his mouth, neck, arms and extremities. His soul continued to fight. He hadn't given up yet. Even after his blood filled the courtroom. Looking down at him from the side of his hospital bed, I knew it was worth it. He was seeking justice for his wife by any means necessary. Though it was not achieved, he still fought. He fought his best fight. Hector knew like we all did that the case wasn't going as planned. I sat by his side for hours anticipating that he would wake after each breath. When it was time for me to go and see Keith, I scribbled a note on a blank card that I bought in the gift shop:

SUPPORT YOURSELF AND
HEAVEN WILL HELP.
—J. Dale

I left before it got awkward. I didn't want to see Naomi.

When court was back in session, we resumed with the closing arguments. The courtroom was noticeably more somber. Nobody wanted to discuss the attempted murder suicide. But it was on all of our minds and all over the news. Judge Graves called me to the stand. He looked at my suit as I approached the bench. Everyone looked at my suit. It was getting baggier each day. I was insecure about it and couldn't afford to take it to the cleaners. It was as though I was pledging a fraternity, wearing the same clothes to set, day in and day out.

"Mr. Dale, are you able to present?" Judge Graves only recently started calling me by name. Like the prosecution, he referred to me as Defense to avoid recognizing my humanity. Every now and then, he would call me Dale or Jamal. I could tell I had earned his respect throughout the trial. Nobody expected this level of hysteria and contention. I nodded back at the judge. "You may proceed."

I took a second to reflect. Keith was in his usual position. We went over the new closing argument yesterday. I walked from the defense table to the prosecutor's table, gently placing my hand in front of Jefferson's laptop. "Mister, I mean, Officer Lucas, may he rest in peace." I made sure to appear like I was not holding a grudge. I paused dramatically to show my condolences. You put a white supremacist in blue and they become a saint. Throughout the case, I made very sure to be apologetic to his widow and his two fatherless children. But it was time to take the gloves off. "Officer Lucas and I had a history."

"Objection, counsel is presenting new information."

"Prosecution called me as a witness your honor. I was unable to cross-examine myself. However, if I had been able to, I would have asked."

"Overruled. Plus, I've been waiting days to hear this."

Judge Graves had not sustained an objection for the better part of two weeks. He had become weary of Mr. Jefferson's practices and lack of preparation. Neal Jefferson thought the trial would be a cake walk, but it quickly turned into lawyer boot camp, and he was ill-informed.

"Do your homework next time, Neal. How'd you let this slip past you?" Judge Graves found it amusing that I knew Lucas. This was the type of information that could change the case, make the attack premeditated and the complexion of the victim changes from white to blue to Black. By showing that Lucas could have recognized me and pulled over for that reason, I chip away at the prosecution's argument that he was acting as an officer. Maybe he was acting as a civilian who hated Black children? As long as the jury is thinking it as a possibility, I win.

"Officer Lucas was a teacher before he became a Police Officer. I knew him as Mr. Lucas, the gym teacher."

Everyone in the court looked confused. Many even brought their hands to their faces, rubbing in bewilderment. They too wondered how prosecution could have botched such an important detail. I had the jury captivated. "And no, he wasn't a bad teacher. He wasn't even particularly difficult to get along with." I shook my head and hand simultaneously. I was waving off the notion that I was trying to discredit his performance as a teacher.

"But Mr. Lucas was a white supremacist. I knew this well. It was evident in his teaching, his voice, and his body language."

I paused again. This time to collect my thoughts. I could feel my hand supporting my chin. My thinking pose.

"But then I saw the Confederate Flag on his car. Then he grabbed me and told me that he should have let 'you niggers kill each other' after an eighth-grade fight. Then he pulled over on the sidewalk as I raced my best friend and tasered me until my one hundred and forty-five-pound body was no longer a threat to his six feet, four inch, two hundred fifty-pound frame. Then, I saw the swastika that was so precisely tattooed in the center of his chest on his autopsy photos."

Again I paused. I held up an image of Lucas' autopsy picture. The four minorities, three Black women and one Latino man, stared at the swastika with disgust. The other eight turned away. Looking at the image brought me joy. Seeing his body lifeless and his hidden tattoo exposed to the world gave me chills like the first time I heard *Illmatic*.

"It wasn't until I saw the final piece of evidence though that I knew who I was looking at. That is the genius of racism. I am not playing the race card in this case. I knew this man. I had several experiences with him. He was my teacher. He taught me not to trust his kind. Our country was founded on certain principles that hold Officer Lucas to be infallible. His very understanding of himself was dependent on me not knowing who I am or what I deserve in this world. His work as a teacher and as a cop was to separate me from my humanity. And in death, he is attempting to do so to my brother."

I had been practicing this argument for weeks. I knew it by heart. This was my best effort to free my brother.

"Keith Dale, my brother, has endured great suffering while being wrongly imprisoned. He has been beaten. He has been starved, tortured in solitary confinement, and held behind bars like an animal."

I paused to make eye contact with my brother, but he was praying. He had heard it all. God was all we had now. Only God could change their hearts.

"You have watched my brother deteriorate throughout this trial, and it has been by the hands of those who were supposed to protect him, the correctional officers. We have consistently been let down by those who are supposed to protect us." I looked at my brother. A tear was brought to my eye. I let it sprint down my face, never to be remembered.

"But we are not talking about a proclaimed racist. We are not talking about a cop killer. We are not talking about a female officer supporting her partner. We are talking about a bully. We are talking about someone who chose to use two noble professions, teaching and policing, to intimidate and limit the freedoms of people who do not look like him. The aggression that Officer Lucas showed to three young men racing home after purchasing groceries for the house was unwarranted and completely prejudiced. You have watched the same dash cam recording as me. The video recording proves the hostility on the parts of both officers while also showing the direct danger that all of us were in. Not only could the officers have run us over with the car. Their guns were immediately unholstered, and they in fact threatened all three of our lives." I stopped.

I didn't want to mention the past because I was already hounding on the race card. But I had to. I had to mention the fallen soldiers and the evidence that we gave supporting our fear.

"Please also note the similar videos of police brutality that were shown. Take into account how similar those incidents were to this one. The only difference being that instead of my brother lying in the street for ten hours, or in a jail cell for two days, there were two officers lying on the ground."

I didn't want to say the names: Ezell Ford, Mike Brown, Eric Gardner, Sandra Bland, Trayvon Martin, etc. Police Lives Matter. But ours are not given equal weight. They are the Americans, we just live here.

After the closing arguments, the jury was excused to deliberate. The court was dismissed. I thought it was going to be quick. I thought they were going to have a decision immediately. I didn't know how they were going to side, but I thought they knew. They didn't. The ruling took four days. The longest four days of my life. They were confused. The video only made them more confused. The evidence supported their preconceptions. It was sad. We were all looking at the same oppression, but we all saw something different.

Some still thought we should have listened to the cops and Keith should have let them taser me to death. While others knew that Keith was in the right, and his place was saved next to Jesus. The truth resided somewhere in the middle. We lost two lives, almost three, because some people think they are better than others. Nobody in the scenario acted like Christ. Keith shot until no more rounds came out. For that, I was eternally grateful.

In the four days that it took for the jury to make a decision, I was overwhelmingly nervous. I couldn't keep any food down. When I could, it came out the other end like soup. I wasn't able to focus on school work. I couldn't help it. The entire family was nervous. Stress is a powerful thing. I went to school that Tuesday. As the lead lawyer, the judge knew to call my school if the jury came to a decision. I received no call on Tuesday. I figured the jury would be tired of talking about this eventually, so there would probably be a decision soon. I was wrong.

On Wednesday, I went to my locker between Chemistry and English to grab my bag and notes from the case. I was leaving the school to meet with Keith. We needed to work out the contingency plan, just in case they ruled guilty. I knew they would move him far away from the city and I wouldn't be able to check in when needed. To be honest, I liked the contingency plan much better. When I got to my locker, there was a little black Cabbage Patch doll hanging from a noose.

Some of my new classmates were really following the case. They were from Bridgeport, and their fathers were cops. I expected them to do something. Up to that point, I had only received a printed picture of a swastika on my locker. White supremacy has really lost its sting. Now they are just bullies. I wondered why other Black teachers, janitors, or students let it stay up for me to find. Maybe they were white supremacists too.

The doll was a much more creative expression of racism. It was so racist I almost found it funny. Not funny enough to let it go. I took pictures on my phone and sent a strongly worded email to the principal of the school. The principal never replied but the next semester, the entire student body and most of the staff received racial tolerance training from the ACLU. As though that's how we rid our institutions of racism. But I wasted their time and energy. They hated me for it. Bigots.[23]

Court was called into session on Thursday. The wait was over. When I got to the courtroom, however, it was empty. Not even Jefferson or his team. The bailiff instructed me that the lead lawyers needed to meet with Judge Graves in his chambers. Until then, I hadn't considered the irony of his name, a judge named Graves. We met in chambers. The judge looked very disappointed. Jefferson was already sitting in his typical seat. I assumed they had been discussing, but the moment the door opened all I heard was silence, then the door closed.

"I apologize to you gentlemen. I know both of you have worked hard."

Judge Graves looked at me with a sense of wonderment. He didn't understand me, he couldn't. He took a deep breath and sat back in his chair. Exhaling he let out, "The jury is hung." I was surprised. I had no idea that he could reveal the jury's decision to us. But I was even more shocked at what that meant. It meant I had been a good lawyer. If my goal was to be a lawyer, I was a good one. I saved my brother. But he wasn't free. That's what I needed. I needed to be God Himself, not a lawyer.

"What the hell Chuck!?!" Jefferson spouted off. "What the hell!?!"

He was a total asshole. For the duration of the trial he held back, but now the pleasantries were no longer necessary. I remember when he called me to the stand and tried to discredit me as a lawyer by discussing my disciplinary record.

---

[23] A wise enemy is worth more than a stupid friend.

"It says here that you were suspended for fighting . . ." It was clear that he was wasting his time, if he thought he had to discredit me as a lawyer to win. I was seventeen years old and related to the defendant. The case was all but his for the taking. A Black Man killed not one, but two cops. He couldn't seal the deal. Maybe it was time for a new profession?

"What the hell Chuck?" Judge Graves shouted back. "You lost to a kid. You let this kid hang the jury with his one suit. One black suit."

People noticed that I was wearing the same suit the whole time, especially as it loosened as the trial wore on. But he didn't have to say it. I looked down at my baggy sleeves, the ones that used to fit, showing off my nice silver jewelry store watch. It was reassuring knowing the Judge thought I had won the case. But in these situations, a hung jury is futile, a loss. My brother would stay in prison until the next trial. How fair is that?

They continued to argue. I was lost. I didn't know what to say or what I could say. They went back and forth. Jefferson was heated.

"How did you pass the bar? You didn't even research this high-profile case. Of course Lucas was his teacher," Graves said. "You made no attempt to explain the swastika tattoos. Two cops were killed, and we are sitting here with a hung jury because of incompetence." The judge was irate at this point. All I could think was, *the closing argument did work.*

"He is not a lawyer." Jefferson muttered off. He was ashamed. He should have been. The judge shook my hand dismissively, as Jefferson ran his mouth. His shake was firm. Too firm. Disingenuous. He didn't make eye contact.

"The jury will announce the verdict tomorrow. This is enough for one day."

Jefferson refused to shake either of our hands. He stormed out, butt hurt. He probably cried in the car.

I met with Keith that day. They moved him to the South Loop for the verdict. It was just outside the center of the city. I was relieved that I didn't have to make the two-hour hike to his prison.

Keith understood what needed to be done. We had to go with Plan B.

CHAPTER 14

The Promised Land

On the tenth day, I met with the Council. It was understood what we needed to do now. We had grown exponentially. The Melanoid Nation was ripe, and our country awaited us. New Africa was going to be a lot colder than old Africa. But it was still paradise. It wasn't a coincidence. Keith and I dreamed of the Nation long before she existed. We dreamed of a place where dark people could be free. Where we didn't have to be lynched daily: the new crucifixion. But what we got in return for our faith in Their plan was unimaginable. The Nation swelled to 8,231,987 citizens. What we thought to be random occurrences turned out to be our way of life. There was no disease, trash didn't accumulate, we made no pollution, people didn't die, people didn't fight, and everything existed in abundance. We had arrived at the Garden under a new covenant, **SUPPORT YOURSELF AND HEAVEN WILL HELP.**

It was understood what we needed to do. We needed to claim what was ours. Bill started the Council meeting. He was the official Oracle of the Nation. Maybe he was a griot, I don't know. But I grew to love Bill as a brother.

"Hakkum," Bill cleared his throat. We were all listening to what he had to say. He began to give a testimony. He looked around the table, making eye contact with everyone before he began. Shannon gave him a nod. He began to talk.

"We have broken ground on our nation."

We all cheered. We were excited. No longer were we acting on faith alone. No longer did we have to wait for signs. God was in our presence. Rather we were in Their's. We were one with Them.

"Our Nation grows with Melanoid Empowerment, Melanoid Love."

I smiled at him. He smiled back. My shadow. My man. The citizens were listening intently. They were awaiting instructions. Bill was an icon of the movement. He had metamorphosed into a dapper gentleman. His hair well groomed. He had an afro with a precise part on the left side. The fro was perfectly round, with the Black Power fist standing on the pick in the back. He wore the traditional Baye Fall multicolored gown, of the Senegalese peoples. His pantalon buffon, loose like a Dragon Ball character. His shoes black, shiny, and pointed. Everyone wanted to see the Promised Land. He was our omen.

"Now we must march out and claim what we have worked for. Bled for. Loved for. We must work the lands that our ancestors tilled and continue to grow. We are free. After centuries, we are free."

The exuberance in his voice was equal to when he jumped on the tank during our siege of the city or when he fought Toews.

Keith then spoke to the Council. The Council had grown to view Keith as the leader. When he spoke, there was no doubt that we were to follow.

"This movement was centuries in the making. From the murder of the first Zulu Warrior, from the destruction of the first Mayan Temple, from the murder of Fred Hampton, from Toussaint Louverture's struggle for humanity. We have been brooding. We have been conspiring with divinity. Today we walk into our Truth."

He, too, was overjoyed and feeling the victory. We all were excited. The world was anew to us. It was ours. As God had promised. The oppressors were scattered. Identities and languages lost to them. All they had were their lives. The lives they cheated and stole so willingly to preserve. Now they were wanderers, trespassers in our world. A different species all together. Begging for the mercy of the Savior.

I looked around the Council. Everyone was there. Chris and Ferris were whispering. I looked onto the Melanoid Nation. There wasn't a face without a smile. It was time. Addressing the people, I prayed. It was my first time praying in days.

"Guide our steps and our hearts, Creators, as we take claim to this new world. This world that You have promised. We will never turn our backs to You because You have never forsaken us."

I turned away from the Council. Journey on my left. Bill ran to my right side, appropriately, holding the Melanoid Flag. It waved proudly in the wind.

I motioned to the people. As one body, we walked out of Soldier Field. The sun followed us. As our feet hit the land, foliage began to sprout anew. Everyone explored the new world. They understood it. Felt in tune with it. The Earth spoke to us, and us to it. We were the hands of this Earth. After years of being denied our own purse, we got our reparations. All of them. Even the blood reparations. We belonged to the Earth once more.

For a long time, I wondered what it might take for Blacks to be equal in America. The answer that God whispered in response was unexpected.

"Support yourself and heaven will help."

We took our birthright. We took back the nation we built with our own hands. The Creators rewarded us for it.

"There's no looking back," Journey whispered in my ear as we trailed the citizens, hope dancing on her voice. She took my hand and placed it on her stomach. There was movement inside of her. Life was on its way to bless our new kingdom.

"Inshallah." My heart was whole.

Further Reading/Listening

Artist	Work
Ralph Ellison	Invisible Man
Richard Wright	Native Son
The Clipse	Grindin
Nipsey Hussle	Dedication (ft Kendrick Lamar)
Medina Green	Crosstown Beef (ft Mos Def)
Patrick Chamoiseau	Texaco
Marcus Garvey	Letter from Atlanta Prison
Outkast	Gasoline Dreams
Georgia Mass Choir	Come On In the Room
Martin Luther King, J.	Letter from Birmingham Jail
Paulo Coehlo	The Alchemist
Edgar Allen Poe	Purloined Letter
Sojourner Truth	Ain't I a Woman (Speech)
Bob Marley	I Shot the Sheriff

CPSIA information can be obtained
at www.ICGtesting.com
Printed in the USA
BVHW031409190819
556217BV00002B/236/P